MAI

poet, mystic and lover of nature was born in 1881 in Leighton
Cressage, Shropshire, the county were she spent most of her life,
which she passionately loved and about which she wrote in all
her novels. Educated mainly at home, she began writing at the
age of ten, and her verse and prose were published in many
papers and magazines in both America and England. *The Golden
Arrow*, her first novel, was published in 1916. *Gone to Earth*
followed in 1917, with a collection of short stories, *The Spring of
Joy*. Her other novels were *The House in Dormer Forest* (1920), *Seven
for a Secret* (1922), *Precious Bane* (1924) and, posthumously, *The
Armour Wherein He Trusted* (1929).

In 1912 Mary Webb married a schoolmaster, Henry Webb:
they moved to London in 1921, living in Hampstead until her
early death in 1927, her short life one of struggle against illness
and near-poverty.

Admiring contemporaries – who included Rebecca West,
Walter de la Mare, Arnold Bennett – described her as a 'strange
genius' and 'one of the best living writers'. But despite the fact
that *Precious Bane* was awarded the Prix Femina Vie Heureuse in
1925, it was not until six months after her death, when Prime
Minister Stanley Baldwin read and publicly praised *Precious
Bane*, that her work began to reach a wider public. But though
she enjoyed a posthumous success, it is only in recent years that a
new generation has recognised again the unique magic of a
novelist whose literary achievement stands firmly in the
tradition of the Bronte sisters, and of Thomas Hardy, but whose
style and voice is nevertheless utterly her own.

Virago also publish *Precious Bane*, *Gone to Earth*, *Seven for a Secret*
and *The Golden Arrow*.

If you would like to know more about Virago books, write to us at 41 William IV Street, London WC2N 4DB for a full catalogue.

Please send a stamped addressed envelope

The House in Dormer Forest

Mary Webb

With a new introduction
by Michèle Barale

Virago

London

Published by VIRAGO PRESS Limited 1981
41 William IV Street, London WC2N 4DB

Reprinted 1983

First published by Hutchinson & Co Ltd 1920

Introduction Copyright © Michèle Barale 1981

British Library Cataloguing in Publication Data
Webb, Mary
  The house in Dormer Forest. – (Virago
  modern classics)
  I. Title
  823'.912[F]   PR6073
  ISBN 0-86068-180-7

  Printed in Great Britain by litho at
  The Anchor Press, Tiptree, Essex

CONTENTS

BOOK I
THE HOUSE

BOOK II
THE FOREST

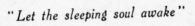
"Let the sleeping soul awake"

INTRODUCTION

It is not common to view Mary Webb as a writer whose focus was the lives of women; certainly her contemporaries did not view her thus. They saw her, rather, as a celebrator of the rural, a depictor of those homely virtues of simple cottage life and charming romance which had been lost in England's urbanisation. She herself seems to present no jarring biographical incident to mar this picture. She married late in life and most happily; she pined in London until her return to the Shropshire of her girlhood; as child and adult she delighted in the friendship of her rural neighbours. Those who remember Mary Webb describe her as painfully shy, perhaps a trait resulting from a disfiguring goitre, evidence of the disease which was to kill her. But they remember as well her extraordinary kindness. Thus she seems the embodiment of the cricket singing on the hearth, chirping in sweet abandon, hardly noticed until no longer heard.

This life which seems to unfold itself amid cottages, primroses, and Shropshire landscape had its darker side. When she was fourteen her mother, Alice Meredith, suffered a fall while hunting and took to her bed for the next five years. Although the exact nature of her injury is not known, a recent biographer notes that such invalidism was more likely emotional than physical, the only means of escape and refuge "from a circumscribed existence in a small country town which she disliked, her young family, or the prospect of future childbearing." (Dorothy Wrenn, *Goodbye to Morning*, Shrewsbury: Wilding, 1964, p.18) As the oldest child, Mary

The House in Dormer Forest

Webb was brought home from boarding school to care for her father and the five younger children. Though it was a task which she fulfilled with great pleasure, when Alice Meredith finally arose from her bed to resume control of household, children, and husband, her role of invalid was taken over by Mary. No longer the centre of her domestic world, Mary, who had taken upon herself both the duties and the privileges of mother, was now herself replaced.

For the next two years, listless, moody, painfully thin, Mary lay propped by cushions on the sofa. Gladys Coles identifies this period of her life as heralding the onset of Graves' Disease, an illness which would explain her collapse, her moodiness, her thinness (Gladys Mary Coles, *The Flower of Light*, London: Duckworth, 1978, p.52). While this may be the case, certainly the relationship between Alice Meredith's sudden recovery and reclamation of household – Mrs Meredith quite literally appeared one morning at the breakfast table, her instantaneous return to health un-announced – and Mary Webb's immediate decline cannot be ignored. The daughter who had been mother of her own house became once again daughter. And in that return to daughterhood, she found herself not only minus the inde-pendence of self-rule and the singularity of attention of her adored father, but subject to the stern demands of her most proper, religious, and critical mother. Rambles in the woods, bike rides to distant vistas, long hours spent lying in sunny meadows while observing wild-life were now continued only in the face of her mother's vocal disapproval. Mary the free agent became Mary the wilfully disobedient daughter.

During the rest of her life she is to be found, with in-creasing frequency, to have "taken to her bed". It is a posture so prevalent among women of her time as to be a convention. We hardly pause to consider its implications, such women as Elizabeth Barret Browning and Florence Nightingale having nearly beatified the recumbent position. But I would like to suggest that this posture of helplessness can be seen as physical metaphor for what such women perceived as their world's expectation of them. Socially powerless to extend their world, they diminished their

Introduction

physical confines as well – to a world the width of a bed.

This is not to make either the metaphor or the posture one which was consciously created. While the sense of enclosure, or even of impotence, may have been consciously acknowledged, it is difficult to believe that the consequent act of self-immurement was willed. Yet it cannot be denied that the sick-bed provided a certain freedom from the endless duties of wifehood, motherhood, country life, and church. But if the role of invalid made such activities impossible, it did not result in a creative paralysis. Elizabeth Barrett Browning and Florence Nightingale were prodigiously productive while prostrate; Mary Webb both read and wrote avidly. It was while recumbent that she formulated her philosophy of mystical pantheism and wrote many of the essays and poems which would later fill two volumes.

Such an analysis of her early history has not been made in order to paint the portrait of a neurotic woman haunted by inadequacies and morbid with unresolved guilt. Certainly I would like to dispel earlier and all too prevalent pictures of Mary Webb as the cheerful little rustic, tripping through the dappled Shropshire sun, communing with the flowers. She *did* see nature with an amazing clarity: her description of leaf, cloud, insect, bird song are accurate and reveal an unerring eye for detail. She *did* prefer the rural to the urban, the simple to the sophisticated, and the mystical to the orthodox, but her insights were themselves complex and most astute. She turned her vision not only upon the caterpillar's cocoon but upon the domestic scene and structure of her world. The portrait which she creates of that world is to be found in *The House in Dormer Forest*. It is a portrait which is utterly believable and utterly awful.

Lacking the sensual warmth of *Precious Bane* or the sensual vitality of *Gone to Earth*, *The House in Dormer Forest*, Mary Webb's third novel, details the suffocation of body and spirit which occurs when human feeling is made secondary to social ritual. It is a novel of domestic entombment in which the only escape possible comes through the transgression of social codes and by a pulling apart from the "mass-ego that constructs dogmas and laws" (p.11). It is, in particular, the story of maternal domination and a feminine will to power. Each of the women in *The House in Dormer Forest* has or seeks to have control over her world. But it is only Amber Darke who knows that love confers more power than do wealth, sexuality, subjugation. And it is Amber who, with this knowledge, experiences the life of passion and feeling which evades all who reside in Dormer House. Amber and Jasper, as much her *doppelgänger* as her brother, are the live beings trapped in the charnel house of Dormer.

The five women of the Darke family span three generations and offer contrasting portraits of powerful women. Grandmother Velindre uses religion and age to dominate all in Dormer House. Her spirit, vampire-like, broods over the family, killing life, hope, happiness. In her, "the herd panic, which drives man to be more cruel to his brother than are the wild beasts, held undisputed dominion" (p.18). Having erased all the vestiges of her own personality in the name of propriety and religion, she has become less than human. As matriarch, Mrs Velindre is allied not with the honoured traditions of the past, but rather with "the ancient gods of vengeance and slaughter" (p.18). Using Biblical texts as support for every cruelty, "she could have refused without a qualm the request of a dying man, if he disagreed with her religious views" (p.18). In both *Precious Bane* and *Gone to Earth*, Mary Webb created characters of no small evil – men whose need for vengeance or possessions destroyed all around them. But in Grandmother Velindre she has created a character of almost satanic power.

Grandmother Velindre dominates through her use of Biblical texts: Mrs Darke uses her silence. Her wordless spirit weighs upon Dormer "like an iceberg silently pressing upon a ship" (p.27). She is the silent power of the house, using Grandmother Velindre's pronouncements for her own ends: "it seemed as if she were a ventriloquist, and talked through her mother" (p.27). Apparently passive, obedient, the epitome of docile daughter and wife, Mrs Darke is a puppet-master. But at night in the mausoleum-like house, Mrs Darke talks ceaselessly in her sleep, in a voice "expres-

Introduction

sionless and secret" (p.44). Though she controls by day, by night she is herself the pawn, a mere mouthpiece for the hidden forces of her repressed psyche.

A distant relative living with the Darkes as a paying guest, Catherine Velindre is a near Pre-Raphaelite portrait. She is pale, golden, aristocratic, her hair intricately bound, her hands long, white, and graceful. Both teasing and aloof, princess and saint, Catherine is nearly worshipped and nearly raped. She uses her beauty and sexuality to gain her ends, attempting to master her world by mastering its men. Catherine's madonna-like appearance contrasts with Ruby and Amber, making one seem nearly tawdry and the other duller still. Ruby is ripe, sensual, beautiful in an over-blown, too blatantly physical way. She is both good-natured and passive, too naive to see Ernest's pious rhetoric and grandiloquent chivalry as masks for a small mind and lusting heart. She is pleased to be Ernest's ruddy bride, certain that the mantle of motherhood will confer status, as wifehood will bring new dresses. Like Catherine, Ruby discovers the dark side of sexual passion. Catherine finds that her teasing power nearly results in the loss of her virginity, her greatest bargaining power. Ruby learns that chivalrous words and social institutions do not assure tenderness within the marriage bed.

Amber, like the brown gem for which she is named, is dusky and plain. MaryWebb repeatedly describes Amber in terms which relate her to living nature, as amber itself is not a mineral but a fossil resin – not stone but the product of a life process. In an early scene Amber stands at the open door of Dormer, clad in white, a "thin, insignificant figure between the large brown hall and the large blue night" (p.28). The pose is nearly emblematic: she stands at the door of her entombment, her back to the Darke past as she faces the natural night. A mystic, Amber understands both love and sex. She goes to Michael Hallowes' cottage without shame, and she expresses her love with forthright passion. Among the Darke women it is Amber alone who finds what she seeks. She alone has gained power over her own life, while the other Darke women remain enthralled.

The House in Dormer Forest

I began by claiming for Mary Webb a place in that tradition of women writers and critics of the female condition. It is this novel, perhaps more than any of her others, which gives the evidence for this claim. Mary Webb understood her society in terms of its power structures. She understood with analytic clarity the drive for control – self-determination – as a natural human desire which, when perverted by social or religious pressure, destroys life rather than enables it. And she understood the complex process by which women are forced to seek their power through the role of victim. Mary Webb is, I would suggest, a most bleak feminist for she seems to find no possible solution for the process of victimisation, by society or by self, within social institutions. A relationship of love and equality is possible only beyond social boundaries: within there is either worship or rape, use or abuse. Thus *The House in Dormer Forest* is no rural tale of rustic love. And if its author is a cricket singing on the hearth, then we should listen very closely to her lyric: she is singing devastating things about our lives.

Michèle Barale, North Carolina, 1980

The House in Dormer Forest

BOOK I

THE HOUSE

I

DORMER

DORMER OLD HOUSE stood amid the remnants of primeval woodland that curtained the hills. These rose steeply on all sides of the house, which lay low by the water in the valley. This was called Oolert's Dingle, and there were plenty of owls to justify the name. On a moonlit night, passing, high up, from side to side of the cuplike valley, they looked like breeze-blown feathers. Higher still, on the very rim of the cup, the far-travelled winds shouted across to one another, all winter, news of the world. When the bats slipped from their purlieus in the cobwebby out-buildings and climbed toward this rim, they had to ascend step after grey step of the windless air, and only attained their ambition after long flying.

From these heights, in fine weather, the house and its gardens lay open to the view, small but clear, beside the white thread that was Dormer brook. The place had been patched and enlarged by successive generations, very much as man's ideas are altered, the result in both cases being the same—a mansion to the majority, a prison to the few. On clear evenings, when

the westering sun struck up the valley and set the
windows on fire, one could see the centuries in the
house, like ferns in a fossil. There was the timbered
black-and-white centre, once the complete house, with
diamond lattices and the unassuming solidity of an
Elizabethan manor ; there was the small Queen Anne
wing on the left—one room down and two up—built
by a rich ancestor of the Darke family ; there was the
solemn, Georgian porch with its rounded, shell-like roof
and Grecian pillars. The right wing, hideously
stuccoed, consisted of one large room with many-paned
sash-windows and a steep red roof, and had been
built by the father of Solomon Darke, the present
owner. At the back, perilously clinging to the Elizabethan farm, was an ancient cottage, which seemed to
be the nucleus of the whole, and was built of stone
and thatched. When the ambitious Elizabethan set
about building his manor, no doubt the two bottle-
glass windows of this cottage eyed him reproachfully,
as a Vandal and a despiser of his ancestors. It was
neglected now, and remained, weighed down by the
large-leaved ivy, haunted by its whisper year after
year, and used only by Enoch, the gardener, who stored
apples there, and by the mice, who consumed the
apples. The house, as a whole, had something of a
malignant air, as of an old ruler from whom senility
takes the power, but not the will, for tyranny.

All these things you could see in clear weather ;
but when it was misty—and mist lingered here as of
inalienable right—the house was obliterated. It
vanished like a pebble in a well, with all its cabined
and shuttered wraths and woes, all its thunderous
" thou shalt nots." At such times it did not seem
that any law ruled in the valley except the law of the
white owls and the hasty water and the mazy bat-
dances. Only those who slept there night by night

could tell you that the house was overspread with a
spider's-web of rules, legends and customs so complex
as to render the individual soul almost helpless. It
is the mass-ego that constructs dogmas and laws ;
for while the individual soul is, if free at all, self-
poised, the mass-mind is always uncertain, driven by
vague, wandering aims ; conscious, in a dim fashion,
of its own weakness, it builds round itself a grotesque
structure in the everlastingness of which it implicitly
believes. When each unit of humanity merges itself
in the mass, it loses its bearings and must rely on
externals. The whole effort of evolution is to the
development of individual souls who will dare to be
free of the architecture of crowd-morality. For when
man is herded, he remembers the savage.

Round the House of Dormer stood the forest,
austerely aloof. The upper woods had never known
the shuddering horror of the axe, the bitter and incurable destruction of the day when gnomes of ugly
aspect are let loose with flashing weapons among the
haughty sons and daughters of the gods, hacking and
tearing at the steadfast forms of beauty, until beauty
itself seems to have crashed earthwards. Successive
Darkes had threatened to fell the forest ; but there
was always plenty of wood from the reaping of the
storms and from trees that fell from the rottenness of
great age ; so they had let it alone. The trees looked
down upon time-shattered hulks of others in every
stage of gentle decay. There were some mouldered
trunks yet standing with a twig or two of green on
them, especially among the yews, which must have
weathered the winters of a thousand years. Others
were of such antiquity that only a jagged point showed
where once the leaf-shadows flickered on the wolf
litters. Among these giants in their prime and in their
dignified dissolution rose on all sides in supple grace

the young trees and saplings. From the lissom creature that only needed the gradual massing of maturity to make its beauty perfect, down to the baby stem with two absurd, proudly-waving leaves, all took part in that slow attainment of perfection through stages of beauty on which all Nature seems intent. They stood, rank on rank, with rounded or pointed tops, their foliage sometimes heavy and solemn, as in the yew and the oak, sometimes fluffy as in the elm, or transparent and showing the sky through its traceries as in birch and larch. They seemed to peer at the house over one another's shoulders like people looking at something grotesque, not with blame or praise, but in a kind of disdainful indifference.

For it does not seem that Nature, as some divines would have us think, was built to stage man's miracle plays, or created as an illustration of his various religions. Nature takes no account of man and his curious arts, his weird worships, but remains dark and unresponsive, beetling upon him as he creeps, ant-like, from his momentary past to his doubtful future, painfully carrying his tiny load of knowledge. But indifference is not hampering, as interference is; therefore those that feel within them the stir of a growing soul prefer the dour laws of earth to the drag of the herd of mankind, and fly from the house of man to the forest, where the emotionless silence always seems to be gathering, as waves mount and swell, to the disclosure of a mystery.

II

THE Darkes had just finished supper, the event of the day. The red woollen bell-rope still swung from Peter's onslaught; for when, at Mrs. Darke's morose order, "Ring for Sarah," he kicked his chair aside and strode across the room, he always seemed to wreak a suppressed fury on the bell-rope, and more than once the tarnished rose to which it hung had been torn from the wall.

"The room. Drat it!" said Sarah in the kitchen, like a person proposing a toast.

Armed with a large tin tray, she burst into the dining-room. Clearing was, in her hands, a belligerent enterprise in which her usual sulky manner in the presence of her mistress gave place to more open hostility. She wrested the plates from their owners, and had been known to leave Ruby, who liked two helpings, stranded, with no plate for her last fruit stones. To-night it was Mr. Darke who cried, "Howd yer, Sarah!" and clung to his plate.

"Don't say 'Howd yer!' like any old waggoner, Solomon!" Mrs. Darke spoke with exasperation.

"Waggoner, Solomon!" echoed a less irritated, thinner, more tiresome voice, that of Mrs. Darke's mother, Mrs. Velindre.

Solomon Darke, a man of sixty, sat with his shoulders bent; his jaw, of the kind sometimes called "jowl,"

13

rested on his Gladstone collar and large " made " tie.
The expressionless heaviness of his face was redeemed
by something of the patience of oxen, and rendered
intimidating by a hint of the bull-dog in the mouth's
ferocious tenacity.   It was obvious that his one idea in
any crisis would be to resort to physical force.   Between
him and Peter sat Catherine Velindre, a distant relation who lived at Dormer as a paying guest, calling
Solomon and his wife " uncle " and " aunt " as terms of
respect.   Her pointed face, her chestnut hair, demurely
parted and pinned round her head in a large plait,
her small and thin-lipped mouth, might have belonged
to a Chaucerian nun.   But her eyes were not those
of a nun ; they were too restless.   They were peculiarly
long, of the type called almond-shaped, with very little
curve in them ; the lids, being large and heavily-
lashed, added to the air of secrecy and awareness that
was Catherine Velindre's chief expression.

In extreme contrast with Catherine were Ruby
Darke, a tall, plump, pretty girl of eighteen who was
sprawling across the table, and her elder sister, Amber,
who was in no way a success according to Dormer
standards.   Her manner, when she was at ease, had
charm, but it was spoilt by shyness.   Her hair was of
an indeterminate brown, and her complexion was ruined
by ill health, due to the perpetual chafing of the
wistful mind longing for things not in Dormer.

Peter, black-eyed, silent in the presence of his
parents, and—for all his twenty years—full of the sul-
lenness of early adolescence, had the look of a creature
gathered for a spring, but he was without sufficient
concentration to know in what direction he wished to
go or what he wanted to grasp.   The air of repression
which brooded over the family, putting a constraint
on emotion and impulse, seemed to act as an irritant
to Peter.   He was vaguely aware of something inimical,

as animals are, but he knew nothing about atmosphere and would have flushed scarlet if anyone had spoken to him of emotion.

Peter, Ruby, Amber and Jasper—who was not here to-night—came by their names in a curious way. Mrs. Darke had been so bored by the advent of each child (for she had married Solomon not because she loved him, but because she hated the Velindre household) that she had refused to think of any names for them. There had been many long silent conflicts when her husband sat, moody and obstinate, staring at the mute bundle in the majestic cradle which was a Darke heirloom, and saying at long intervals : " Give it a name, Rachel ! "

Mrs. Darke, equally obstinate, on her large sofa with its uncomfortable ornaments of carved mahogany leaves, silently tore calico. The argument, wordless on one side, always ended without a name having been found ; and, though Solomon's nerves were those of a ploughman, they at last became irritated by the harsh, regular tearing, and by that in his wife's character which lay behind the tearing and caused it.

" What are you making, tearing so ? " he would ask angrily. And she would reply, like scissors snapping, " Binders ! "

Afterwards Solomon generally took his gun and strolled towards the Rectory, which was at some distance from the church and the House of Dormer. The Rectory, a few cottages and an immense, overbearing rookery made up the village. Entering the Rector's study with a couple of rabbits pendant in his hand, Solomon would say sheepishly :

" Give it a name, Rector ! "

Now the Rector was an authority on seals and gems. Nobody knew why he had given his life to this study, but it was generally felt at Dormer that he was an honour to the village and must be known all over the world. As Mr. Mallow, the constable and chief member of the choir, said with unintentional irony, " The Rector's got a powerful burden of learning, and he's first in that line, no danger ; for who else ever wanted to know about a stone ? "

After these visits of Solomon the Rector would spend a happy morning, poring over his lists of jewels, and —having dined frugally on the rabbits—would write a long, allusive letter to Solomon in beautiful pointed script. Solomon, having extracted the name from it, would light his pipe with it and say to his wife in an off-hand tone :

" What d'you think of Amber, Ruby, or Jasper ? "

Whereupon Mrs. Darke said :

" That's the Rector ! " and Solomon was very crest-fallen.

Rachel Darke was grimly amused that her children should be called by the names of precious stones ; but to protest would have been to upset her attitude of aloofness. Three gems headed the family, but, when the Rector suggested " Garnet " for the fourth, Solomon rebelled and said :

" Call him Peter. It was good enough for his grandfather."

The Rector comforted himself with the reflection that Peter, a rock, was only a jewel in the rough, and Peter had been true to this from his cradle. As Mrs. Cantlop, the Rector's cousin, said with one of her helpless sighs, " Peter's such a *knobby* baby ! " Mrs. Cantlop knew the children's idiosyncrasies far better than Mrs. Darke did. She knew that Ruby could absorb the crudest paint from her toys and still flourish ; that Amber, though an ailing child, was always ready to gurgle into laughter ; that Jasper, even at the age of three, required reasons for obeying an order, and that he would, after pondering on them, behave " like a Christian lamb." She knew also, though neither Mrs. Darke nor Mrs. Velindre noticed it, that Catherine, from the moment of her first arrival—white-pinafored, reserved—ruled the nursery. Of all the children, Peter was most like his mother. He had the same long, obstinate chin and the same smouldering black eyes.

To-night, while Sarah clattered at the sideboard, Mrs. Darke sat staring at the tablecloth, drumming on it with her long, restless fingers. She was just beyond the circle of lamplight, and the dimness made her seem even taller than she was. Her thin lips, very pale and straight, were closed with almost painful firmness. Her forehead was covered with lines, both vertical and horizontal, and an expression of frigidity combined with exasperation made her face sinister.

Away from the table, in an armchair by the fire, sat Mrs. Velindre. She was grotesquely like her daughter. She had the same close-set black eyes, long pale face and lined forehead ; but her eyes had no expression. If one penetrated them, there seemed to be something stealthily in wait behind them. It was like walking in a lonely wood and becoming aware of something running in and out among the trees, silent, invisible, and gradually being convinced that it is a ghost. There was a ghost hiding in Mrs. Velindre's eyes—a cadaverous, grisly thing which had looked at her out of other people's eyes when she was a child ; slowly possessing her in womanhood ; finally absorbing her whole personality—eating into it like a worm into a rotten fruit. As she sat, hour after hour, in her high, straight chair, with her white cap and black ringlets, two on each side, this ghost brooded with batlike wings above her failing mind and endowed her with something of awe, something that proclaimed her

kin to the ancient gods of vengeance and slaughter.
For in her, more than in any other at Dormer, except
her daughter, the herd panic, which drives man to
be more cruel to his brother than are the wild beasts,
held undisputed dominion. As a young woman she
had known generous instincts, but now, at eighty,
she could have refused without a qualm the request
of a dying man, if he disagreed with her religious views.
Yet she could scarcely be blamed. She had lived so
long by fear and not by love, that her capacity for
cruelty had grown in proportion to her capacity for
panic. She had for so many years been trying to be
like other people, that she was now like nothing in
heaven or earth. For the more a soul conforms to
the sanity of others, the more does it become insane.
By continually doing violence to its own laws, it finally
loses the power of governing itself. Mrs. Velindre,
who was the oracle of the family, never used either
intellect or intuition in giving her verdicts. She simply
echoed her ancestors. If anything occurred without
precedent in her tradition, she was flustered and
incompetent, until she had found some text which
could be made to bear on the question. Then she
would give her ultimatum.

Beneath the hanging lamp, which lit the large room
vaguely, the six faces, drawn in heavy chiaroscuro
against the brown wall-paper, shone out dimly as
from an old picture. They might have belonged to
a pre-renaissance Italian family or a household newly
converted to Calvinism. But though they might have
belonged to any country or period, they could only,
it was clear, belong to one spiritual atmosphere. Perhaps it was the weight of this atmosphere that gave
the room its medieval gloom. For the kernel of
medievalism was fear—of God, devils, man, and all
the laws, customs and fetishes invented by man.

And this antique negation seemed to find in the House of Dormer a congenial dwelling. Thick shadows clung to the ceiling like hovering night-birds, eliminating the corners and all furniture not within the lamp's radius, obscuring detail and giving the room a measure of gloomy dignity.

" I wish Jasper would come ! " said Amber suddenly. " He's late."

" It would be almost better," said Mrs. Darke, " if Jasper never came at all."

" Wicked ! A wicked boy ! Never came at all," muttered grandmother.

" He isn't, grandmother ! " Amber was all on fire with wrath and love.

" Don't contradict your elders," said Mrs. Darke. " It is very tiresome of Jasper, with Ernest taking the curacy here, to come home an infidel."

" D'you mean to say we've got to have that fool Ernest living here ? " queried Solomon.

" I do. He is to be a paying guest."

" Lord ! The house'll be like to bust."

" *Burst ! Burst !* " corrected Mrs. Darke in exasperation.

" *Burst !* " echoed grandmother from the fireside.

" Bust ! " repeated Solomon.

Peter guffawed. Any defiance of authority was a refreshment to his tethered spirit. Amber was pink with suppressed laughter. Her grandmother's voice was so like that of a distant, ruminative bird answering a near bird, and her father's explosiveness was so funny and excusable that her perpetually simmering glee at the humours of life almost boiled over. A strain of what Mrs. Darke called vulgarity in her husband was one of his most lovable qualities in Amber's eyes. She always suspected it of being at least half compounded of humour.

Catherine looked pained.

" Really, Solomon, I wish you wouldn't be so vulgar ! " said his wife.

" What've I said ? Bust. Well, the house *will* bust. It won't hold Jasper and Ernest together."

Sarah, at the sideboard, gave a smothered chuckle.

" Sarah ! I said, clear ! " Mrs. Darke spoke with incisive anger.

" Clear ! " came the faithful echo from the hearth.

Sarah, with subdued passion, concluded her enterprise and was heard dealing hardly with the crockery in the kitchen.

" Aren't you going to have any supper left, mamma ? " asked Ruby.

" I am not."

" What a welcome ! " cried Amber.

" Is it a time for welcome ? "

" A time to dance and a time to weep . . ." quoted Mrs. Velindre, with the buoyancy given by the knowledge of having made a quotation to the point.

" I don't see that poor Jasper can expect a very cordial welcome, after his behaviour," said Catherine.

At that moment Sarah was heard roaring (there was no other possible description of Sarah's voice when raised), " The gun-dogs' supper's ready, sir ! "

" The dogs get supper—the very dogs ! " Ruby spoke obstinately.

" The dogs eat of the crumbs ! " said grandmother, again buoyant.

" The dogs will enjoy their supper, won't they, father ? " asked Amber.

" Ay, ay. They mop it up."

" Jasper will be hungry, father."

But Solomon had gone. He would not be drawn into open hostilities with his wife.

" Jasper deserves to be hungry," said grandmother.

" Why must a fellow starve because he's expelled ? "
cried Peter angrily. " If the old fools expel him, it's
their look-out ; it's not his fault."

" What *is* Jasper's fault," said Catherine softly,
" is the sin of denying his Maker."

Peter was silenced. He was susceptible to physical
beauty, and, in the absence of more obvious charms,
those of his cousin held him. The devout air, the
" preachy " sentence that he would have ridiculed in
his sisters, he admired in Catherine. By one of the
ironies of things, Catherine's religious words and looks
were acceptable, not because they were real, but
because she looked and spoke with the eyes and lips
of a courtesan. Not that Catherine was anything but
innocent and ignorant ; she was virginal to the point
of exasperation ; but there was something cold in the
allure of her eyes, something knife-like in her smile, that
recalled the loveless sisterhood. Grandmother spoke
again :

" A jealous God ! " she said in her most sepulchral
voice. " A jealous God ! "

" If he doesn't think there's a God, how can he say
there is ? " Peter asked irascibly. It was easy to
see that he did not argue for a principle, but because
arguing was an outlet for his volcanic dislike of things
in general.

" Why not just say there is and be comfy ? " murmured Ruby sleepily.

Mrs. Darke turned and looked at her, and the look
was enough to wither her. But Ruby was not of the
easily wilted souls. She was a complaisant creature.
She returned her mother's look contentedly, ruminatively, and went on eating apples. Catherine watched
her.

" You eat a great many apples," she remarked.

" That's why she has such a lovely complexion," said Amber.

Catherine's eyes, narrow and lustrous, came round upon Amber, who immediately became conscious of her own bad complexion.

She looked round the room, wishing she could make it more homelike for Jasper. Dormer was not a comfortable house, though there were plenty of material necessities. No one need ever be hungry; but no meal ever partook of the nature of a sacrament. Amber often thought wearily that here food and drink were only so much solid and liquid matter put into the body in order to strengthen it so that it should once more acquire solid and liquid matter. In many a poor home she had seen a light that never shone at Dormer; seen the chalice lifted in whose mingled wine is agony and ecstasy; heard those bells pealing out into the rainy, windy night of time which swing only in the mysterious belfries of the human heart. Sometimes when she came late through the village she would see an oblong of crocus light that seemed to come not only from the cheap lamp and the carefully tended fire. It might be a young wife who stood in the doorway, while the eldest child, with stern concentration, wielded the toasting fork. Or an old woman strained her faded eyes to embrace with their love the old man coming heavily up the path. When these vanished into the soft glow that was their rightful country, Amber was filled with a strange, wild longing. Once she talked of this to Ruby, and she was so wistful that Ruby cried: " I'll make *you* toast, Ambie! Yes, I will—scold who may!" In her childish way she strove for the inner grace by first attaining the outer sign. The toast caused trouble, but Ruby had a capacity for obstinacy, and the war of the toasting-fork became an institution. But the Dormer meals still failed to be sacraments.

To-night the room looked exactly as usual. Catherine had brought out one of her hobbies, a device by which ink was sprayed through a wire comb by a tooth-brush on to white cardboard where ferns had been pinned. The resulting white fern silhouettes were varnished and made into blotters for bazaars. Catherine pinned the ferns on with great precision, but Amber preferred Ruby's blotters, which were blotters in every sense. The ink, in Ruby's hands, seemed to become exceedingly wet, and the spray, which should have been fine as pepper, ran into pools. Amber, seeing Ruby's large hands doubtfully poised over the work, her indeterminate mouth slightly open, sometimes thought that Catherine—neat, competent, her dark eyes slanted amusedly towards Ruby—willed her to make blots. To-night the regular, metallic brushing worried Amber. She wanted to think about Jasper, but the room was full of small irritating sounds. Listening to them, it seemed to her that they were the essence of the people that made them—each little noise the complaint of the spirit within. Peter was whittling elderwood for whistles, drawing his breath through his teeth meanwhile. Mrs. Velindre's four steel knitting needles made a nervous undersong to the brushing. Ruby's regular munching was occasionally drowned by a rending noise as Mrs. Darke tore rags to stuff cushions. This sound predominated over the others because of its very relentlessness. Each tear was a momentary shriek. No one spoke for a long time. They seldom talked over their evening employments. When Solomon came in, Amber felt grateful to him because his amusement was a silent one. Every evening except Sunday he read *The Golden Chance,* a paper consisting

chiefly of puzzles, graded for varying intellects. Some
required the creation of a complete couplet of verse.
Solomon looked askance at these. Others only needed
an intuitive knowledge as to which lady would marry
which gentleman in a line of pictured heads. But
by some black decree of fate Solomon was never able
to win a prize. Each Saturday, when he depressedly
ascertained that he had again failed, Amber loved him
more passionately. She resolved that next week he
should win if she had to sit up all night. But she was
not good at puzzles. She thought the man with a
box-like chin would marry the hectic lady ; Solomon
was sure he loved the lady with the excessively
developed figure ; whereas the perfidious young man
really burned for her of the diamonds. " We might
have known ! " Solomon would say gloomily, and Amber
always wished that she wasn't too reserved to throw
her arms round him. She used to wish the same when
Peter came home from school as a tiny boy with a
bad report. To-night she wished it more intensely
about Jasper. For he had made in the eyes of Dormer
a signal failure. None of his puzzles had come right.
His riddle remained unguessed. She remembered him
as a small boy having been placed on the stool
of repentance by Mrs. Cantlop—who had taught them
all till they outstripped her in knowledge, which happened early—and standing there insecurely in a curious
little yellow tunic, his shoulders humpy with a sense
of injustice. When she remembered Jasper's keen
love of fairness, the wild rages that shook him at the
lack of it ; when she thought how he would come home
to-night, already frayed to breaking point by the failure
of the world of college to see his side of the question,
she felt dismayed. She knew exactly how they would
all look at Jasper, how the souls would lean out from
their faces like crowds watching a criminal—grand-

mother peering, Mrs. Darke glaring, Ruby and Peter curious, her father glowering, Catherine hypercritical. Her hemming grew large and wild.

" Father ? " she said questioningly.

" Um ? " Solomon looked up from the page he was poring over.

" When will he be here ? "

The question had been quite different, but the room was too strong for her ; she fell back upon time. Time was a god at Dormer. Clocks ticked in every room with fury or with phlegmatic dogmatism, and their striking cut through every conversation. Mrs. Velindre's grandfather clock was especially dictatorial. At five minutes to the hour it hiccupped, and, when people had just forgotten this, it gave forth the hour in deliberate and strident tones that only ceased at five minutes past ; so that it cynically took ten minutes from every sixty in order to preach the fleetingness of time. Mrs. Darke owned a black marble timepiece like a tomb, which ticked irritably on the cold black marble mantelpiece in the dining-room. In the hall was a tall clock which chimed and would have been pleasant if the chimes had not been slightly cracked. Sarah possessed a cuckoo clock, which shouted as unemotionally as if it knew that here at Dormer its cry did not mean summer. In all the bedrooms were alarums, bee clocks, carriage clocks. To anyone standing in the hall on a quiet afternoon, the multiple whisper of all these time-keepers was very ghostly. They rustled like autumn leaves ; they hushed the living into the sleep of death. They increased Amber's feeling that Dormer was too full of people ; for, where man is massed, there he seems doomed to live by rule and by time. Those who dare to be themselves are not so bounded. For the lover time is changeable ; a moment of absence wears on him like a year, and a year with the beloved is gone like a falling star. For the mystic also time does not exist ; already he dreams into eternity. When man is self-poised, he awakes from the hallucinations of time and law, and stealing out into the silence of his own being hears a voice sound beyond mortality, telling him that place and time are but bubbles ; that the nervous counting of moments and years is foolish ; that he is free and has never been in prison, since the walls that he thought loomed about him, strong and opaque, are nothing ; that he is, even now, one with the immense freedom in which these bubbles float.

Solomon looked at the marble clock. " Not for twenty minutes. Enoch's slow," he replied. " And what I say is, the lad should have thought of the family. What's it matter what *he* thinks ? God's God. The Saviour's the Saviour. Anyone that denies it— tar 'im and feather 'im ! "

Amber was puzzled. She herself would have been willing to assent to any dogma for the sake of one she loved, for she felt that to sacrifice the human being who was dear to her for a creed, an idea, would be criminal. In her, love had a way of flaring up like a beacon, changing the world and consuming even herself. But she knew that Jasper would regard this as lying. As she recalled his sensitive, scornful face, the heinousness of what he had done faded before a sense of romance. He had been out into strange places. He had fought a ghostly warfare on the shadowy slopes of the soul. Had he lost or won ? Lost, was the verdict of Dormer ; but Amber dared to think not.

" I admire Jasper for not being afraid to say what he thinks," she said, conscious of temerity.

" Admire ! " cried Catherine, with pretty horror.

" Admire ! " echoed grandmother subterraneously.

Mrs. Darke said nothing, but her spirit seemed to weigh on them all like an iceberg silently pressing upon a ship. Her silence was alarming. The less she said, the more she seemed to say. Sometimes it seemed as if she were a ventriloquist, and talked through her mother. So when Amber, almost in tears, beating herself against the blank wall of their imperviousness as the winter robins would beat against the Dormer windows in terror at finding themselves in prison, cried : " Yes ! Admire ! It's brave of him to tell the truth ! "—it was grandmother who looked bleakly across the room, gripping her needles of polished steel with fingers of polished bone, and said : " Jasper, until he repents, is damned." Her voice, with its metallic lack of emotion, seemed to hack the air and leave it jagged. Solomon breathed stertorously over his puzzle ; even Ruby felt the tension, and sighed. No one contradicted grandmother. The room, with its heavy shadows, fell again into silence.

Sarah's activities had died away in the kitchen, and the house lay dumb under the night. To Amber it seemed that its quiet had the quality of the spider's, mutely awaiting the faintly vocal fly. As she thought it, a soft regular sound became audible, the fateful sound of a horse trotting. She sprang up with a defensive feeling and went into the hall. As she pulled open the heavy door, the voice of the stream, swollen by the autumn rains, smote upon her suddenly, full of sad foreboding. It was deepened by the low, sonorous sound of the Four Waters, half a mile away—a monotonous and bee-like note that seemed to have been struck before the beginning of time. Dormer, in its cup at the bases of the hills, was always full of damp air and the sound of water. Besieged by this grievous music —and what is there in nature sadder than the lament of falling water ?—she felt as if she had opened the

door not to the night and the stream, but on to a
future full of doubt and dread, veiled in mist.

She went back into the hall. Jasper could not be
here for a few minutes, and she found the light reassuring. From the dining-room came Mrs. Velindre's
voice reading passages from *The Lion of the Tribe
of Judah*, a paper which dealt exclusively with the
vexed question of the lost tribes. She persisted in
regarding the Jews not as one of the finest nations
the world has seen, but as people requiring a missionary. This paper was her spiritual and intellectual
fodder, and she read it nightly, with praiseworthy
perseverance, to a totally indifferent family. She also
read it to Sarah while she lit her fire on winter mornings, and Sarah had been heard to say that " if the
tribes must be daft and mislay themselves, she wished
they'd mislay themselves for good and all, and not
like hunt the thimble—no sooner lost than it's werrit,
werrit, werrit to find it." But it was useless for Sarah
to rattle the fire-irons ; useless for the family to talk
in raised voices ; for grandmother had a voice of great
carrying power when she liked, and she was not afraid
of using it. The good seed was sown. To-night it
was being sown. Jasper's arrival was unmarked,
whether by design or accident Amber did not know.
She opened the door again and heard the wheels suddenly muffled as the gig turned into the sandy drive.
She had put on her best frock, a white cashmere, old-
fashioned in make, and she showed as a thin, insignificant figure between the large brown hall and
the large blue night.

So deeply had her genius for loving been stirred by
Jasper's forlorn condition—she knew he would be un-
speakably forlorn at Dormer ; so greatly had the
innate chivalry of the individualist (who believes in
the essential beauty that is beneath the froth of action

speech and motive) been aroused by hearing the absent abused, that it almost seemed as if she might triumph over the constrictions of Dormer and express herself to Jasper.

" My dear ! oh, my dear ! " she whispered, as Enoch, with a " Be good, pony ! " drew up at the door, and Jasper jumped out.

He kissed her perfunctorily, looked restlessly past her into the hall, and said :

" Where's Catherine ? "

Amber, alone in the porch, twisting her hands together with a crushing sense of failure and futility, murmured with a kind of smouldering passion : " Oh, I *wish* I were his mother ! "

She was realizing the perpetual denial of spiritual truth by crude fact. She was feeling that it was of no avail that she loved Jasper maternally, protectingly, perceptively. He would neither expect nor welcome these things from her. From Catherine he would expect them ; but would he get them ? From Mrs. Darke he would not even expect them. Amber raged, but her rage consumed herself only. For in the House of Dormer, with its hollow-echoing chambers, ascendancy is given to bodily and not spiritual ties ; to propinquity and not affinity ; to the shout of the crowd and not the faint, far voice of the soul.

Jasper disappeared in the gloomy doorway, and Amber, with the second-sight that always comes to those who ponder anxiously upon a loved one, knew, at least in part, what he must endure ; she guessed also that her conflict for his happiness with the personality of the House, with the thing that hung, like a haunting demon, from the old roof-tree, would be long and hard and would perhaps bring defeat in the end.

III

JASPER stood in the dining-room doorway and thought that the room looked like a cave—a dark cave from which anything might emerge, devils or angels. As he thought this, he was gazing at Catherine. As a little boy, he had adored the tall white resurrection angel on its golden background in Amber's Sunday book. He had been unusually fond of church and of Bible pictures, and, while Peter was busy in the kitchen, salting the raisins with which Sarah enlivened her Sabbath, he would be wrapt in contemplation of the resurrection angel. Now, having discarded angels, he needed something to put in their place. His mind had not yet cast away the old religious phraseology. Perhaps the hardest thing from which to break free in being born to the life of individual honesty is this protecting caul of ancient phrases and observances. To Jasper's temperament these were peculiarly dear. At his first communion, when the Rector had read the plaintive " In the same night that He was betrayed . . . ." Jasper had sobbed, and Mrs. Velindre, who was there in an armour of solemnity that frightened him, had eyed him suspiciously, thinking that he had a secret sin.

The dark sweetness of eucharistic dawns, the spiritual vitality of Christianity's best ideals—these he had resigned. But there, in the restricted lamp-

30

light, with demure, down-bent head and bright hair,
bound in the manner of religious art, was Catherine
Velindre, tangible and beautiful. Her white hands,
just plump enough to be graceful, moved to and
fro quietly. Her shoulders, which sloped a good deal
beneath her dark silk blouse, gave her an air of
fragility and gentleness. It seemed to Jasper that her
face broke upon him like a radiant landscape seen
from a forest, or a flower thrown from a dark window.
He had always been rather sentimental about Catherine.
That Peter also was, though only by fits and starts,
encouraged him. So also did the fact that his elders
thought it " very suitable " that she should marry
Peter ; for Catherine possessed a small independent
income which would help the Dormer property, to
which it was arranged that Peter should succeed,
Jasper having chosen the church. Her money was a
barrier in Jasper's eyes. He wished she were a beggar
and he the lord of the manor. He thought her face
would be adorable in a ragged setting, like the crescent
moon on a wild night. He had always been eager to
be her lover, but to-night he began to care for her in
an intenser way. He put her in the empty niche in his
spiritual life and took her for his guardian angel, who
was to lead him along hard paths by the fascination of
sheer whiteness. She would smile down at him in his
tourney for Truth ; she would be proud of him when he
gave up material welfare for conscience' sake.

He had an idea that they would all be proud of him,
though possibly deprecating his views. During the
uproar at the training college, which followed his
outburst, during the sleepless nights when he mourned
his cherished future (he had wanted to be a scholarly,
cultured, yet practical vicar of some huge, wicked
parish which he was to convert) in the midst of exas-
perating misconstruction of his motives ; in all these

he had comforted himself with the thought that
Catherine, and in a lesser degree the rest of the home
people, would know that his motives had been of the
highest. He had thought that they would all agree
that honesty was the one course open to him. So little
do we know the personalities with which we are most
intimate !

Jasper looked very handsome, very vital, very young,
and therefore very pathetic, standing in the dusk
beyond the furthest lamp-ray. His eyes dwelt eagerly
and dreamily on Catherine, until he suddenly remembered that he had not, in Dormer phraseology " been
the rounds." The curious coldness of his reception
was rather lost upon him, he was so dazzled by the halo
he had just created for Catherine, the beauty of which
he ascribed entirely to her, and not at all to his own
imagination.

Mrs. Darke silently suffered his embrace ; but so she
always did. Ruby gave him one of her indifferent,
wet kisses. Peter said " Hullo ! " which was, for him,
demonstrative. Then, just as he reached Catherine,
his father looked up and said the sentence he had
hammered out as being suitable.

" I'd have been better pleased to see you for a better
reason."

Grandmother raised her head, and Amber, tearful
in the hall, thought that she looked, with her small,
bright eyes, like a snake about to strike.

" Why hast thou brought down my grey hairs ? "
queried grandmother rather inappositely, for her ringlets were as black as sloes. This was by courtesy of
a certain mixture called " Uzit," or through lack of
the emotions, for the emotions turn more heads grey
than does old age. It is not the Isouds and the Teresas
of the world that conserve their youth, but the Aphro-
dites.

" I've done nothing to be ashamed of," said Jasper.
Mrs. Darke looked up.

" You have sinned against the Holy Ghost ! "

" Ghost—ghost ! " muttered Mrs. Velindre.

" There's no such person," said Jasper, defiant
because he was alarmed at his own daring.

" Blasphemer ! " Mrs. Darke eyed her son with
what an onlooker, who did not know their relationship,
would have called venom.

Jasper stuck out his chin ; it was long, like his
mother's.

" Blasphemer against what ? Sinner against
what ? " he asked with exasperation. " You can't
blaspheme against a lie."

Solomon flung *The Golden Chance* across the
room and banged his fist on the table.

" Silence, sir ! " he shouted.

" Father," said Jasper, his voice shaking with
passion and disappointment, " I won't be silent. It's
lying to say I believe the idiotic hotch-potch of the
churches."

" Silence ! " roared Solomon again.

" Oh, why does Jasper rub them up the wrong
way ? " whispered Amber.

" I won't be treated like a naughty boy ! " said
Jasper furiously.

" A naughty boy ! Yes ! A very naughty boy ! "
said grandmother. " When I was young, caning was
the cure."

Grandmother had been brought up on " Cautionary
Tales for the Young."

" Yes, a good stout stick'll find God for most of
'em," remarked Solomon, adding with an air of great
reasonableness, " God's God."

" Oh, can't you understand ? Won't you understand ? " Jasper's voice was pleading.

" We understand," said Mrs. Darke, " that you must have done something wicked and don't *want* to believe."

Jasper's lips quivered. So they thought all his spiritual conflicts mere fleshly lusts! This misconception irritated him as much as it hurt him.

" You're not angry with me because I don't believe in God," he said, " but because I'm different from you."

He had hit upon the truth. What they hated him for—and Mrs. Darke's feeling, like Mrs. Velindre's, did reach a silent vindictiveness—was that he had disparted himself from the gelatinous mass of the social ego, as the one live moth from a heap of dead larvæ. Their quarrel with him was wholly material, though it was disguised as a spiritual warfare. (Grandmother often referred to herself as one of a militant band warring against " Midian," an impersonal and mysterious foe as to whose identity no one ever evinced the slightest curiosity.) It was the inchoate obstructing formative power ; the inert pressing down upon life. They were not aware of it, but Jasper saw it, and it made him miserable. If he could have felt that his father and mother and grandmother and all the hostile faces he glimpsed beyond them were really fighting for an ideal, however dim and rudimentary, he would have been able to respect them, and even like them, though they tore him to pieces. There would also have been the chance that they were right, that they might convince him. He would have liked to be convinced of some of the things they professed to believe. Failing that, a definite adversary, a hope of either victory or defeat, would have been welcome. What more could a young man ask ? Jasper asked it, but he did not get it. An amorphous mass is not definite ; it gives no hope of anything but

blind, aimless struggling. He was horrified at his
sudden vision of the vast crowd-egoism which says :
" You are not as we, so we crush you." He felt this
in grandmother's eyes when she gazed owlishly upon
him out of her twilight. Still more he felt it reaching
out to him from his mother's mind. She had no need
to speak or look. It was enough that she was in the
room ; the silent air grew sinister with an unspoken
threat.

" Different ? " said Solomon slowly. " Ay, you are,
more's the pity."

" Well, father, that's how the world gets on. You
go a step higher than your father. I go a step higher
than you."

" Conceited ass ! " Peter spoke roughly. He
was annoyed that Jasper could talk above his
head.

Jasper turned on him furiously, and their eyes met
across Catherine's bent head with mutual antipathy.
Jasper despised Peter as a reactionary and a lover of
the fleshpots of orthodoxy. Peter disliked Jasper
because he had more imagination than himself. Each,
feeling the atmosphere of the house lowering over him,
mistrusted the other. Left to themselves, they would
probably have been interested in each other's differ-
ences. At least, they would have been tolerant. But
an inimical atmosphere creates quarrels.

Catherine raised her eyes to Jasper's.

" Who put those dreadful ideas into your head,
Jasper ? " she asked. " You can't have thought of
them yourself."

" Why not ? "

He looked at her pleadingly with his brilliant hazel
eyes. As she watched him, Peter slowly lost his lustre
for her. Yes. Jasper was distinguished. There was
something in his face that had not been there a few

months ago, that was not in any of the other faces
round the table. She could not exactly name it, not
understanding that it was the essence of Jasper's being
unveiling itself to her. What she did see very clearly
was that he would have been a great success in the
Church. " Not a miserable little backstairs curate,"
she reflected, " nor a fat fool like Ernest Swyndle. He
would have been asked everywhere. He would have
ended with a bishopric. Idiot ! Theatrical idiot !
He *shall* end with a bishopric ! He shall give up this
nonsense, or else——" the tip of her tongue just
moistened the corners of her pointed mouth—" or else
he shall be punished. He shall suffer."

" You are too nice for such silly ideas," she said
" Tell me who talked to you about them ? "

" I thought things out for myself," said Jasper
patiently. To anyone else he would have been
haughty. " But I have got a friend whose views are
in most ways the same."

" Is he expelled, too ? "

Jasper shrank into himself at her tone. Then he
reflected that Catherine could never be intentionally
unkind, and pulled himself together.

" It's no disgrace to be expelled for an idea. He
would have been glad to be expelled with me, only he
was a lecturer, not a student. He left of his own
accord because he disagreed with the Head."

" What about ? "

" Everything. He hates all the things the Head
likes, only he keeps his temper better than I do. He's
older."

" Age always tells ! " cried grandmother. " Quality
and age go together."

" A fine chap! " Jasper flushed with enthusiasm.
" He's all for the anarchic state."

" Anarchists ! " Solomon was irate almost to

apoplexy. "Look you, my lad, no more of that. Your thoughts are your own ; if you want to be damned, you will be damned——"

"Be damned !" said grandmother, but without expletive intention.

"—But I can and will stop you fouling the house with such talk. Board and lodging you can have, but no more argufying. Behave and stay, or argufy and go. See ? "

Jasper saw only too well that life at Dormer was going to be unbearable. He was in the white-hot missionary and martyr stage. His message might be one of negation, but it was none the less precious to him.

"I won't be muzzled !" he cried violently.

"Mad dogs always are," remarked Peter.

Jasper glared at him.

"I'll go !" he said. "I'll go clean away and never see any of you again." He choked. The first crepus-cular oncoming of the fog of misunderstanding and misconstruction is very hard to bear. When the black-ness has engulfed and numbed the soul, rebellion dies and the soul sinks into painless despair.

Catherine laid down her comb and tooth-brush, straightened herself, and looked at Jasper. It would not suit her at all for him to go away. How could she, if he went away, save his soul ? She rested her chin on her hands and let her eyes absorb him. He was, for the moment, saturated with, engulfed in her will. He was fascinated and rather alarmed. She had never looked at him like that before. No one seemed to observe them, all being intent on their own interests. Mrs. Darke was tearing a piece of linen in a way that was reminiscent of a cat tearing feathers out of a bird. Catherine's eyes remained steady, and Jasper, as if drawn by a cord, slowly leaned towards her till, with elbows resting on the table, he almost touched her.

" Cathy ! " he whispered.   " Cathy ? "

His lips moved and remained parted. The first feverish glow of passion swept over his face, leaving it troubled.

" Stay—with me ! " she whispered

" I can't, I can't ! "

" I want you."

" They'll drive me mad if I stay."

Once more, Catherine submerged him under her gaze. The room was quite silent at the moment.

" Jehovah ! " said grandmother suddenly. She believed in ejaculatory prayer, and her style was coloured by her literature.

" Tch ! " said Catherine irritably. But Jasper had heard nothing.

" I want you to stay more than anything in the world, Jasper. Will you ? "

" I'll stay if I die for it," whispered Jasper.

He knew that there was nothing more solid, iron and soul-destroying than an inimical atmosphere. It kills more quickly than fire or sword. It is more ferocious than a wild beast. To live among people who have a false and unfriendly estimate of one's character, who misconstrue motives, against whose changeless prejudice the wretched spirit flings itself in vain—this is a refinement of torture with which few sympathize. Then Catherine smiled up at him and the room seemed to grow peaceful again. The sudden outbreak, thunderous and threatening, had sunk to calm. He knew it would come round afresh in the manner of tempests ; for the people of Dormer could see only one point of view—their own. This is the hot-bed from which strife, national and individual, always springs—narrow mentality, shrivelled emotions, overweighted with physical strength, brooded upon by a still narrower mentality, that of the past. This, because it is effete, is considered immortal, and has been glorified by man into a god of vengeance.

Jasper, on his side, had the roughness of the conscious outlaw, the élan of the growing plant, the necessitated fierceness of a creature outnumbered. He could see their point of view, but he was afraid to put off his armour of combativeness, and if he had done so there was no common ground where they could have met, for the family never would see his. His virtues were crimes in their eyes, his hopes a madman's raving.

" Ring for prayers ! " said Mrs. Darke suddenly.

Peter plunged at the bell. Ruby yawned. Solomon woke up, and in the kitchen " Onward, Christian Soldiers " came to an abrupt end.

IV

DURING prayers Amber could think of nothing but Jasper's footsteps pacing backwards and forwards in his bedroom, which was above the dining-room. Long after everyone had gone to bed she stood by her window, trying to gather courage to go and comfort Jasper. As a consciously plain woman she was deprecatory in action ; as a sensitive woman she was tender to the reserves of others. She knew Jasper would be awake, going up and down like a caged creature. It was pathetic that he should feel so deeply a thing that seemed to her a trifle. That he should be homesick for a God and not able to find a God—this was tragic, terrible. But to-night the main point had been simply that he was expelled. On that everyone had harped. About that Jasper was defiant and wretched. Because of that he was tramping his room. She would go to him and tell him how greatly she admired him and sympathized with him. But no ! The reserve that chained them all at Dormer and that often binds members of large families (so that the legends of chains rattling and fetters clanking in their haunted houses seem to have an allegorical significance) held her now a prisoner. Yet she could not sleep. The strange clashing of antagonistic temperaments, more obvious to-day than ever before ; intuitive fear for Jasper, since she saw that his nerves were inadequate to the

40

life before him—these things troubled her. She knew,
because she loved him, that Jasper was one of those
who need the woolly wrappings of convention—small,
ordered thoughts, bounded desires, mediocre faiths,
safe, communal rights. These would have kept his
too sensitive spirit and easily frayed nerves warm and
intact. She knew also that Jasper's tragedy lay in the
fact that he could not have these safe things. His
passionate love of truth sliced them away and left him
shivering in the cold air of individual effort ; committed
him to wild adventures in quest of God, to insensate
hopes and black despairs. Jaded by these Alpine
wanderings, he was unfit to bear the strain of life at
Dormer, and was, as he once said with bitterness,
" any man's fool."

Amber looked out into the chill moonlight. On the
silver lawn there lay, black and sharp as carved ebony,
the shadow of the House of Dormer. Its two heavy,
rounded gables of dark red brick topped with grey
stone, the solid, massed chimneys and the weather-
vane (a gilded trumpet supposed to be blown by
the winds) were painted, large and far-spreading, on
the grass. The house gave a sense of solidity even by
its shadows. From outside came the muttering and
crying of the weir and the Four Waters. Through this
continual plaint broke, at times, the muttering of the
herds that peopled the low, misty meadows, their dim
shapes moving portentously in the vague moonlight.
Their inarticulate *malaise* with autumn or the night,
with their unknown destiny or the quality of their
herbage, burst forth at times into a smothered bellow,
an incipient roar, broken and muffled as a tide on
rocks.   Sometimes one would startle the air with a
high note that was almost a shriek ; sometimes there
would rise a deep, low chorus akin to the melody of
milking-time. Never, for long together, was the

round, hollow Dormer valley without some rumour of
their calling, like the herds of humankind, out of their
tentative darkness, for they knew not what. The mist,
which lay lightly on the fields, thickened along the
stream into an opaque curtain, standing about the
domain of Dormer like the bands of an old enchantment.
Mist always haunted Dormer. Sometimes the house
stood knee-deep in it, like a cow in water ; sometimes
it was submerged far below, like a shell on the sea floor,
the mist—white, weighty, stirless—brimming nearly
to the tops of the surrounding hills. At these times,
when the morning cocks crew sharp and sweet from
the rickyard, the plaintive sadness of their thin music
pricked Amber to tears. It was as if a city long dead,
for infinite ages forgotten, were summoned from
ancient oblivion by a resurrection trumpet so faint
and inward-sounding that only the eager spirit heard,
while the clay-bound sleepers never knew that the
moon had slipped down behind the western hill and the
grey world flushed for dawn.

Amber listened to the faint night-sounds that came
and went beneath the singing of the water and the
grumbling of the herds. There was the sea-murmur
of the woods that climbed the hills and chanted in
winter a song more mysterious, though of less volume,
than that of summer. There was the lisp and rasp of
dry leaves that came about the house on the doubtful
night-wind. There was the sibilant whisper of large-
leaved ivy that clothed the walls in heavy layers. And
within the house, from their bedroom across the landing, Amber could hear the voices of her father and
mother uplifted in their evening prayer. They always
said their prayers aloud, perhaps for the sake of
example, and their voices—lugubrious and penetrating
—seemed to Amber to issue from their room like her
father's setters from their kennel, dour, passionless,

acquisitive. She felt shocked at herself for having had the idea, but with each rise in their inflexion the resemblance grew more distinct. At last they were still, and silence fell upon the house. Amber waited, hesitated, sought for some pretext for going to Jasper.

The time crept on to midnight. She opened her door, and straightway it seemed that the house was alive with noise, muted, but none the less noise. The echoing whisper of the clocks seemed very loud and full of meaning. The ticking of the one in the hall was like the falling of heavy drops of water. Then the grandfather clock hiccupped, and in a few minutes a storm of sound came up and along the passages. All the striking clocks gave out the hour, and from the kitchen —far down, as if from a cavern—the hoarse cuckoo shouted. Afterwards, in the comparative silence, as if in satiric jest, began a new ticking—the ticking of the death-watches. The old walls, hollowed and tunnelled by rats and mice, were so full of these little beetles that nobody took any notice of them except Sarah, who put cotton-wool in her ears nightly. But this was more than half in plain physical fear of earwigs, which she thought would penetrate to her brain. She had even been heard to say (in daylight) that " death-watches were poor feckless things, traipsing and yammering like a blind beggar with a stick." As Amber listened to these eerie tickings she was reminded of the sound of grandmother's watch at night, and of the curious ebony watch-stand on which it hung. She thought whimsically of all the death-watches ticking busily, each on a miniature stand, carved with an hour-glass and a skull.

As if at the signal of midnight, there now began a new sound, more disturbing and grotesque than the noise of the death-watches—a human stir and murmur, probably started by the sound of the clocks. But the sounds were those of sleep, not of waking life. It was as if the spirits of those in the house, slumbering during the body's activity, half awoke, and tried to pierce the silence around them. Amid a continual stir of restless movement, tossing and turning and creaking of beds, there began a low murmur from which at intervals a stray voice would emerge. Amber could hear Mrs. Darke talking, as she generally did in sleep, with a ceaseless monotony of self-expression. It was the reaction from her unnatural waking life. She who preserved all day an iron control of word and look and impulse committed herself all night. But even in unconsciousness she spoke with characteristic reserve, in a voice expressionless and secret. No one outside the room could ever have distinguished a word, and her husband, who might have heard, slept heavily and stertorously, his snores resounding through the walls. Amid Mrs. Darke's indistinct babble and Solomon's snores, Amber could hear Peter, whose door was ajar, grinding his teeth. This came at more or less regular intervals, and at other intervals, from the far end of the passage, came grandmother's voice, thin but awe-inspiring, crying " Gideon ! " and " Jehovah ! " Only from Catherine's room no sound ever came. Amber wondered what she herself contributed to this concert, and was smitten with silent, irrepressible laughter. But she became serious again when Ruby cried out in some dream terror. There was something wrong here, she felt, something sinister and unwholesome. Lost voices came along the tortuous passages, uplifted as if in complaint from amid murky dreams, and as if in baffled longing for some undiscovered good. Even so the nations sleeping, drugged by tradition, among the bones of their ancestors, stir restlessly and utter vague scattered cries, mutterings, a low lament, a sudden far shriek. The midnight house seemed like a graveyard where the tremendous " I say unto thee, arise ! " had been spoken and then revoked ; where the dead stirred and uttered strange plaints and groanings, but could not cast aside their cerements nor rise up into the light of morning. Under the panic of the thought that they were like people in a vault, and that she and Jasper were the only ones alive, Amber fled along the passages to Jasper's room. She heard as she came near, with great reassurance, his restless tramping, comfortingly commonplace. Its very wrathfulness and irregularity brought relief. He seemed to her like the watchman in some ancient lightless town, where goblin hosts crush in from every side upon the shelving air, which strains and is fissured under the weight of evil until, to the terrified people in their nightmare chambers under the threatened roofs, comes the watchman's voice, querulous with reality, telling them that the night is cold and rainy.

Amber, with her mouse-coloured hair and her face grey with weariness, looked, as she stood in the doorway, wrapped in her brown dressing-gown, like the priestess of some occult worship. Jasper did not see her. At the moment when she came in he was kneeling in front of a little table on which he had placed a photograph of Catherine with a vase of flowers in front of it. In the shock of this discovery, Amber's face at first expressed disgusted surprise, then, as she saw that he had, from very exhaustion, fallen into a doze on his knees, her look melted into pitiful love. At such times the intensity of her expression was so great that the outer self melted, like the crust of rock when fire breaks through, and was fused in the inner self. No matter what the face is, when the young spirit shines there exultant, it will be beautiful. For the spirit, the centre of the ego, is eternally vital, youthful, free. It has a thrilling life, never dreamed of by the earth-nourished body. So Amber's face in these rare moments was beautiful as are few faces in this world of pale emotions. For Amber Darke was something of a mystic, though not exactly a religious mystic, nor that wilder, sadder creature, an earth-mystic. Sometimes she was deeply stirred by the beauty of Nature, but she did not live for it alone, as does the true child of the weeping god. Sometimes it was music that stirred her, or a stray sentence from the Bible, or the stars, or poetry ; but most often it was the sudden rapture or the sudden pain of loving. Love would leap up in her at a chance touch of pathos in the most unpromising people. At these times she left the shallows of beauty that is heard and seen, and slipped out into the deep sea where are no tides of change and decay, no sound, no colour, but only an essence. In those waters nothing is but the spirit. She alone knows the immortal waste. She only, in a voice lamenting and sweet, cries across it as the curlew cries in spring. She only, circling above its darkling peace, eyes its mystery that haply she may find God.

Amber stood and looked at Jasper for a moment, then softly went away. She was bitterly disappointed to find Catherine thus enshrined as a divinity, when she herself had only asked to be as a servant. It was grievous to see her perception and love refused and herself rejected for one whom, she could not help thinking, had little to give. But stronger than her disappointment was her need of doing something practical for Jasper. For the mystic, whatever received opinion may say, is always practical. He arrives at his ideas more quickly than others, reaching the centre while they grope in a circle. And to grasp the essential is to be triumphantly practical. The world never credits the mystic with quick sight in mundane things, forgetting that, for his long gazing into infinity, better sight is necessary than for grasping obvious and clumsy facts. The mystic understands sex better than the sensualist. He can analyse malice, greed, hypocrisy, better than those who swim obscurely in their own black passions. A saint and not a devil can best unravel the psychology of evil.

Amber's heart said : " Warmth and comfort ! " She remembered that Jasper had probably had no food all day. With careful haste she went down the shallow, creaking stairs, followed by sighs, indistinct words, coughings desolate as the coughing of sheep on the wide moors, welcomed in the hall by the stern ticking of grandmother's clock and its growling, which was caused by some defect in its striking arrangements. In the kitchen the cuckoo defiantly announced the hour of one. This big shadow-ridden place always filled Amber with panic at night. It was all so cavernous ; the house seemed so haunted by broken voices. She hastened her preparations, hearing the autumn wind breathing beneath the door with the soft, long-drawn melancholy with which a horse sighs.

When she got back to Jasper, he was tramping up and down again, and the photograph was put away.

" Hullo ! What d'you want ? " he asked, in the unfriendly tone of those in stress of mind. But Amber knew that beneath the frown and the gruffness was a being who was very glad of sympathy. She saw his spirit like a little weeping boy, round-shouldered with vexation, backing into the darkest corner to avoid condolence, while watching with a concealedly eager eye for the following of love, for the outstretched hand and the carefully ordinary voice. She knew Jasper valued these things, for she had found by chance in his handkerchief drawer, carefully treasured, a letter she had once slipped under his door when he was in durance after falling foul of grandmother. She had comforted

him then, so she could comfort him now ; for whose
nerves are more sensitive in trouble, who is more un-
reachable than a boy ? She made a cheerful wood fire,
put the kettle on and spread the little meal on two
chairs. Jasper, interested in spite of himself, walked
about in a moodiness that showed signs of disappear-
ing when the ingratiating scents of tea and frizzled
bacon filled the room.

" Now, dear ! " announced Amber, conscious of reck-
lessness, for in the atmosphere of Dormer endearments
seemed out of place.

Warmed and comforted, Jasper spoke. Amber
waited, breathless, for the long-desired talk about the
events at college from Jasper's point of view, for a
word of illumination as to his own ideas ; for—possibly
—a touch of affection for herself. She loved both
boys ; but Jasper she idolized.

" Don't you think," said he, " that Cathy's an
angel ? "

That Amber did not burst into tears argued a certain
strength of character in her. That she lied cheerfully,
heartily, and immediately, proclaimed her a great lover.
For if there was a person on earth that Amber mistrusted, saw through and feared, it was Catherine
Velindre.

" So noble and above common things ! " went on the
adorer, chumbling bacon with wholesome relish.

Amber clenched her hands.

" Anyway, he likes his supper," she told herself.
" You are very fond of Catherine, I know," she said
aloud.

The room was comfortably reassuring, Amber re-
ceptive, but not inquisitive (curiosity is a weed-killer
to young confidence). The barriers came down.

" Fond, Ambie ! Fond ! I'd die a thousand deaths
for her. I'm not good enough even to be her friend,

and yet——" his voice went from him in an undignified husk, for it is only in grand opera and in bird-land that the lover's inmost heart is spoken with unwavering tunefulness. In the daily life of man huskiness hovers round the gates of expression with humiliating insistence, and the helpful lozenge is not always handy.

" Jam ? " queried Amber practically. " You like strawberry."

Jam acting as a demulcent, Jasper took up his tale.

" I wish we were back in the old days, and I could gallop away with her colours on my helmet and tilt with everybody in her honour ! "

His face was exalted, flushed with the embarrassment of self-expression, his dark hair ruffled. He looked younger than ever, and he always looked too young for his years. The idealist, if the world lets him alone, keeps his childhood until he dies. He only loses it if some great emotional tempest ravages his being to the depths. Amber thought : " He looks like a dear fluffy chicken ! " She said : " I'm glad you can't. You'd get so knocked about. They always did."

" I want to do hard things for her."

" It seems to me that you have something quite hard enough to do—living here at Dormer with Peter put above you, and not quarrelling with him or with Ernest. Not giving in and yet not arguing, nor irritating them all."

" O Lord ! What a life ! "

" If I were you, I should go out into the world."

" If *she* came too ! " His beautiful eyes had such a look of rhapsody and blazing passion that Amber, flushing, turned away. The old slumbering longings, the old unconquerable desires flamed up within her anew. No ! She would never have a lover. Catherine, with her beauty ; Ruby, with her abundant health—

lovers were for them. But who would ever seek in Amber Darke, so still, of so sad-coloured an exterior, the creature of fire and tears that could feed a man's heart with faery food and call him into Paradise with songs wild as those of hawks on the untrodden snow-fields ?

"Of course," said Jasper, "you don't know how a chap feels. But to me it would be heaven just to pile up everything I had in front of her—if I had anything worth giving."

"She'd take it," said Amber.

"And hell would be—her misunderstanding me."

"You think she understands you now ? "

"Oh, yes ! She doesn't approve, but she under-stands. She's got such a lot of sympathy."

"H'm ! "

"As long as she believes in my motives, everybody else can go hang."

"I believe in you, Jasper."

"Do you ? " His tone was grateful, but indifferent.

Amber sighed audibly.

"Would Catherine, now that they all think you so wicked, marry you ? "

"Marry me ? Marry me ? " Jasper tasted the delicious, commonplace phrase as if it were new honey. "Marry me ? "

All the flutes of the morning were playing fantasias in his head. How soft and persuasive they were ! How sweet and maddening ! They were like the birds in Dormer forest when the April madness had them under its spell. And Amber, commonplace, sisterly, dull, Amber had started them. He looked at her ruminatively. He had never, until now, thought of Catherine as his wife. He had dwelt upon her with the selfless imagination of a poet's first love. Amber's stray words had altered his whole point of view, as stray words will. Catherine Velindre would never again find the completely malleable metal with which she had been accustomed to deal. A hardening alloy had been introduced, and Catherine's clever fingers would find their work no longer easy. Despondency fell again on Jasper.

"No," he said. "I don't believe she ever would."

He was once more wrapped in reserve; the flutes had made him shy, aloof. What should Amber know of them? What could she know of the music of passion? The cries of the Venusberg, so shrill and fierce, were not for sisters' ears.

"And you wouldn't change your views, Jasper? Not even for her?"

Jasper's chin came out. Immediately it seemed to Amber that her mother had impinged on their talk.

"No! Not even for her!" said Jasper. His face took on a sombre and forbidding look—a look that boded ill for his happiness. Then his eyes brightened.

"But she wouldn't ask it. She's too large-minded. Although she's very religious, she'll understand that my way is right for me. She'll be tolerant."

"Like Ernest!" Amber said it with a smile.

"Tolerant, great-aunt, tolerant!" quoted Jasper. His mimicry of Ernest was so inimitable that Amber had to stifle her laughter in the pillow. She had a rare capacity for mirth. Her aspect of controlled gleefulness was continually apt, without notice, to break out into laughter as violent as that of Isoud of fragrant memory, who, as the naïve chronicle remarks, "laughed till she fell down." This whole-hearted laughter and the irrepressible humour behind it had stood her in good stead at Dormer. She had been known, in moments of grave family crisis, when the atmosphere was heavy and electric, and all minds were sternly exercised over a delinquent, to collapse into helpless and infectious laughter. Grandmother would speak of " the crackling of thorns," and Mrs. Darke would say, in her green-ice tone, " I hate a laugher ! " Catherine would merely look pained.

" You know Ernest's coming next week ? " asked Amber.

Jasper nodded glumly.

" And I think, I'm afraid, he wants to marry Ruby."

" Great Heavens ! Can't it be stopped ? " Jasper spoke with such real disgust, as if at something unnatural and indecent, that Amber was again overwhelmed in laughter. But her eyes grew mournful when she thought of Ruby.

" I'm afraid not," she said. " You see, they all want it, and Ruby's such a child. She thinks of things like rings and dresses."

" Don't you ? " Jasper was momentarily curious about his elder sister.

" Oh, no."

" Would Cathy ? "

" No.   She's above *that*."

What Cathy was not above remained unspoken ; for at that moment the cocks began to crow down in the misty morning fields, and within the house the passing of time became audible ; for the clocks struck in every room, and it was as if Time's robe had rustled.

" I must go," said Amber. "Sarah will be down soon."

When she had taken back the supper tray and regained her own room, she looked at her face in the mirror. It gazed back at her, twenty years older for the night of watching. For perceptiveness and emotional beauty, even the gift of humour, must be paid for to the last drop of vitality. Hence the poet very often dies in early youth, the lover of humanity is smitten by disease, those who would be the Christs of the world have " faces marred more than any man's."

" Ah, well ! what does it matter ? " she thought. " Nobody notices what I look like."

Yet the irony of the fact that, in growing nearer to the spiritual ideal hinted by her own face in childhood, she had lost the physical expression of it, was bitter. The spirit, after all its wild burning, had left her face not gaunt and riven (she would not have minded that) but commonplace. Her eyes should have been, according to poetic justice, clear pools for God and His tremulous retinue of shadowy woes and glimmering joys to lean across and watch their delicate reflections. But they were dull and sad. This is often so with minds of peculiar strength or tenderness. The world lays such heavy burdens on them that something must break. The soul is impregnable, so the body breaks. The people whose eyes are clear pools are usually those who, being completely vacant in soul, put all their vitality into physical well-being and have a good digestion.

She leant from her window into the twisted, ancient pear tree that grew round it, watching the yellow leaves floating, hesitant, to the wet, brown soil ; hearing the late pears, left ungathered a day too long, falling with faint thuds, as their stalks, severed by damp and the slight frost, gave way one by one.

" I must tell Enoch," she thought. For out-of-doors Enoch was the providence of the family, as Sarah was within. Amber lay down, but she could not sleep, seeing ahead of Jasper the rocks he could not see, the inevitable conflict that must arise when two entities wish to go linked through life, but are attracted to opposite paths.

" I wish I didn't know Catherine quite so well," thought Amber. " Perhaps I misjudge her."

But cold, smooth as a well-cut mirror, changeless as

fate, Catherine's personality floated up before her. She heard the clash of wills, the baying of the pack of bitter thoughts, warped loves, disillusionments, despairs. The scene was laid for tragedy—not necessarily overt tragedy, but a drama of the spirit, more devastating, more searing. How was she, with her small strength, to avert it ?

She heard Sarah wrestling with the bolts and shutters, and knew that the day had begun. From the pear tree came the courageous shrilling of a robin who, having breakfasted with alderman's pomp on half a pear, intended to give his audience something handsome in the way of music. And from Dormer Woods away across the water, an autumn thrush fluted pensively, like a voice calling from another world, the song of one of the elder gods out of the dædal forest.

V

FAMILY PRAYERS

AMBER was late for prayers. These were an institution at Dormer. It seemed to Amber that everyone
was unwillingly obliged, for fear of everyone else's
displeasure, to take part in them. Even Enoch's
cousin, Marigold, was under orders from Mrs. Darke
to attend and be saved, because she worked daily at
Dormer. His aunt, Mrs. Gosling, however, who
only put in a few hours' work each week, might presumably absent herself and be damned. Enoch Gale
himself, in spite of all representations, steadfastly
refused to hear the Word. He was put down as
" simple " by everyone but Sarah, who would say
to him on Ash Wednesday or Good Friday : " Well,
we've bin through a long sitting to-day. Nigh on
half an hour. There's more sense at the back of
them calf's eyes of yours than a body 'ud think,
Enoch ! "

She hoped that these veiled compliments would lure
Enoch to commit himself as to his reason for avoiding
prayers. Mrs. Velindre said it was secret sin, but
Sarah scouted this, saying : " He inna 'cute enough
to sin." Enoch never committed himself, being,
facially and vocally, as immune from self-expression
as a young owl. It was quite useless for Mrs. Darke
to send for him, and say : " You are expected to attend
prayers, Gale," or for grandmother to add : " Watch

and pray, Gale!" When Solomon said: "D'you
hear the missus, Enoch?" he replied, "Ah, sir, I
yeard the missus." But next day, as usual, he failed
to watch and pray.

This morning Jasper was also absent, and there was
more nervous tension than usual as the family watched
Amber's flurried entrance.

Sarah and Marigold sat apart like lepers on the
other side of a stretch of neutral-tinted carpet.
Solomon read the Bible in the gruff, protesting voice
of a man of action confronted by literature. Every
day he gave them a chapter, and said the same number
of prayers. But he was not the kind of man to make
such gatherings seem a mystic meeting of all the wistful
souls in the House of Life. There are some beautiful
and benignant personalities that can do this, glorify-
ing even a function which has been spoilt by respectability. They can infuse into the forms of Christianity
so grave and sweet a loveliness, as to allure the mind
—even a mind that knows them to be weaving dreams
on the loom of legend, preaching the Godhead of
Christ as the old alchemysts preached the elixir of
life.

On Sundays Solomon went once to church. Once
a month he attended "the second service." On
ordinary occasions he put a shilling in the offertory;
at Christmas, half a crown; at Harvest Thanksgiving,
gold. He was considered a good churchman, and a
good business man. He had been a land agent, but
had retired on his father's death to the ancestral house
of Dormer. Perhaps the most lovable thing about
him was his honest indifference towards every member
of his household except his two setters.

"Praise Him in His name Jah!" read Solomon,
unconsciously hurrying and blurring the words a little,
as the suave scent of hot bacon stole in from the

kitchen. Sarah was the only person who showed any interest in the remark, and she spelt the divine cognomen with an " r." Amber observed that Ruby was asleep, that her mother was busily tearing an envelope into small pieces, that Sarah was chumbling coffee berries, to which she was partial, and that Peter was staring at the isolated Marigold with extraordinary fixity. Marigold's cheeks, always of a bright cherry laid very definitely on the cream, were much pinker than usual, and her whole body drooped. Her eyes had a curious expression for which Amber could find no name. Peter looked older than his years. His rather hawk-like and fierce face had lost its round boyishness, and his quick, imperious dark eyes were those of the born adventurer. Brought up in an atmosphere of things outworn, sent to a school where the same atmosphere brooded, he could find no outlet. He was possessed of the same passion as his mother for impressing his personality on something or somebody, only his mind was not yet warped. But no one had ever told him of the great adventures of the soul ; of the trackless paths of imagination ; of philosophy and its brave search for truth ; of love and its golden abnegations, its supreme rewards. Peter would have made a martyr for any cause that had enough life in it. He was full of the defiant " I will," which in unity with " I love," moves mountains. But his temperament, his abilities and budding promise, had not been discovered or treasured, so he lounged about at home, full of urgent, aimless vitality, and spent the moments of enforced stillness at prayers in staring Marigold out of countenance. This morning Amber noticed that while Peter stared at Marigold, Catherine was watching Peter, intent, yet guarded, with an occasional glance to spare for Marigold, who seemed almost to writhe under Catherine's aloof, cold,

virginal glance, strongly tinctured with criticism.
Once Peter caught Catherine's eye and scowled ; but
she met the scowl with a half smile.

" Let us pray ! " said Solomon, and they all went
down, with more or less grace, on to their knees.

When the others knelt, grandmother remained
seated, like a stone idol which is immune, through its
very stoniness, from human movement. It was
understood that grandmother could not kneel. Only
grandmother and her Creator knew that not her knees
but her pride of years deterred her from this religious
exercise ; that, in fact, she did not choose to kneel.
This remaining upright amidst a grovelling family
gave her a satiric glee. Her gaze, travelling over the
kneeling figures, seemed to say : " Don't you wish
you were older ? " She triumphed in the fact that
her daughter—even she, the cold, the dreaded—
humbly knelt, while, by an unsuspected artifice, she
herself escaped. She enjoyed her leisurely scrutiny
of shoulders and backs of heads, noticing with secret
amusement that Ruby's blouse was undone, Amber's
hair untidy, Rachel's quite white over the ears. She
perceived also that Sarah sat on her heels instead of
kneeling (she often spoke to Sarah about this, but
without effect), and that Peter was making " mice "
with his handkerchief, to the delight of Marigold.

Serene above the array of backs, Mrs. Velindre was
also able, in her leisurely privacy, to have an occasional
game of *solitaire*, for which she had a passion. She
made this right in her own eyes by telling herself
that she was simply passing the marbles through her
fingers as nuns handle their beads, only without the
wickedness of Rome. The lugubriousness of some
of grandmother's *Amens* was not due, as Amber once
pityingly thought, to a sense of the tragedy of age,
nor, as Sarah thought, to indigestion. It was due to

the game going badly. Amber knew the truth now, for since grandmother had decided to sit next the lamp (for the better management of the marbles), her shadow had utterly betrayed her to the two girls sitting near her, and had gone grotesquely mopping and mowing—coal-black on to the dun carpet—like a long-armed imp, first to the feet of Amber, and then to the feet of Catherine, while the marbles made themselves elongated shadows, like little pillars. Amber never divulged this, though she longed to share with Jasper a joke that made her crimson with laughter night after night. Catherine's silence had a different motive. She regarded such chance bits of knowledge as so many trump cards to be kept for moments of need. She was not at all amused, but slightly irritated, that grandmother should consider her foolish ruse successful.

Amber wondered, as her father went through the usual prayers, in the usual way, what they were all there for. When they all joined in a prayer, their voices seemed to her so discordant—tuned by duty and not by love, each going loudly on its own way—that she was reminded of a dog show. She was sorry for a God who was compelled, every day at eight, to hear this, infinitely multiplied, when He might have been listening to trees or running water, or the song of birds created for joy.

" Amen ! " said Solomon, with a note of triumph, and in a moment, as by a conjuring trick, all except Sarah and Marigold were in their chairs, eating.

Mrs. Darke poured out coffee as remorselessly as if it were poison. Perhaps she was bored with the multitude of cups, but she never accepted help.

" What about Jasper ? " she asked, when the cups had gone round.

Jasper looked nervous. He hated these family

discussions that always came at meals. He had manœuvred to sit by Catherine. This was Amber's " place." Everybody at Dormer had a " place," and it was sin to take it. Amber, however, said nothing, but sat down by grandmother. This position no one coveted, as grandmother emphasized her wishes by a very sharp elbow in the side of her neighbour.

" Well ? " said Mrs. Darke sharply.

Solomon looked at his eldest son ruefully.

" I dunno," he said.

" What's he to do ? " asked his wife.

" I don't see that he can have the place now. I can't take it off Peter."

" *From*, Solomon ! " Mrs. Darke spoke with exasperation.

" From ! " echoed grandmother, in a cautionary tone, addressing the lumps of sugar that she was drowning in her cup. When she did this, her parchment face had an expression that might have been worn by a medieval lady drowning another lady in the moat.

" Seeing that Peter's gone straight, and Jasper's gone crooked," added Solomon. Jasper, looking at Peter's self-righteous expression, wanted to spring at him. The two young men, with their straight, rather Egyptian profiles, glared at one another across Catherine's head, gracefully bent. They always seemed to be one on either side of Catherine. This morning the three of them made a striking frieze, like one on an ancient vase, Catherine managing to look like gracious femininity between two types of predatory manhood.

" But Jasper will go into the Church," she said softly. " He won't disappoint us all."

" He can't if they turn him out of college," said Peter, with a loud laugh.

"He can go to another college," murmured
Catherine. "He can retrieve his mistake."

"Retrieve! Ha! Good girl!" said Solomon,
feeling at home with the word.

"I wish you'd talk to me and not at me," remarked
Jasper.

"Why not go for the Army?" asked Solomon.

"Fight the good fight," added Mrs. Velindre.

"Die for your country!" Peter put in.

"Not die, Jasper!" cried Ruby, with great concern.
"No, you must live and get very fat, like the old
sergeant at the Keep, and wear a medal, and remember
battles a hundred years ago."

Mrs. Darke looked as if she thought dying for some
respectable object was the only thing left for Jasper
to do.

"Well, my lad," suggested Solomon, "suppose we
buy you a commission?"

Catherine silently turned her eyes on Jasper, and his
pale, regular face suddenly reddened, like a statue in
a stormy sunrise.

"I'd rather stay at Dormer, father," he said.

"He's afraid!" shouted Peter, and received, above
Catherine's head, what Sarah would have called a clout.

In a moment Peter was on his feet, his chair upset
with the violence of his rising.

Sarah, who came in at that moment to "gather for
washing-up," afterwards remarked to Marigold:

"The young gentlemen's ravening sore; like two
furious cats they be. I never saw the like!"

"I'se reckon Master Peter'll be king o' the midden
if it comes to fisses," remarked Marigold.

"Wringing clothes gives you a very red face,
Marigol'—a very red face it does. Maybe, it's your
'eart!" Sarah spoke with fine irony.

In the dining-room the storm had been quelled by

Solomon's command, and the conversation continued in a highly electric atmosphere.

" If he stays, he'd better work at Arkinstall's," said Mrs. Darke.

" What for ? " asked Solomon. " I can't set him up as a farmer."

" To earn his keep," said his mother.

" In the sweat of his brow," added grandmother. She felt that this work, which Jasper was known to detest, would be a fitting judgment from the Lord.

" But I don't want to be a farm labourer ! " Jasper was dismayed.

" No. The lad must have a respectable trade," said Solomon, who had some rudimentary ideas of fairness. " You'd better be a land agent, boy."

" But I've no gift for such things, father. Can't I go on with my books ? "

" If you go into the Church."

" Never ! "

" Jasper ! " Catherine's voice was caressing. " Jasper ! Think how much good you could do."

" It's useless to argue, Cathy."

" She's a sensible girl," remarked Solomon.

" I thought," Jasper spoke hesitatingly, " I could get a job at the Keep, and bicycle there every day."

" I can't be thwarted ! " grandmother suddenly broke out. She had a theory that, if crossed, she would die. She was fond of saying : " I've got a weak 'eart, Rachel ! "—dropping her " h " not because she could not aspirate it, but because she did not see why, at her age, any letter of the alphabet should be her master. She said it now, adding : " In the sweat of his brow. It is the judgment of the Lord."

" But can you stand such hard manual work, Jasper ? " asked Amber.

" He looks remarkably well," said Mrs. Darke. She

had said the same at the death-bed of each of her early wilting sisters, for she was that curio which one meets very frequently—a stoic to the pain of others.

" Take it or leave it," said Solomon, getting up. " Board and lodging and training at Arkinstall's, or —get out."

Jasper opened his mouth to say he would get out. But Catherine, with a slanting look shot with green fire chill as ice, caught his glance in a cold spell, as the sirens caught the ships of lost mariners. Stranded and fascinated, he felt as the weaker does in the presence of the strong, that there was only one thing to do. Catherine's thin lips slid into a smile that made a dimple in her right cheek ; her hair had a living and conquering ripple, with a sheen like copper-coloured armour.

" I never could have believed," thought Jasper to himself, his eyes dwelling on her face, " that anything could be so white and so warm at once—except a rose, a hedge-top rose, out of my reach."

Then, realizing that Peter was in ecstasies of laughter, pointing at them with a shaking finger, he forcibly withdrew his eyes, and said simply :

" Arkinstall's, then, so be it."

" Amen," said grandmother.

VI

THE ADVENT OF ERNEST

ERNEST was arriving. He was bicycling from Mallard's Keep—the scene of his recent ministrations. It was twelve miles away, but as Ernest said, he was " vigorous, vigorous ! " He believed very strongly in athletics of all kinds, and one of his mottoes was : " *Mens sana in corpore sano.*" Whatever he achieved with regard to *mens*, *corpus* was a triumphant success. Some of the family waited in the hall to welcome him. The hall was large and dusky, with a stone staircase. The walls were adorned with horns, hoofs, heads, tails, feet, fur, and occasionally, with complete corpses of wild creatures. It was a savage spectacle, and when the house had been shut at night it smelt as atrocious as the most indignant ghost of a hunted animal could desire in the way of vengeance. These trophies, and various guns and whips made, with a large dinner bell, the furniture of the hall. Brown drugget ran from door to door, that leading to the drawing-room little trodden, that leading from kitchen to dining-room worn white by Sarah's emphatic feet.

Amber, seeing the group, felt indignant when she remembered Jasper's homecoming. Punctually almost to a moment, Ernest came pedalling up the drive. As he entered, he said : " Peace be to this house," and raised his right hand. He was tall and

64

stout. "A mounting of a man," according to Sarah. He was florid in complexion.

"Yes! His eyes *are* crafty," thought Amber, peering over the bannisters. His hair was very fair, and his head dome-shaped. The sparseness and paleness of his hair helped on the oviform effect. Peter and Jasper had been known, in their youth, to rush kitchenwards at Ernest's arrival, shouting, "An egg-cup!" This joke was greatly appreciated by Sarah, who always flung her apron over her head, placed one hand on her heart and one on her diaphragm, and rocked in an agony of laughter.

Ernest rather waived the clerical in his dress. It was a discreet blend of the ecclesiastical and the sporting. On the expanse of his waistcoat shone a Maltese cross, inscribed with the cryptic remark: "All in one." Why he wore this, what it meant, who first thought of it, were mysteries. Probably the phrase pleased him because of its crowdedness. He was, as he often said, "Gregarious, friend, gregarious!"

Hardly had the first greetings been interchanged, when grandmother's penetrating voice was uplifted.

"Great-nephew! I hear you!"

As a matter of fact, Ernest was so distantly related to the family as hardly to be connected, but they believed in the ties of blood, and grandmother liked to be called "great-aunt." They all repaired to the dining-room.

"You're not so deaf as you sometimes seem, grandmamma," said Catherine.

"Heh?"

"You're not deaf, mamma!" said Mrs. Darke coldly. "At least, you're only deaf when you wish it."

"The wind bloweth where it listeth!" quoted Mrs. Velindre airily. She had a gift for apparently pointless quotations which, by their very inappositeness, quelled her adversary, and were usually found, on examination, to have a sardonic fitness.

" Great-aunt Velindre ! Young as ever ! Wonderful ! Wonderful ! " cried Ernest.

" Too old to kneel," said grandmother, with what Sarah called her " downy " glance.

" When the heart adores," said Ernest mellifluously, " the feeble knee is pardoned."

Grandmother looked pleased. " D'you know," she confided in her sounding whisper, " Jasper's been a naughty boy. A very naughty boy ! He's an infidel ! "

She said it in the tone of concealed glee, with which one child will sometimes speak of another's misdemeanours.

" Ah, yes. Pity ! Pity ! " Ernest replied. " Give him line ! "

He was rather a predatory shepherd. He always spoke of " catching them young," " hauling them in," " spreading the net wide."

" It's a sign of the times," said grandmother.

" What is, granny ? " asked Amber.

" Unbelief. The end is upon us. Day of wrath ! At midnight, or at cock-crowing, or in the morning." This sentence of grandmother's had, in Amber's childhood, kept her awake night after night, afraid to go for comfort to her father, lest he should endorse grandmother's words. When sheet-lightning played across the velvet night, she would be paralysed with terror, momentarily expecting the rending blast of the trumpet. When shooting stars wandered to annihilation across her little window, she covered her head with the pillow and waited tensely, as one always awaits an expected sound, for the terrible stir of resurrection. Terrible indeed it all seemed to her, coming as it did, wrapped in the grave-clothes of grandmother's creed. Her sanity itself might have been threatened, but for Sarah's coming into her room one night, to find her hysterical with fear.

" 's Amber, 'ush your roaring," she said decidedly, when she had heard the story. " Would 'im above finish up the 'orld with all the harvest about so untidy, and the turkeys but half grown ? Not likely ! When He finishes, it'll be done proper. And I ask you, 's Amber, what time o' the year there *inna* summat in the doing ? Come to think on it, I don't see when the 'orld *could* end, for even in January there's the ewes near lambing, and the early rhubarb coming on and what not."

This peculiar theology had greatly comforted Amber.

" Great-aunt," said Ernest, " he *must* find God ! He *shall* find God ! " He had just added : " Persuasion ! Persuasion ! " when Jasper came into the room, not looking very open to suasion.

" A little talk, a quiet little talk, Jasper ! " said Ernest. " That's what we need ; that's what we must have ! "

To do him justice, he meant to help, and tried to be tolerant. But his bedside manner was too much for Jasper.

" A friendly talk ? " he concluded. " You'd like that ? "

" Enormously ! Enormously ! " replied Jasper.

Amber gave an irrepressible little gurgle, which might have passed unnoticed but for Mrs. Velindre, who pointed an accusing finger at Amber.

" Risible ! " she said. " Always was ! Laughed at her baptism. Blessed are they that weep ! "

At this point Sarah rang the tea-bell. She always seemed to enjoy these moments, four times a day, when, instead of listening in silence as she handed dishes, she was able, *ex officio*, to drown the voices of the family in torrents of noise.

Solomon and Peter came in.

" They've spared you from the Keep, then," was Solomon's greeting.

" Yes, my Vicar was kind, very kind. Let me come without a murmur."

" Willingly—willingly ! " muttered Jasper.

Grandmother, who had been watching Solomon carve the game pie, fortunately created a diversion at this point by calling out in a tone of anguish :

" I like the tid-bits ! Give *me* the tid-bits ! I'm so old ! "

" Well, you see, ma'am,"—Solomon always spoke respectfully to Mrs. Velindre. She filled him with an almost religious awe—" You see, Ernest's the guest."

" But he don't *need* the tid-bits," said grandmother argumentatively. " He's as fat as butter already. Now, *I'm* thin ! "

She was indeed cadaverous and meagre.

Amber, with difficulty controlling her laughter, looked to see how Ernest received this. But he was talking to Ruby and had not heard.

He was saying in his usual cumulative style :

" Cousin Ruby, pink is your colour. You should always wear pink. You *must* always wear pink ! "

Ruby was looking flushed and pretty. Colour was her one claim to beauty, and the pale, chiselled face of Catherine looked scorn at her on this account.

" Last piece," said Peter, pushing the bread-and-butter plate towards Ruby, " last piece and a handsome husband."

Ernest blushed.

Ruby was pleasantly aware that he admired her. To her eighteen years, this was sweet. She began to

dream of wedding cake and dresses ; to imagine how
the three church bells would ring—*Ting Tang Tong!
Ting Tang Tong!* She could see the lines of villagers
(very sparse lines, for the parish was small) watching
her triumphant progress to the carriage. Amber
and Catherine would be her bridesmaids (Catherine
would not like her being married first), and they would
help her to dress. Then her father would say something funny, and the Rector something solemn, and
her mother—(No. On second thoughts, it was quite
impossible to imagine her mother crying). Then they
would drive away, and she would have " done well
for herself." She would be a success according to
Dormer ideas. It did not occur to her that this con-
ception of marriage was like an elaborate box with
nothing in it.

She decided that Ernest's forehead was intellectual ;
that the egg-cup joke was unjust. She giggled so much
at everything Ernest said—and he said a good deal—
that Mrs. Darke frowned ominously. Then, being an
astute woman, she considered the matter and frowned
no more.

Ernest was patronizingly absorbed, and his cold
eyes rested on Ruby. Amber, from her unnoticed
corner, saw in them an expression only to be described
as greed. She could not help thinking of a toad
travelling over a strawberry bed. If Ernest had
known her thoughts, perhaps he would have modified
his summing-up of her personality, which was :
" Colourless, great-aunt, colourless ! " It was a trick
of his to sum-up people in this way. Having done so,
nothing but a portent would shake his belief in his
own decree. Amber felt more and more, that, in
spite of his good nature, she did not like Ernest. Her
eyes wandered to Jasper, sunk in gloom because
Catherine was talking to Peter. She wondered why

none of them were happy at Dormer. It occurred to
her that they were apt to treat each other as society
treats the poor—as criminals. Especially was this
so if the inner self of any member of the family dared
to peer out of its hiding—dared to show what it was,
instead of remaining concealed in what they all thought
it was. It was seldom attempted, for there are few
things so strong as mass-atmosphere. Half a dozen
people can build about a soul walls stronger than those
that were built around erring nuns ; in that prison the
living is as helpless as if he were dead. Let these
people decide that a sane man is mad (he being different
from them) and his most reasonable actions will be
twisted to madness. If he is sensitive, he will probably
be driven mad in the end, from a consciousness of
injustice, antipathy, and of the hopelessness of all his
struggles for understanding. So at Dormer Amber
was colourless, Jasper had a secret sin, Ruby needed
moulding, and Enoch was " simple."

Amber's further reflections were cut short by the
ringing of the front door bell, and by the appearance
of Sarah, who remarked in her usual stony manner :

" The Rectory ! "

To Sarah, the man without his house was a poor,
flaccid thing, like a snail without its shell. She,
therefore, made a practice of announcing houses and
not people. To such as Sarah, bricks and mortar
mean a great deal, the mind very little. So in the
village it was never " Mr. Darke's lugging the hay,"
or " Arkinstall's cutting ; " it was " Dormer's lugging,"
and " The Wallows is cutting."

" I've put 'em in the drawing-room," Sarah
remarked.

" Light the fire," said Mrs. Darke.

" Done ! " replied Sarah, who loved to be able to

meet a command in this way. It was one of her few
satisfactions in a life of drudgery performed for people
to most of whom she was indifferent, while some she
actively disliked, and one—her mistress—she hated.

A crowd of people shut up together in one house,
one creed, one strait view of life, must eventually
wear each other out. Good nature is ground down
by constant friction. Hatred leaps out like sparks
from flint and iron. Society thinks that mistakes are
made and crimes committed through the human soul
being too much itself, going its own way. But crimes
really happen through the soul being too little itself,
striving to conform, or being crushed into conformity.

The family adjourned to the drawing-room, where
the Rector stood, hands behind him, examining the
one picture in the room (excepting portraits) with the
critical, astute air of one at an Art exhibition—the
same look with which he had regarded the same picture
on every visit to Dormer in the last twenty years.

Mrs. Cantlop sat by the fire. Her hair, snow-white
and always untidy, was crowned by a lace cap adorned
with a tremendous ultramarine bow. These bows of
Mrs. Cantlop's desolated Mrs. Velindre, for she could
not wear such things herself. She had once, in emula-
tion, donned a large velvet bow ; but her daughter
had heaped such bitter scorn upon it, that the poor old
lady had given up the attempt, almost in tears.
Tears were difficult to connect with grandmother
Velindre ; one expected them to be less like rain than
hail. Since that day, grandmother's small, round,
hard head was always decked with the unambitious
caps that suited her best. She confided to Amber
how much she felt this, and how greatly she resented
the fact that Mrs. Cantlop (a younger woman ; a
much less important woman) could outshine her in
cap-wear. Not that Mrs. Cantlop did exactly *wear*

her caps. They seemed rather to have alighted un-
expectedly, like birds in a high wind, on her hair, and
they were always on one side. About all her clothes
there was this air of separate volition, as if she were
perpetually saying to them, in the words of her
favourite hymn, " Thy will, not mine, be done."

Mrs. Cantlop was engaged in tatting—a curious and
ancient occupation, which seemed to have for her a
peculiar fascination. Every blind at the Rectory
was edged with it ; the legs of the armchairs were
decently veiled with it ; cushions bristled with it ;
her own room might fairly be said to reek of it ; and
things had come to such a pass that the Rector had to
lock up his dressing-gown.

" Well, Rector ! " said Ernest, entering boisterously,
" I've come ! "

" Yes," replied the Rector depressedly. He did not
like Ernest very much, and he had been more or less
forced, by Mrs. Darke's representations, Ernest's
bland bullying and his own good nature, to give him
the curacy. Pulling himself together, he endeavoured
to infuse into his manner an air of delight, for he was
a kindly man.

" Welcome to our little community, Swyndle," he
said cordially. " I look forward to hearing you read
many a good sermon in our ancient pulpit."

" Extempore ! Extempore ! " Ernest corrected.

" As you please, of course."

The Rector himself managed to preach excellent
sermons, and to keep people awake, through being a
first-rate raconteur. By virtue of this gift he could
make the most insipid, dull or coarse narrative seem
cultured and interesting, with a gentle aroma of the
walnuts and the wine.

" I should like," said Mrs. Cantlop in her crooning
voice (it was always a croon except when, under the

visitation of heaven, it was a wail), " to add my mite of welcome, Mr. Swyndle. And so, if he were here, would Keturah's father." Here Mrs. Cantlop's voice faltered, and grandmother eyed her with contemptuous interest.

The gentleman alluded to was Mr. Cantlop. He was not, as might be supposed, defunct. He was, to use his wife's words, " looking for gold in the wickedest place in the world." He had been thus engaged for the past thirty years, but so far there was no indication of his having found any. In their early married life he had set up as a tea merchant at Dormer. He and his Maker alone knew why he thought he could get a living in this way. He did not make a living. Solomon's father, a very arbitrary old gentleman, rated him soundly and told him if he couldn't make gold he'd better " go and scrat for it." As Mr. Cantlop afterwards told his wife, " Incompetence was mentioned, and the name of California." It was useless for Mr. Cantlop to say he did not want gold, or for Mrs. Cantlop to say she wanted Mr. Cantlop. Public opinion was too strong for them. They tried to be cheerful.

" My dear," said Mr. Cantlop, " I'll seek it. I'll find it. I'll bring it." He had a gift for terse and energetic expression ; but there it usually stopped. Under the stern eye of Solomon's father the poor little man did really set out with a carpet bag and a red pocket-handkerchief and eyes even redder from the parting with Amelia, and a ticket provided by the Rector. Mystery had flung her curtains over his doings after this, though from his yearly letters it was known that he had arrived in California. In these letters he always spoke of the gold as being just at hand. Mrs. Cantlop nearly always alluded to him as " Keturah's father," seeming to feel that his personality, taken alone, was rather misty. Keturah had ceased to exist a few hours after she began her earthly race (during the tea period), so her personality was, at best, doubtful. But taken together, rolled into a ball and shaped by her imagination, they became quite intimidating and attained a kind of ghostly awfulness, a spook-like majesty. With them —or, rather, with it, for Mrs. Cantlop had made out of two nonentities an entity—the timid old lady was even able to enter the lists with grandmother. That lady held her in unutterable scorn, because she was " nesh," and because she was not a grandmother. To Mrs. Velindre her own life seemed eminently right and laudable. She was a mother and a grandmother. It did not occur to her to wonder, before engaging in these occupations, whether she was fitted for them. Nor would she ever have thought, as she looked at her daughter's face—chill, secret and expressionless as granite—that perhaps she was a greater failure than Mrs. Cantlop.

The two old heads nodded at one another across the large, chilly room. They were like generals in a battlefield many times contested. The Dormer drawing-room was, in some curious way, reminiscent of a mausoleum. The vault-like air ; the white marble mantelpiece recalling tombs ; the wreath of wax camelias made by Mrs. Velindre in early youth and by her jealously treasured ; the heavy curtains of purple cloth and the immense valance, weighted with balls and fringe, that concealed their union with the curtain rod as if it were an indecency—all these, and the solemn hush that pervaded it, slowly gathering Sunday by Sunday like a rising sea, made it less like a sitting-room than a grave. It was obviously furnished out of the bequests of a great many people with tastes that agreed, as a rule, only in being execrable. The room seemed full of the waste products of ineffectual lives—full, indeed, to repletion. The wills had been thorough ;

everything had come. Great-Aunt Darke's two emu eggs, her alabaster vase and its red wool mat were here as well as her Chinese cabinet and her own harsh portrait. Another great-aunt, who seemed to have been gentler than most of them, and not well-dowered with this world's goods, had left a sampler and three shells with " the sea in them," as Amber used to say. " You mean, the mighty sea," Catherine corrected, for she liked things on a grand scale. And Jasper, Sunday after Sunday, irritated his mother and suffered severe slappings by reason of his unceasing question, uttered in a low but obstinate voice : " Why is the sea in the shells, Mamma ? Who put it there, Mamma ? Who made it sing ? "

There were a few beautiful things in the drawing-room, but they were obscured by the rest. An exquisite Chinese plate hung among a crowd of others painted with flowers by ladies of Dormer ; a delicate French fan was nailed up between two of grandmother's home-made ones, constructed of fowls' breasts and wings not always very perfectly cured. In these, which appeared all over the house, were immortalized many excellent dinners, when the Plymouth Rock or the Dorking had given its flesh for the physical and its feathers for the æsthetic well-being of the family. A small carved chest, that looked as if it might once have sheltered love-letters, held grandmother's feather duster, with which she daily stirred the ancient dust that settled on all these things as of indisputable right. On a work-table near the fire were a few silver trinkets, which caused great vexation to Mrs. Cantlop. This good lady had become, perhaps through ceaseless concentration on the desirability of Mr. Cantlop's finding gold, a harmless kleptomaniac. She was what Sarah called " a magpie to metal." Though she was the most transparently honest soul in Christendom, it always happened that her large black silk apron was quite lumpy with things concealed beneath it by the end of the evening at Dormer.　Sometimes Mrs. Velindre pounced upon the first offence ; sometimes she waited. To-night she pounced.

" What are you doing with my grandson's christening spoon, Amelia Cantlop ? "

" Doing ? " said Mrs. Cantlop, very flustered, and obviously extracting it from her apron, " I was just minding me what a sweet baby Jasper was ! "

She melted into tears.　She did this as naturally and easily as snow melts in a warm spring.　The feat was very mysterious to Mrs. Velindre, whose emotions were in perpetual cold storage.

" Not your baby, any way," said Mrs. Velindre.

" And eh ! how the poor child cried when the Sign was put on him !　It seemed like something boded."

" That was Sattan coming out ! " said grandmother complacently.　" He's in all young children."

" Not in Jasper, I'm sure !　For Keturah's father said——"

" He couldn't say.　He'd gone to look for gold ten years back when the child was born.　You've no head for dates, Amelia Cantlop ! "

" I was always thought a great one at my book," said Amelia valiantly.

" You can't mind the big holly being felled ! "

" I can !　And I mind Keturah's father picking a leaf off it and writing with a pin : ' Love, honour and cherish ! ' "

" H'm !　Fine words !　But he didn't act up to 'em."

" We are all weak mortals," said Mrs. Cantlop. " Only the Spouse never faileth."

While Ernest said " The Captain," Sarah—" 'im above," Mrs. Gosling—" the Lamb," and grandmother —" the lion of Judah," Mrs. Cantlop said " The

Spouse." She let it be tacitly understood that in Mr. Cantlop's place, the Spouse would long ago have found gold.

Ernest came softly up to Jasper, leaning over him, laying a large white hand on his shoulder, murmuring with his slight lisp—

" My dear fellow, remember your baptism ! "

Jasper flung round. " What the deuce has my baptism to do with you ? "

" You cannot annul it ; you cannot spoil it ; you cannot get away from it. What we have, we keep."

" Shut up ! I won't argue."

" I hope we shall be fast friends," said Ernest. He held that a clergyman's work was threefold—to persuade, to punish and to pardon. At present he was trying the first.

" You only want to be friends in order to convert me to your peculiar superstition."

Ernest waived this. " I am gregarious," he said.

This was so true, as all Ernest's acquaintances knew to their cost, that Jasper smiled. Encouraged by this Ernest added :

" Also, I am responsible, dear lad, for your eternal welfare ! "

" Who gave you authority over me ? "

" The voice of ordained authority," said Ernest, in what he judged to be the typical tone of that authority, " is the voice of God."

" What did you get ordained for ? " Jasper inquired.

" I took Holy Orders because I was called."

" You took them," said Jasper, " because Great-Uncle Swyndle left his money to the first relation to take orders."

Ernest was saved the necessity of a reply by the departure of the guests. This was always thrilling

when Mrs. Cantlop was present. To-night grandmother suddenly shouted " The Rector's going ! "
in her sleepy ear, and then waited eagerly, her eyes
fixed on Mrs. Cantlop's apron. There was a silvery
clatter of spoons, paper knives and matchboxes and
Mrs. Cantlop departed, drowsy, tearful and under a
cloud, leaning on the Rector's kindly arm. The
Rector himself was depressed, for he found conversation with Ernest a great strain.

" Great-Aunt," said Ernest, when they had gone,
" you may like to see my little paper on hymns. I
read it at the Keep. Comprehensive, we hope. Tolerant,
we know. I have included the hymns of other churches
as well as Mother Church." (He had given a quarter
of a page to all hymns other than those of the English
Church.)

" They are outside salvation," said grandmother.
" They can't write hymns."

" Well, well, great-aunt, they try. We must not
quench the smoking flax. We must sympathize even
with them that are without."

" Without are dogs ! " said grandmother succinctly.

VII

HARVEST PREPARATIONS

It was the vigil of the Harvest festival, a week after Ernest arrived. The days preceding Harvest or Christmas were red days at Dormer—a time of fluttered hen-roosts and agitated pig-sties, when the air was full of shrieks and the yard ran with blood. In Sarah's calendar they were called " skriking-tide." Sarah's calendar was peculiar. She had red-letter days unknown to the churches. She was accustomed to say : " When the geese go a-stubbling, I take to my linsey petticoat. When the last chick cracks out, I cast my cross-over." In the harvest preparations she stalked about the yard grimly, her shoes reinforced with pattens, accomplishing, with Mrs. Gosling's help, feats of skill and muscle—hacking pork into joints, trussing the goose, dressing fowls.

Mrs. Gosling dressed fowls with the air of important resignation with which she always brooded over death, whether that of a near relation, a king or a spring chicken. She was " layer-out " for the neighbourhood. Dressing poultry was only her secondary gift, but she surrounded it with the same pomp and ceremony.

She would murmur : " A beautiful corpse in the coffin, Mum ! The tidiest I ever laid out." Or : " A grand bird on the table, Mum ! The best I ever drew." And in both sentences her voice was exactly the same. She was small and quiet. She seldom made a direct statement. It was a symbol of her apologetic attitude to life that the most obvious fact was modified in deference to the listener. She " liked a drop of something heartening " and was down in the Rector's private parish book as " oinos." There Solomon figured as " sound ; " Peter had a capital D, for difficult ; Jasper only possessed a large query. This book was jealously guarded by the Rector. He locked it with a silver key which he regularly left in his trouser pocket when he changed into his Sunday suit, thus enabling Mrs. Cantlop to have some interesting reading.

Sarah sat by the kitchen fire. She was expecting Mrs. Gosling, Marigold and Enoch, who lived across the water at the foot of the woods and sometimes came in when they had " cleaned " themselves. This was the happiest moment of Sarah's day, for she was exercising her artistic faculties. On the table stood a large stone ball, such as ornaments old gateways. Beside it was a heap of broken crockery. On the hob simmered a pot of glue. Sarah was affixing bits of china, reduced to the required size with a hammer, to the stone ball. This she called her " world." It was, so far, her most ambitious effort. She had done a seven-pound jampot, a " pair o' vawses " and other works, which shone with varnish on the mantelpiece. The kitchen, dusky and draughty, was paved with large grey flags, cracked and chipped at the corners. In the centre of the high mantelpiece stood a mortar and a pestle, round the white end of which the mouths of all the young Darkes had been stretched. Flanking this were the vases. To the right hung the cuckoo clock, with which Sarah found herself very much in accord, for it startled the air like a summons to battle, and the kitchen was the scene of a deadly daily battle between Sarah and inanimate things. Opposite the clock was Sarah's one picture—the photograph of the grave of a little girl (unknown to Sarah) who had distinguished herself by dying from the effects of pushing a bead into her ear. This lugubrious oddity suited a vein of religious fatalism in Sarah and Mrs. Gosling. They were never so content as when, over cups of very strong tea, they solemnly regarded the photograph in its frame of varnished chestnuts and remarked, shaking their heads : " Ah ! Poor thing ! It was to be. 'Im above was 'ware of that bead afore ever it was blowed. Some met think it was for this. Some met think it was for that. But *'e* knowed as it was for Jemima Onion's ear and a summons to glory ! "

As Sarah hammered, conscious of a large batch of successful cheesecakes in the oven, she heard Enoch come across the yard from milking. Then he rubbed one shoulder against the door, which was his way of knocking. Having taken the pails to the dairy, he sat down and began to steam, diffusing an atmosphere of manure, and watching Sarah from this shechinah with a wondering stare.

" Well ? " said Sarah, operating on half a tea-cup.

" Well ? "

" Enoch Oddman ! You'm the most aggravating man. All eyes and no tongue ! "

" Eh ? "

" There he goes ! ' Eh ? ' Words met be gold the way you 'usband 'em."

Enoch's contemplative gaze wandered round the kitchen.

" What dun you want me to say ? " he asked. His voice had a sing-song tone which always made Amber think of wind in the pine-tree. Enoch was a silent soul. Solomon chose to consider him daft, and acquired him cheaply on that account His name was

Gale, but he was called after his profession, as is often
the case in the country. Sarah did not reply to his
question, but opened the oven door and took out the
cheesecakes.

" When I wed," she said dreamily, breaking off a
bit of crust for Enoch, " 'im as I choose'll get a plenty
of these—a plenty."

" Dear now ! " Enoch spoke in the midst of
chumbling. " It eats short."

" Short ? Ah ! I'd as lief some folks 'ud be as short.
They take as long, some folks do, axin to wed, as if
they were saved in Paradise with all eternity to sing in
under their wings."

" Serious things," said Enoch slowly, " inna able to
be done quick. They mun be gone into in good
sadness."

" Mr. Ernest inna of your mind."

" Eh ? "

" Any oonty can see he's after 's Ruby. Nor 'e
wunna let the time pass like some does. Tick, tack !
Tick, tack ! and the hours hooting and nought done.
And Mr. Ernest's an example to go by, seeing he's a
surplussed clergyman (and a good few yards it takes
to go round 'im) and seeing as he can preach the
whiskers off a cat."

" Oh ! "

" And I'll tell you this, Enoch Oddman, though you
dunna deserve to know ought, for Mr. No-eyes is your
name. I'll tell you this " (she lowered her voice to the
awed and mysterious tone in which one might speak
of elocutionary marvels such as the self-expression of
Balaam's ass), " 'e'll speak to-morrow ! Ah ! I seed
him telling it over to himself very solemn, not out loud,
but talking to 'is mommets ! Sarah, my girl, I says,
to-morrow in the flush of words (for it's like a cloud-
burst when Mr. Ernest preaches the Word) his tongue

being oiled, and the words boiling in his yead, he wunna be able to stop, and he'll speak ! "

" Ah ! " Enoch was still indifferent.

" Eh, oh, ah ! " mocked Sarah. " Eh, oh, ah ! You're like the Christian Minstrels Rector got down to liven us up, choir treat. It was twang, twang ! and eh, oh, ah ! and thrum ! thrum ! like 'earts at a Hiring Fair, till I was fair melancholy."

Enoch smiled, but his eyes did not lose their wistful, rather bemused expression—the look of one just awakened from sleep-walking. This made him kin to the animals, for it is in their eyes, from the humblest to the fiercest. What are animals but souls walking in their sleep—personalities still overdone by matter, prisoned in the early stages of evolution amid the necessities of lust and blood ? Yet there, even in the eyes of a cat as it laps the blood of its victim, you may see the disquieted spirit looking on with the startled wonder of a child that has set the house afire. It is as if the animals saw, confused as the reflections in running water, what they are and what they would be ; as if they glimpsed the possibility of breaking loose from the vast machine of multitudinous physical bondage—from bloodshed, wrath, the competitive struggle for life—and saw their little spirits, shivering and afraid, but free, on the dark hills of futurity. Anyone who cared to study Enoch came upon a mystery, discovering a being so near the animal world that he could easily interpret the vague half-thoughts of a sheep or a cow, yet so far advanced along the road of psychic development that most of the other inhabitants of Dormer were pigmies compared with him. None of them, except Jasper and, perhaps, Amber, were conscious of their own souls ; they were still asleep, and in their sleep they mouthed the old righteousness of their forefathers. Enoch was awake.

Though he had not been roused by the sharp, clear trumpet of intellect, he had heard in the twilight of semi-consciousness the drowsy bell of intuition.

Enoch was never quite at his ease in Dormer. He liked to be out on the huge purple hills under the towering sky, where the curlews cried out strange news to him in passing, and the little brown doves murmured of a hidden country, a secret law, more limited than those of man, yet more miraculous. For there, to dream a nest is to build it. To desire the sea, or an orange tree in Africa, is to obtain it. Genius and love are the nearest approach we have made to this wholly mysterious life. They are akin to it, though they are at once greater and more subject to mistakes. There is something in that blind shaping of nests and cocoons and cells, in that strange swinging out in sightless faith into the limitless air that we have not yet understood.

Sarah stirred her glue like a dark-browed witch. She was what is known as hard-favoured.

" What's Master Jasper lay tongue to when he comes round along of you ? " she asked.

Enoch contemplated her in silence. Sarah stamped.

" Deaf as a post and dumb as mutton ! What a man ! "

There was a soft fumbling at the door.

" That's ours," remarked Enoch. This was his usual way of indicating his aunt, while Sarah was " the 'ooman." Mrs. Gosling entered, saying that she partly thought it was seasonable weather. Sarah was beginning work on a vase that seemed quite intact.

" You're never going to take and break that ? " said Mrs. Gosling. Enoch looked from the vase to Sarah with an expression that said, " There's nothing she won't do ! "

" It's 's Catherine's," explained Sarah. " I'm obleeged to break more things for her than for any of 'em, though the old lady runs her pretty close."

" I partly think the old lady's grave-ripe, poor thing," said Mrs. Gosling, " 'er's looking very middlin'."

" She's looking what she is," remarked Sarah, " and downy's the word. The things she'll do ! Ah ! There's a good few of 'er Uzit bottles on the World ! But this vawse of 's Catherine's I'm obleeged to break along of her making game of me in that letter to her auntie. ' Poor Sarah ! ' she says. ' Poor vawse ! ' says Sarah."

Sarah was obliged to break people's china when they offended her. It was not spite. It was a judgment, inevitable, just, as the judgment of God. You offended Sarah—you lost a vase. And, by the poetry of things, your loss was Sarah's gain, and your forfeited ornament went to the building of Sarah's *magnum opus*.

" She's sleek, is 's Catherine," continued Sarah. " But she's got sharp claws, like a little cat ! I can't abide cats ! Out, you cats ! "

She seized the broom and dislodged a tabby cat and kitten from the fender. Then the dining-room bell rang, and Sarah, after some grumbling, answered it. Returning she said : " They're ravening sore in the room. Master Jasper red as a layer's comb, and 's Amber roaring crying."

" What ails 'em ? " asked Mrs. Gosling.

" 'Im above knows ! But it's always passion-tide in this 'ouse, I'm thinking."

" There'll come a day," said Enoch in a low and singing voice, " when this bitter old 'ouse will fa-a-al."

" Fall ? " said Sarah. " When the walls are six bricks through and solid as my aunt Sophy, that weighed fourteen stone on her wedding day, so when it came to ' 'ave and 'old ' the bridegroom looked right

scared. But the best man nudged and the parson
gave the word, so he spit on his 'ands and said it like
a man."

" It'll fa-a-l," said Enoch, " like a waspy apple.   It'll
fa-a-al like rotten leaves.   And it'll fa-a-al in the night
with a weight of shadows on it."

" But that dunna tell us why they're chevy-chasing
the lad," Sarah said, fetching refreshments as Marigold
came in.

Marigold was very young, very dewy, a limpidly
sweet nonentity—a soulless fairy still asleep in the
dawn-cold flower of youth.   She sat down by her
mother and began without more ado to eat pig's chitterlings and onions.   As nobody thought of chitterlings
with anything but respect, nobody thought Marigold
was doing violence to her beauty.

" I partly think," said Mrs. Gosling, " as Master
Jasper's taken on soft and got religious.   There's a
tidy few does.   Old Lady Camperdine got it and went
for a Catholic.   The last Sunday she ever come to
Dormer Church, she took and shied the gathering bag
at the Rector's yed, with folks' money in it and all.
A beautiful corpse she made, too !   Maybe Master
Jasper's found God all of a sudden ! "

" Oh, God."   Sarah spoke with an air of indifference.
Her religion took the colour of her mind—materialistic.
Like a pool, it received whatever was dropped into it.
Every Sunday she tolerated the Rector's sermon.   She
understood that if she committed no overt act of dis-
obedience against certain arbitrary laws, benefit would
accrue to her.   Heaven would, she felt, be difficult,
but worth while, because so many people wanted to
get there and never would.   God, in her eyes, was a
person who dispensed limited favours for the pleasure
of observing the antics of humiliation in which the
recipients were obliged to indulge.   Respectability was

the end and aim of life. To be in comfortable circumstances was a great credit to anyone. Such things as love, sacrifice, spiritual beauty, when mentioned in the Bible, must be taken with a grain of salt, as being written by men who lived in a very hot place and were nesh. The kind of love that meant arms round waists, smacking kisses and an eventual wedding was, of course, different.

"To my mind," she said, "it's more like love than religion."

She privately thirsted for love affairs, though usually denouncing them in public.

"Miss Catherine?" asked Marigold.

"Maybe yes. Maybe no. But she wunna stay true to Master Jasper. She's for Master Peter and the 'ouse."

"That she never is!" Marigold spoke suddenly and violently.

"You know a deal," said Sarah.

"Where you bin since you cleaned yourself?" asked Mrs. Gosling. "And what'r you bin doing?"

"Nowt."

Marigold's cheeks were very red.

Enoch's eyes, dwelling on her, were troubled.

At this moment the prayer bell rang. Marigold got up to go with a light in her eyes. Sarah also got up with "Prayers, drat 'em!"

But before they could go, Ernest entered.

"My man," he said, "how is it I never see you at family prayers?"

Enoch preserved his far gaze and his silence.

Sarah, anxious to get the day's work done, said in commiserating tones:

"Seems like he's got a lattance in the speech, sir. He'll sit the daylong mum as a Luke-tide fly. The mouth-mauling as I give un! And all wasted!"

Ernest looked at Enoch with the interest of a doctor diagnosing a difficult case.

" An impediment ! " he exclaimed, and added with militant cajolery, " A man in the Bible had an impediment. It need not frighten you away. Keep together ! All in one ! "

These encouraging phrases beat upon Enoch's placidity like waves on a granite promontory. Sarah's stern mouth so far relaxed as to smile at the cheese-cakes.

" Remember," Ernest concluded, with authority tempered by benevolence, " I shall look for you. I shall expect you. Don't be afraid. ' Just as I am,' you know, ' just as I am.' "

Ernest retired, confident of victory.

" Got 'im ? " queried grandmother sharply, as she would have questioned a rat-catcher.

" I think so—I trust so," said Ernest blandly, looking out for the evening's reading the chapter about the man with the impediment.

" I think *not*," murmured Jasper. He wandered out to the kitchen and sat down opposite Enoch. He found rest in the company of this being who neither asserted nor denied, but remained aloof, a soul crude and simple, but its own.

They had the kitchen to themselves, for Mrs. Gosling had gone to take her nightcap in luxurious solitude. Enoch was waiting for Marigold. He knew that these walks through the star-fruited wood were soon to end, for now that the Dormer family was larger, Marigold was to " live in," sharing Sarah's attic.

The kitchen door was open and that of the dining-room ajar. A hive-like murmur came along the passage.

" Enoch," said Jasper, " are we astray or are they ? "

" Master Jasper, if Mr. Ernest was astray he wunna'd stray far. They'd find un by his blaating."

" No, but, Enoch, seriously, what do you think ? "

" Oh, if it's to be in good sadness, Master Jasper! canna say fairer than—' I dunna know.' May-'appen we'm all strays. Maybe we'll ne'er find out ought till Time's gone by. But I canna see as it's to be found out," he nodded sideways towards the murmur, " that-a-way. Nor yet from a bit of a four leaf clover on Mr. Ernest's belly."

VIII

When Ruby woke next morning, the early harvest bells were ringing up the valley, the rooks were loquacious in the upper woodlands, and Sarah was thundering on Ernest's door.

" Mr. Ernest shanna say Sarah Jowel started 'un late the day he's askin' to wed ! " she said to Marigold. " For ask to wed he will, afore dark."

Soon Sarah appeared with an unwonted cup of tea for Ruby, and Ruby's happiness increased. For she loved a cup of tea, strong and creamy, and a picture book and a soft pillow ; and at the back of her mind was the thought that Ernest would certainly " speak " to-day. She raised her beautiful and indolent body sufficiently to drink.

" Has Miss Catherine had some ? " she asked.

" 's Catherine's not," was the reply. " For she's gone to the seven o'clock, and when 'er goes to that 'er clems. Though why 'im above should take it unkind if she went full, is more than Sarah Jowel knows. I'm as earnest after religion as most, but my stomach's my own."

So saying, she flung back the curtains, and there was Ruby in a flood of yellow sunshine, friendly to her young splendour, but cruel to Amber, who was leaning from her window drinking the golden day.

Ernest also was up, looking very pink and clean,

reading in a new little manual he had brought with
him, which was a service of prayer for those contemplating marriage. It began with a prayer before the
proposal, and went straight on, as it were, on the
crest of the wave, to the banns, the wedding, and the
children. What happened if " the answer was no,"
as Enoch would say, did not appear. Only the
successful were catered for. To do Ernest justice, he
meant very well in reading this book. He nearly
always did mean well. He wished to do right and he
wished others to do right in his way. What would
have happened if his church, instead of telling him
that what he wanted was right, had told him that what
he wanted was wrong, it is not easy to say. Fortunately, it had never yet happened. Ernest knew
it was right for him to marry Ruby, and rear a large
family. Ruby's point of view never occurred to him.

" Well, 's Ruby," said Sarah, " you do take the eye ! "
She felt romance tingling in the air. Romance, to
her, did not depend on anything so ephemeral as love.
So long as the dresses, the cake, and some sort of a
bridegroom were got together, what else mattered ?

And Ruby, sipping her tea, basking in the sunshine,
idly admiring the texture of her skin under the light,
and the full curve of her breast, was of very much the
same opinion.

That which Sarah had prophesied duly came to pass.
After the service Ernest hurried out of the vestry in his
cassock and detained Ruby, who was lingering rather
expectantly. They wandered beneath the swart yews,
which canopied the churchyard mournfully, shadowing
the grotesquely shaped tombs—obelisks and sarcophagi,
needles of stone, an immense triple-tiered round erection
of fluted marble, like a wedding cake, and a stout stone
boy, apparently of negroid extraction. All these

tombs were greened over by lichen, and as Ruby and Ernest walked under the trees their faces took a greenish tint, as if upon them also it had gathered.   Keturah Cantlop's grave was smothered with waxen wreaths in glass cases, for Mrs. Cantlop added a new one every Easter.   She thought them far more beautiful than real flowers.   The little mound, thus decorated, lying so darkly by the water under the heavy yews, had given Ruby a great distaste for white flowers.

When they came to it she shivered and turned away. Ernest did not notice.   He was flushed and heated with the service and with the consciousness of having preached a successful sermon.   As Sarah would have said, he was " flown with words."   Mrs. Cantlop, who enjoyed many a half-hour's nap under the mellifluous ebb and flow of Ernest's self-expression, said, when Ernest's preaching was criticized in her presence : " Ah, well !   He has a gift for imparting knowledge." To this Catherine had rather tartly replied :   " If only he had any to impart ! "

Ernest was, therefore, pleased with himself, Ruby and their background of the world in general.   He was only waiting to gravitate again to the scene of his triumph until Solomon and Mr. Arkinstall had gone. These two found the vestry convenient for their weekly talk.   Before church they argued.   During the service they seethed.   Afterwards they quarrelled bitterly.

When they came out, Ernest said : " Come into the vestry, cousin Ruby."   She was not his cousin, but Ernest liked what he called the homely ties and titles of relationship, and if they were not there, he invented them.   The atmosphere of the vestry, though not so sacrosanct as that of the church, was still sufficiently hassocky.   Ernest sniffed it and found it very good. The vestry was under the belfry at the west end, and was curtained off from the church, so that the choir (who came in humbly one by one in ordinary dress, conscious of their inferiority as mere men) might robe in decent seclusion and emerge suddenly, surpliced and looking quite different from their week-day selves, when the sexton flung back the curtain with his dramatic gesture.

"Sit down, Ruby," said Ernest, proffering the sexton's carved chair and himself taking the small one with the rush seat (a great concession).

Ruby felt embarrassed and alarmed, and rather as if she were going to have an operation.

In the dark-stained window above, blue-bottles buzzed, drunk with the fruit of the harvest decorations. Ruby's eyes strayed upwards. She caught herself thinking, as she watched them crawling, so tight and well-found, that they looked as if they wore cassocks.

Ernest did not hesitate. He knew what he intended to say, and he said it.

"Cousin Ruby, you must be mine! You *shall* be mine!"

"Why?"

Ruby was pleasantly conscious of a very pretty openwork yoke, and she looked up disconcertingly through a long, loosened strand of bright hair.

"Is it because you think I'm pretty, Ernest?"

Ernest moistened his lips.

"Looks are nothing, Ruby. It is a meek and quiet spirit that I ask in woman."

"Would you love me if I was like Mrs. Gosling?"

"Don't be flippant, Ruby."

"But don't you like people to be pretty?"

"If looks are an index to the mind. But bodily beauty interests me very little."

He looked long at the bright hair, the cream-and-roses skin, and licked his lips again.

" Amber says, if you love a person, you love them
because of the *me* in them.   Because they're them and
nobody else.   Will you love me that way and never
say ' clumsy ! ' or ' stupid ! ' or ' foolish ' ? "

Ernest thought it best to refrain from all mention of
moulding, and not to give her any hint that her value
lay in her ductility to the hand of the potter.

" So it is yes, Ruby ? "   He took her hand in his
large white one.

" Oh, it isn't real," cried Ruby, suddenly.   " Amber
said you felt all different, and I don't.   It will be dull
being married, if I feel just the same as I do now."

For a moment Ernest's soul, or his conscience, or his
essential self was pricked into a mistrust of itself.   The
" sense of tears " which, in a world brimful of tears,
must visit the most self-satisfied at times, stirred in
him as he looked at Ruby's childish face and heard her
callow questionings.   Then he pulled himself together,
cast aside his doubts and fell back upon custom and the
letter of the law.   Once more his spirit lay inert, a
partially atrophied organ embedded in the fatty deposit
of expediency.

" Of course !   Of course ! " he said comfortably.
" We feel different.   Quite, quite different."

This was true.   He was feeling uncomfortably warm
and was perspiring a good deal.

" Yes, Ruby ? " he suggested helpfully.

Ruby indicated that it was yes, and Ernest kissed
her.   Ruby edged away.

" Oh, your mouth is hot, Ernest !   Hot and slow
like——" she had almost said—" like a blue-bottle."
She felt as if the row of surplices that hung in folds
characteristic of their wearers, watched and criticized.
There was the Rector's, straight and spare, seeming
to deprecate tatting ; Mr. Arkinstall's, long, with a
kind of smug droop ; Ernest's own, starched and

robust ; Mr. Dank's (he was organist) almost hidden beneath that of Mr. Mallow, the constable. Mr. Mallow's was the largest of all. It was his astral self. It hung in the swelling folds admired of Sarah. It was like a football from which the inside is removed —a touch will collapse it, but until the touch comes, it seems to be the same round, hard ball as ever. By virtue of it Mr. Mallow's presence, breathing Law, still haunted the vestry.

Ernest was huffy, with some excuse. He took off his cassock and said " Home ! " while Ruby still eyed the blue-bottles with fascinated disgust. Going out, in her confusion and hurry she stepped on one of the trailing bellropes, and down from the belfry came a tiny mournful toll. Going out between the sheaves of corn, Ruby's eyes, which had been vacant and asleep, took a gleam of wakefulness, and within the wakefulness was a seed of fear.

When they told their news to the family, grandmother smacked her lips. To the old, or the mentally unoccupied, or the spiritually slumbrous, events are a stimulant—almost their only stimulant. Grandmother was not at all interested in the thoughts of those she lived with, but she was absorbedly interested in their doings. Let them fall from heaven to hell in the life of the soul—grandmother would not be aware of the slightest change in their condition ; but let them cease to take sugar in their tea—grandmother was all agog in a moment. So now it was she and not Mrs. Darke who questioned as to the date of the wedding.

Ruby giggled.

" Soon, great-aunt, soon ! " said Ernest.

" Where'll you live ? " asked Solomon, who, as he said, scented mischief.

" Well, if convenient——" Ernest looked at Mrs.

Darke, with whom he had already prudently arranged matters.

" They'll live here," said she.

" Until I attain my vicarage."

Ernest always spoke of this vicarage as if it were abuilding for him in some terrestrial foretaste of Paradise, and were his for the taking. This attitude annoyed Catherine, her contempt for Ernest being extreme.

" You've had one offered you then ? " she asked, in the smooth, Persian-cat manner which made Sarah so wrathful.

" Well, to be accurate, not yet, not exactly."

Ernest generally went to pieces when in conflict with Catherine. Then he reflected that Catherine was perhaps jealous of Ruby ; he rallied.

" Though, until I get my vicarage, I shall not need a helpmeet, I do want a companion," he explained. " It is not good for man to live alone."

" Alone ? In this house ? " Jasper spoke with a kind of bitter wonder. His eyes, travelling round the room, were so full of mingled disgust and half-comic dismay that Amber with difficulty kept her gravity.

" Never alone ! " said grandmother. " There is an Eye that watches. There is an Ear that hears."

Ernest adjusted his collar, beaming. " I'm gregarious—gregarious," he said.

Jasper groaned.

" I love my fellows, and I hope—I may say I think —that my fellows love me."

He had the unconscious conceit of those temperamentally gregarious people with whom companionship has become a lust ; who think they are always wanted ; who mistrust and hate the lonely soul that does not want them. Eventually, these people become exasperated with the non-social being and (by way of a cure) shut him up with a great many other people in some prison of the body or of the mind. Very often the first time in his life when the unfortunate being is allowed the privilege of loneliness is when he lies, at last, in his grave.

"Yes, I am sociable—very sociable. But one needs more. One needs, in short, a wife, one with whom to share the lifelong eucharistic sacrament of marriage."

"No popery!" cried grandmother suspiciously. The word eucharist always annoyed her. She and Ernest did not agree very well, he being "High" and she "Low," he saying "Ah-braham," while she said "Ay-braham." Such a difference even religion could not bridge. At this point Ruby, who had been staring at Mrs. Darke like one hypnotized, suddenly burst into a torrent of words.

"Live here? Live here? But when people are married, they have their own house, and furnish it and have presents and a storeroom——"

"When Ernest gets his bishopric you'll have all that, dear," said Catherine. But Ruby took no notice. She was stirred to the depths of her not very deep personality.

"If I can't have a house and a storeroom and a trousseau, what's the use of getting married?"

She burst into loud crying. Ernest came forward and laid his well-kept right hand on her shoulder.

"You will have *me*," he said with suave simplicity.

Ruby looked up at him with an expression that seemed to Amber to say that Ernest was the fly rather than the ointment. She cried louder. But grandmother saved the situation. She tapped her stick with authority.

"Clothes! The child must have clothes for the credit of the family. She's gotten what she has in a pretty pickle! Hey! She's a tomboy, and so you'll find, great-nephew!"

Ernest looked as though he were prepared to mould any quantity of tomboys into patterns of wifeliness.

"Gowns!   She shall be brought unto him in a raiment of needlework.   I must have a new one too, and a cap." She eyed her daughter, conscious of temerity.

"No bow," said Mrs. Darke.

"I *will* have a bow! My grand-daughter's being married, ain't she?"

"You're too small, mamma."

"Son-in-law!" cried grandmother.

"Ma'am?"

"You must have out the closed carriage and Enoch must drive us to the Keep.   There are some nice new caps at Mrs. Griffin's, with *small* bows"—this with a pleading glance at her daughter—"for Sarah saw 'em last time she was there.   When was it, Sarah?"

"Monday was a week, mum," said Sarah, sweeping crumbs with the action of a mower.

"So you'll order the carriage, son-in-law?"

"I suppose so, ma'am; eh, Rachel?"

Mrs. Darke nodded.   At once the closed carriage, Enoch and Mrs. Griffin became enrolled in the book of destiny.

Ruby brightened.   Edging away from Ernest's hand, she sat down at her grandmother's feet with a confiding air.

"Will you buy me frocks, granny?"

Among Mrs. Velindre's good qualities was a certain generosity which, though perverse and variable, could always be counted on at an occasion like this.   For she loved a merrymaking almost as much as a funeral. She was just going to assent when Mrs. Darke said: "You will have what's proper, Ruby."

"There! Kiss your mother, Ruby," said Ernest. Ruby did so, murmuring:

" White satin and a veil ? "

" Is white satin suitable to a country girl ? " asked
Catherine non-commitally. She had a way of managing people through these vague questions. " Why
not muslin ? " she added.

" Ruby would look very nice in satin," said Amber,
" and not nearly so nice in muslin."

Mrs. Darke hesitated. It was really a satisfactory
match. The economy of it pleased her, for it was
only a case of telling Sarah to move Ruby's things
into Ernest's room, and of having Ruby's food paid
for by Ernest. Yes. It must be encouraged. But
white satin was absurd.

" What does great-nephew say ?" asked grandmother.

" I don't care what he says ! " cried Ruby, stamping,
and drowning a murmured—" Not in putting on of
apparel "—" if I can't have satin, I won't marry you,
Ernest. There ! "

Ernest moistened his lips slightly. Decidedly
moulding was required. But for the present——

" Well, great-aunt, I think Ruby would look well,
very well, in satin. It would do for parties after,"
he added frugally.

" At the Palace," murmured Catherine.

" Very well, Ruby," said Mrs. Darke. " White
satin and no nonsense."

" No nonsense ! " echoed grandmother firmly, but
with a sneaking fear that caps with bows—even small
ones—were nonsense.

" Can we go soon ? " Ruby's spirits were rising
fast. " Can we have the band to dance with, and a
knife and fork tea ? "

" I don't see why not," said Solomon. " The first
to go and all."

" Only I'm not going ! " Ruby's lips trembled again.

" Very well," said Mrs. Darke, seeing another outbreak imminent.

Ruby was pacified, and Solomon and Ernest were
able to retire and discuss the financial side of the affair.
For in respectable houses marriage by barter is still
the fashion instead of the much more interesting
marriage by capture and the rare, seemingly almost
unattainable, marriage for love.

Ruby fixed the day, early in November, after very
little persuasion. She was dull and her mind was not
sufficiently furnished to be any entertainment to her.
So the prospect of excitement, a stir, new possessions,
was very attractive. As Sarah said, it was all fixed
up as neat as egg-and-bread-crumbs.

It never occurred to Ruby that in her passion for
the acquisition of goods she was losing herself.

IX

IT was beneath one of the grieved skies of early October that the five women set forth to buy Ruby's finery. Amber noticed how the clouds lay in long bars of faded lilac on a background of pale, irradiant yellow, wherein faint veinings were visible, like those in a sweet pea. Across the lilac and the yellow and the pale golden lines floated on the damp westerly wind small tear-coloured clouds.

Amber's thoughts were sad-coloured also, as she looked out of her window at grandmother's piercing call :

" Grandchildren, I'm waiting ! "

Ruby was so boisterously gay, so full of song, so lavish of confidences and childish hugs, that she seemed pathetic, almost tragic. Amber reflected that Ruby lived on the smooth surface of life—a surface that covers all the griefs, the boiling hatreds, the wild impossible loves and the white-hot despairs under a decent exterior. But for all its smoothness, Amber thought, it was only a lava crust. The volcanic fires might break through at any moment, consuming, terrible. She was afraid for Ruby. She felt, as she had felt for Jasper, a creeping dread of something sinister, not coming from without, but lying dormant—a seed of evil—somewhere in the ghostly recesses of the house itself. She hastily counted up her pocket money, destined to be spent at the jeweller's on a watch for Ruby. For, as if there were not enough time-pieces at the Keep, Ruby wanted another. Ernest suggested silver; Catherine gun-metal. But Amber was determined that whether Ruby's life were golden or not she should at least have a gold watch.

Grandmother's voice being again uplifted, Amber ran down. The closed carriage was drawn up before the door, and revealed itself as a small brake, to which had been fastened a frame with a brown waterproof top, and curtains all round. Thus was attained the maximum of convenience with the minimum of extravagance. On the box sat Enoch, arrayed for the occasion in his fawn livery coat with silver buttons, and a kind of baby top-hat, rather rough in the nap, trimmed with corded ribbon. The horse-rug discreetly hid his corduroy trousers. Amid all the changes and chances of Enoch's upper garments—working coat, Sunday coat, livery—his nether garments remained immutable, as if to symbolize his scornful attitude towards these ceremonial robes.

" I'm up, and in ! " cried grandmother, peering like a brown bird through the brown curtains, rustling from side to side across the straw-covered floor, leaning on her tall stick. She wore her winter cape, a creation of Mrs. Cantlop's, made of multitudinous flounces of brown wool. It was really a charity to give Mrs. Cantlop work of this kind, for without tatting or crochet she was as restless as a sugarless canary. Instead of the usual black satin sunbonnet, Mrs. Velindre wore her state bonnet, a helmet of net and beads tied under her witch-like chin with a huge purple bow.

Ernest, Solomon and Sarah came to " send " the

party, while Marigold and Mrs. Gosling hovered in the shadows of the hall.

"Well, Marigol'," said her mother, as Ruby dashed downstairs with ribbons, veil and scarf flying, "I'm in behopes the poor thing'll live. She eats hearty and she looks hearty, but I partly think the strapping uns go quickest. There was Polly of the Mill, and there was Mary Anne of the World's End Public, as faded with the fading of the first year, and died at Tummas-tide. But they do say she laughed at a blind man at the lych-gate as stood to bless the bride, so it served un right, seeing the poor fellow was dark."

"Dunna crake so, Mother. It's easy talking for you with troubles done and nought in mind but dressing poor folk for Judgment. But for them with their troubles to come——"

Mrs. Gosling meditated. Then she said:

"Enoch looks grand to-day! The livery sets him off, and that majenty tie."

Marigold tilted her nose scornfully, muttering: "Enoch, indeed!" and a burning blush ran from neck to forehead.

"'s Ruby!" commanded Sarah. "Wait till I fettle you, or they'll say at the Keep as Dormer folk goes to town with their things daggly all about. But it's Mr. Ernest as ought to tie the laces, for luck."

Ernest did so with no very good grace; for when he knelt, he liked a hassock.

"I wish Sarah would know her place," muttered Mrs. Darke.

"Know your place, Sarah!" piped grandmother, who was very much excited.

Sarah folded her arms.

"I thank 'Im above as I know my place as well as most, mum," she said, mentally selecting one of grandmother's Spode vases for oblation to the "world."

Solomon, who had watched them get in and who now
scented a domestic disturbance, said : " Gee-hup,
Enoch ! "

" Up, Solomon ! Not ' hup,' " said Mrs. Darke.

" Up ! Up ! " shrieked grandmother, like Deborah
arousing the Israelites. They swung out of the gate,
the curtains flapping ; Ruby chattering, losing her
purse and finding it again ; Catherine sitting, very
cool and polite, opposite grandmother, who indulged,
at every declivity, in ejaculatory prayer, and took
the more mundane precaution, at the worst hills, of
prodding Enoch with her stick to remind him to be
careful. Meanwhile Solomon took the gundogs into
the dining-room, which was forbidden, and sat down
with a stiff whisky and soda to concoct a letter to
Mr. Arkinstall which should, without bringing him
under the law, convey to that gentleman exactly what
he (Solomon) thought of his proposed fee for teaching
Jasper to farm.

Sarah, Mrs. Gosling and Marigold retired to the
kitchen, where they revelled on cold pie, colder prog-
nostications and green tea, which Mrs. Griffin procured
especially for grandmother. Mrs. Velindre always
drank this, not because she particularly liked it, but
because it reminded her of her youth, which had
receded so far into the past that she revered it almost
as much as the Bible. If ever Mrs. Griffin was " out
of " green tea, being a very complaisant person, she
hated to say so. She, therefore, put down " green
tea " in the bill. But, being very honest, she only
charged the price of black. Whereupon grandmother
cried jubilantly : " Green tea's gone down ! " and
enjoyed the black inordinately.

Ernest went to his room to touch up a little book
of sermons which " friends at the Keep " had asked
him to publish. No one could ever find out who

these friends were. Catherine suggested that they must have been his landlady, who couldn't read, and her son, who was deaf and had not heard them. It was to be called " Gleanings from the Sermons of a Parish Priest." Sarah, dipping into it while doing Ernest's room, remarked to Marigold : " If this is only the leasing, God save us from the stooks."

Meanwhile the equipage trundled along through the lonely, deep, dim-burning countryside. First through the outer precincts of Dormer forest, where the tall beeches and the mountain ash trees, slender and haughty in their flaming scarlet, seemed to give as little heed to the passing of the carriage, with its tumult of human tongues, as to the crawling of a brown beetle in the grass, but remained, wrapped in their age-long meditation. Here the road lay beside Dormer brook, which flowed—mute, brown, and covert—beneath trees so close and heavy that they plunged the road into green twilight. Tall, early-tinted poplars pricked up, covered with beaten gold, like spires belonging to a worship secret and remote. Sparsely in the hedges grew the pale, infragrant flowers of early autumn—wild snapdragon, scabious, purple and blue, wan yarrow and the forlorn harebell. Amber gathered some of these for Ruby as they walked up the long hill at the foot of which Jenny always stopped, looking round with an appealing air and the expression of a reasonable person putting the case to another reasonable person.

" Tabor on a bit, Jenny, my girl ! " said Enoch, and the carriage meandered up the hill.

Amber thought : " It's autumn with me, cold autumn ; and it's never been summer." It was of the sadness of autumn that she thought—of the tearful harebell and not of the golden spire. For a

moment she envied Ruby.   She was, at least, plunging
into life of some sort. Then suddenly the affair
appeared to her startled mind exactly as it was—a
compact between ignorant vanity and calculating
lust.

" Do you love Ernest ? " she asked in a tremor.

Ruby was not offended.

" Well enough," she said.

" Oh, turn back ! Turn back ! It's not too late."

" Too late for what ? "

" To save yourself."

" But I don't want to be saved. I want to be
married."

" Oh, you don't know—you don't think——"

" How do *you* know ? "

Amber paused ; she tried to find the explanation
of what she knew, how she knew it.

" It's something deep down," she said, " far down,
like a pool in a mountain hollow. I look down ;
I see things pass there, faces looking up, hands beckon-
ing. It's as if the things other people have felt come
and lean over me. And I see them, far down and
faint——"

Ruby laughed, startling the little birds that feasted
in the hedges.

" I suppose that's some of Jasper's stuff," she said.
The family always took it for granted that Amber's
remarks must be derivative.

" Oh, Ruby ! Don't laugh. Think ! Wake up !
Marrying a man you don't love is being hired at a
hiring fair for wives."

" What things you say !   But Ernest does love me."

" How much ? "

" As much as his nature lets him, I expect."

" Then tell him to go away and increase his
capacity."

Once more the little birds fled up before Ruby's laughter.

" How could he go away when he's curate of Dormer ? What would mamma say ? Oh, Ambie, it's a good thing you're going to be an old maid ! You would give your young man an awful time ! "

An old maid—an old maid ! Ruby was unconscious of the sharp pain she had given ; of the passionate rebellion she had aroused.

" Yes ! She is right," thought Amber. " She is marrying. Catherine will marry. Marigold, even Sarah, will marry. But never Amber—who would want Amber Darke ? "

She knew her limitations. Yet in some occult way she knew herself sad, not with the grief of emotional sterility, but with the sorrow of the honeyed flower that no bee visits.

" Still," she said aloud, " better be lonely for ever than marry without love."

" Do stop croaking, Ambie, and be nice ! "

They walked on in silence, eyed from the leafy layers above by wood-pigeons who lamented in tones impersonal yet impassioned, monotonous yet arresting. It seemed as if that for which they mourned were too old to be remembered, and had vanished, leaving nothing but a moan.

" What are you thinking of ? " asked Amber, hoping that Ruby was repenting of her decision.

Ruby looked dreamy.

" I was thinking," she said, " that Catherine will be talking mamma into muslin, and I *will* have satin ! "

Amber sighed, looking away across the plain that was rimmed with sorrowful blue—the blue of swallows that flash and are gone ; the blue of drowned forget-me-nots ; the faded blue of old men's eyes ; the blue, lucent and pure, of a child's veins ; all mingled, running into one another beyond the cloud shadows, all gathered into one sad, perfect circle.

" She wants gold for the maids' dresses ! " cried grandmother, gesticulating wonderfully.

Catherine had evidently made good use of her time. She never walked uphill. Her theory was that Jenny was a beast of burden and should therefore have burdens. As for the dresses, gold would not suit Amber. It would show up all her bad points. But herself it would suit. It would make her look like a richly-jewelled Madonna.

" Get in ! " said Mrs. Darke. " Let's get there and get done."

They climbed in and sat in an atmosphere of displeasure, knowing, without Mrs. Darke saying it, that Mrs. Griffin ought to have come to Dormer, instead of Dormer taking an unnecessary outing and going to Mrs. Griffin. Four times a year, in the spring, at midsummer, at the turn of the year, at Christmas, Mrs. Griffin's head young man visited Dormer in his gig, bringing an evangel of fashion—designs, rolls of material, all kinds of feminine gear. Mrs. Gosling still called him " the outrider."

As they neared the Keep, they met gigs and various cows and sheep, the latter wearing the expression of nervous tension which attendance at an auction gives to animals. They adopted the sensible plan, at the Keep, of doing all their buying and selling on one day. The farmer brought his cattle and the wife her butter and both invested in such things as farm and family needed—a sack of flour, a pig, a roll of scarlet flannel. The latter would be purchased from Mrs. Griffin after a sitting of half-an-hour or more. As Sarah said : " Mrs. Griffin never stinges words. Whether you lay out ten pound or ten farthings it's all one, she'll talk till your yead sings." When they passed Mrs. Griffin's on their way to the inn, there she was in the midst of a crowd of ladies buying for dear life, while their husbands had a final glass.

Dinner was awaiting them, for Mrs. Darke was no niggard where her own dignity was concerned, and liked to order things in style. They sat down in a panelled parlour with so many corners that hardly a panel was of the same size. This had been a great coaching inn, and in Mrs. Velindre's youth, several times a week, it blossomed with high-born ladies in delicate dresses.

" I mind," said grandmother, " how my Aunt Deborah brought me here to buy a white gown to be bishopped in. I was but eleven. The Bishop didn't come often, and you had to get rid of Sattan when you could. I hid an apple-cob in my pocket (Sattan being in me at the time), and the grease showed. Aunt Deborah said : ' Bishopped you *may* be. That's the will of the Lord. Birched you *shall* be. That's mine.' A very brisk woman was my Aunt Deborah."

When dinner was over, they went down the short, steep village street to Mrs. Griffin's. When Ruby had emerged from her congratulations (like a strong swimmer from a high sea) business was begun. Then those who came for buttons and those who came for pins were little accounted of ; everyone gathered round the Dormer family.

" I want," said grandmother, " a purple gown and cap with a purple bow."

From the window three caps were fetched. Mrs. Griffin's windows were very fascinating. They were many paned, high up from the ground, and bent very slightly into a gentle bow. Within, everything, from boots to velvet, from sugar to sheets, was arranged in neat boxes piled in pigeon-holes. Nothing

disdained the neighbourhood of anything else on the
counter, and there was a delicious scent of new calico,
soap, tea, apples and leather. It was, in fact, the
thing dearest to Mrs. Griffin's heart, a blend. From
tea to shot silk, from coffee to wine, she loved a blend.

Grandmother sat on a high rush chair, like a thin
little bird, balancing one of the caps on her head.

Mrs. Griffin looked at the others.

" A thought—just a thought—too large ? " she suggested.

" It would suit Mrs. Cantlop," said Catherine.

" Ah ! Mrs. Cantlop's a fine figure," said the
milliner.

Mrs. Griffin frowned at her. Grandmother was here,
and Mrs. Cantlop was not.

" Bulk ! " she murmured reassuringly. " What is
bulk to brain ? "

" The cap is too large," said Mrs. Darke. " Take it
away ! "

Finally the right cap was found, the yellow silk
and the white satin chosen, and all the other fineries
bought. They left the shop with a conquering air,
conscious that there was comparatively little that they
had not bought. The assistants, worn and exhausted,
bowed them out. Mrs. Griffin, fresh as ever, talkative
as ever, bowed them out, looking at Ruby—cause of
all this honourable outlay—with the tranced admiration with which Mr. Cantlop would have looked at
a gold mine, could he have found one. Enoch, without
emotion, loaded up. Jenny, without emotion, watched
him. Only, as she started, she shook her head sadly,
patiently, as the Rector might have shaken his over
some choirboy's peccadillo. So much useless lumber
to be dragged to Dormer ! And Amber, tired and
quiet in her corner, thinking of Ruby's reason for
marrying, and of the bridegroom, central figure to

all this pomp, and of her own dreadful appearance in the yellow dress, was inclined to agree with Jenny.

The trees, dark, leafy still, but with the rasping music of autumn in their withering boughs, leaned and muttered above them as they passed. As the night wind rose, they seemed to shout a message, a message with no words, a thought expressed in music and moanings. But the voices were so loud within the carriage, raised in altercation about the purchases, that Amber could not listen to it. She only thought : " The forest is a great artist. It is never paltry, never mean." Then she drew her coat more closely round her, for coldly with the cold wandering wind came the thought :

" The forest will sing like this when I am dead. I shall die, but I shall not have lived."

X

THE WEDDING

THE great day dawned, as such days often do, in a tumult reminiscent of spring cleaning, preparations for a family holiday, and sudden death. At seven, by way of adding her mite to the confusion, grandmother rang for Sarah.

" What is it now, mum ? " asked that sorely tired prop of the household.

Grandmother nodded sideways at her new cap, which sat on a knob at the foot of the bed in much the same way as it was to sit on her head, so that knob and cap together looked like grandmother's elf.

" I don't like it," said Mrs. Velindre. " My great-niece chose it, and I don't like it. I don't like her either."

" She's as 'Im above made 'er, mum, but I doubt He didna give full mind to the job. Seconds she is, like the teaset she gave 's Ruby."

" Is the mistress up ? "

" Not yet, thank God ! "

" She don't like a merrymaking, Sarah ! She pretends she does, but she don't, Sarah ! "

Her daughter was the one person of whom she did not speak possessively. It was always " Rachel," or " the mistress." With others it was, " my great-niece once removed," " my husband's nephew." These people, she tacitly implied, had no place in the world

except in relation to herself. Possibly the sinking
of the possessive in her daughter's case was an unconscious act of homage to an egoism even stronger than
her own. These two had been meant for individualists.
This not being allowed, they had become egoists, which
always happens on the principle that if you deny
a child sugar it will steal from the sugar basin. The
human mind, unless it is to remain nescient, must have
itself, must develop and explore itself. The more
vital, the more awake it is, the more it must turn
inwards. For within, deep in the tenebrous recesses
of sub-consciousness, man hopes to find God. Not in
churches, not in his fellows, not in nature will he find
God until he has seen all these things mirrored in that
opaque and fathomless pool lying within his own
being, and of which, as yet, we know nothing.

" Tell my eldest granddaughter to come and furbish
it up," said Mrs. Velindre.

" 's Amber's along of 's Ruby in the attic.   's Ruby's
roaring crying."

" What ?   What ?   What ?   On the wedding day ?"

" It met be she likes the taste of salt, but I know
my place too well to inquire, mum."

" Sarah !   Has Mrs. Cantlop got a new one ? "
Sarah clicked her tongue.

" 'Ow should I know, mum ?   I'll send 's Amber
to you."

She departed, arriving in the hall just as Enoch
staggered up to the door with a huge wedding post.

" Well, you've lugged us a power of things ! " said
Sarah, arms akimbo.

" I do sweat," remarked Enoch.

" Ho !   You've not begun yet.   Come you in and
lend a hand ! "

Enoch's eyes took on their most cryptic, most bee-
like expression, and he was just beginning to say :

" It wunna be able to be done," when Marigold appeared. She rushed from the kitchen, all dishevelled pink and gold, yellow hair waving, rosy print dress flying.

" Oh, Enoch, Enoch ! You mun put the leaves in table for us, they'm going to have the wold big cloth with the farmyard border, and sit down seventeen all told ; and there's the trestles in the barn and the yurns to lug from the Rectory——"

Beneath that bewildering smile Enoch became as wax, and spent an hour labouring devotionally.

" Enoch can work as well as one here and there when he likes," Sarah remarked, pleased with the activity though not with the cause. She turned to Marigold.

" Now, Marigol' Gosling, what ails you, smiling at Master Peter's picture ? You met clean the mantel brasses. Anybody 'ud think you'd been to Gauby Market and lost yourself."

" I've done 'em. They wunna come better ! "

" I'll show 'em to come better ! " cried Sarah. " From rust to dust, from vardigris to kettle-collow, every dirt's 'ware of its own master. Go and get the kitchen breakfast. I'm clemmed."

So the battle raged, above and below, the kitchen fire roaring ; Sarah shouting ; the cuckoo striking every hour too soon ; Rectory-Lucy and the other helpers rushing about like frightened hens ; Sarah turning out the cats ; Enoch bringing them in again ; the gundogs howling ; Peter lying in wait to startle Marigold, making her drop the Crown Derby sugar-basin ; Sarah saying " it was to be," and storing fragments for the " world " ; Mrs. Darke seven times frozen ; Mrs. Cantlop seven times thawed ; Marigold in tears for fear she would have to leave ; Ruby in tears for fear she wouldn't ; Ernest, Solomon, Peter and Jasper all fetching hot water for shaving

at different times, each taking, as Mrs. Gosling said,
" the one poor drop I kep' to scalt the gizzards " ;
grandmother ringing, unanswered, till the bell broke,
when she took refuge in the imprecatory psalms ;
Amber trying to keep her temper, which was always
apt to be hasty, and greatly desiring someone to laugh
with ; and Enoch, huge, silent, calm, like some carved
figure of a god contemplating the hot fury of a market
place.

When Amber went to Mrs. Velindre's room, the
trouble of the cap was not abated. Box after box
had to be pulled out from under the vast bed in the
search for cap decorations. Grandmother kept innumerable boxes stored in this way, imagining that
the dark green valance would discourage burglars.
Sarah knew of the treasures, but as she always freely
and openly alluded to them as bonfire fuel, grandmother did not fear for her honesty. What with the
boxes, the Christmas-card screens, the feather fans,
old gowns, and stacks of *The Lion* tied up with
wool, the room was quite stuffed with possessions,
which seemed to elbow grandmother's thin body almost
out of existence.

When the cap was done, it was time to dress, and
then, before she had half finished, there were the
carriages—lent for the occasion by various neighbours—and there was Ruby with her veil half on and
a very red face refusing to go downstairs unless she
could have a definite promise from Ernest as to her
dress allowance. Ruby was no weakling, and she
seized the strategic hour. So Ernest had to be fetched
from the drawing-room, where, before the greenish
mirror, he was practising the saying of—" I will "
—soft, loud, modulated, mellifluous, gentle, virile,
stentorian. He tried it all ways, and had almost
decided upon stentorian, when in came Peter, very

sulky, saying " The little fool says you're to promise
a dress allowance or she'll chuck it." Poor Ernest
felt that perhaps " modulated " would be best. He
went up.

" Dear Ruby," he said, " such thoughts must not
trouble us in this solemn hour. Nay, they shall not."

" Fix it ! " cried Ruby dramatically. " Fix it,
or no wedding ! "

" She seems unstrung ; she *is* unstrung," said
Ernest.

" Obstinate ! " said her mother.   " Obstinate as a
mule."

" A mule—a mule ! " sang grandmother.

" The price of a good woman is above rubies," said
Ernest helplessly.

" Fix it ! " cried his bride.

So fixed it was. But Ernest was so much dis-
heartened that he could scarcely remember whether,
after all, it was to be stentorian or mellifluous. Everything, however, went well in church. Mr. Mallow
sang " Oh, that I had the wings of a dove, for then
would I flee away." This was always a serious strain
on Sarah's allegiance to Enoch. On the way back
to the house Catherine remarked—" He sings that
same thing at every festival, and every time he sings
it louder."

" And better," said Amber, for though Mr. Mallow
amused her, she did not like Catherine's bitter humour.

" And every time he sings it he is fatter, and his
dream more impossible," finished Catherine.

She was looking even more attractive than she had
hoped. The dress was one of those that for some
unknown reason endow the wearer with new mysterious beauty. Jasper thought she was like a gold-
encrusted, richly jewelled saint in a niche in some
dim cathedral. She had seemed (as she intended)

much more like a bride than the bride, much more
full of charm and tenderness and delicate femininity
Her figure had a slender grace that made Amber's
mean and gave the bride a kind of brawny truculence
The lurid colours of the East window, which repre-
sented Death and Hell with gloomy realism, were
powerless to sadden her cowslip-tinted gown, but
they fell on the bride's white dress in wan, forlorn,
and gloomy purples, and as the mid-day sun shafted
in through the Southern facet of the East window,
it laid a derisive bar of corpse-like blue across her
hot, red face and on her hand, stretched out to receive
the ring. Jasper thought : " How lovely my dear
is ! How sweet ! The devotion of a life, of a whole
life, is not enough."

Catherine thought : " What a cow-like creature
Ruby is ! She'll give herself such airs, being a bride.
She shall not." The white teeth snapped.

Peter thought, " Marigold would look nice in a
veil—all that yellow hair—I'll try and get hold of
Ruby's veil and put it on Marigold for fun."

Ruby thought, " Ernest's hand is too hot, and I
wish he wasn't so stout."

Ernest thought. " She must learn not to pant. I
must tell her about it this evening. Still, she has a
well developed figure. That is good. She has a
better figure than Amber or Catherine." He was
able to say with truth and placidity, " With my body
I thee worship." Fortunately the wedding service
says nothing about the love of the soul.

The tremendous wedding breakfast, with its mountains of flesh, its rows of little corpses of various sizes
—turkey, goose, duck, chicken, pheasant—all taste-
fully laid out by Mrs. Gosling ; its rather solid cake
and its rather hollow gaiety ; its health-drinking,
with Solomon's heavy mirth, the Rector's cultured

compliments, Ernest's fulminating eloquence and
Jasper's shy and flowery little speech to which nobody
listened, was not over till well on in the afternoon.

The party separated for a short time before tea,
and Peter took his opportunity to fling the veil over
Marigold. Ernest also took his opportunity to give
Ruby his caution as to panting. Jasper decided that
the moment had come for the presentation to Catherine
of the wreath of yellow jessamine that he had persuaded
Marigold to make for him. He sought for Marigold.

" Here, Master Jasper," came a muffled voice from
the dairy, and a very pink Marigold emerged, leaving
Peter behind the door with the veil.

" The wreath ! " whispered Jasper.

Marigold fetched it.

" Don't tell of me, Master Jasper," she implored.

" Tell what ? " said Jasper, in a lover's dream.

" He's daft about Miss Catherine," said Marigold,
to the cautiously emerging Peter.

" And I'm daft about you ! " said Peter with a
smacking kiss so loud that Sarah, getting tea in the
kitchen, cried :

" Enoch !   Enoch ! "

But hearing that Enoch was not present, she sub-
sided. The whole world might give smacking kisses
to all and sundry if Sarah's " intended " was not
among them.

The day wore on. Tea was over. The villagers'
knife and fork tea in the barn was over, and the
dining-room cleared for the dance. Ruby, trying not to
pant, sat expectant by her mother awaiting the guests.

First came Mr. Arkinstall, followed by his family in
Indian file.

Mr. Arkinstall taught Peter and Jasper to farm,
Solomon to keep accounts, and the Rector to manage
the parish. He was Solomon's fellow-warden. He had a

broad pale face, drooping moustaches, which Catherine
said gave him a Chinese look, and a sniggering
laugh. He also had a gift for devious conversation
which concealed undeviating views. He had proved
undeviating about his daughter's engagement. Alice
had been engaged to the new organist for fourteen
years. He was still the new organist; no one was
considered even a moderately old resident at Dormer
unless he had lived there sixty years. When Charles
was really new, being a florid young man of twenty,
he had "asked for" quiet Alice Arkinstall. Mr.
Arkinstall had immediately forbidden it, with devious
reasoning. Charles, on weekdays, was clerk to the
solitary lawyer at the Keep. But as no one ever
went to law there (not because they did not quarrel,
but because they were economical) there was not very
much for the lawyer, and there was very little indeed
for the clerk. Mr. Arkinstall said that financially
the marriage was impossible; that Charles must
have saved at least a hundred pounds before he would
even consider it, and that, in short, he'd die before
he'd hear of it. Charles' father—a very much more
scarlet exaggeration of Charles—really did die; for
when he interviewed Mr. Arkinstall, he was so exasperated by the Chinese expression, the snigger and the
devious talk that his old enemy, apoplexy, overwhelmed him. All this discouraged the young couple.
They only had spirit enough just to keep on being
engaged. Alice collected vast quantities of d'oyleys
and antimacassars, and became a victim to Mrs.
Cantlop's tatting. Charles looked for a house. That
is to say, he looked at the only house that fell vacant
during the fourteen years, but it was beyond his
means. Every Sunday Alice listened a little more
quietly, but always with the same admiration, to his
rendering of the voluntary. This became, every

Sunday, a little more explosive. Alice knew exactly the places where he went wrong and where he missed a few bars, for his playing had now lost the variable elasticity of youth. As the Rector said with his accustomed tact, it had matured. Like Charles it had gone to seed before it reached perfection. The denial of love and fulfilment and the heart's desire will cause even a genius to run to seed. Charles in maturity was more pathetic than Charles in youth, and he was most pathetic of all when he played dance music, which he was to do to-night. He was to be at the piano, Mr. Greenways had taken an evening off in order to play the flute, and Mr. Mallow was to manage the clarionet. Amber, as she looked at Alice, whose plain, unlit face wore the vaguely jaded air of a woman who nears forty and has never lived, thought that Mr. Arkinstall had much to answer for. Then she reflected that Alice was happier than she was herself, for someone cared whether Alice lived or died. Certainly, it was a muted love. They met once a week, at church, and walked circumspectly back to the Wallows. There, as no one invited Charles to tea, they parted. Charles did his duty in both walks of life. He sat in the office all the week, and was greatly admired by the vague, infrequent old ladies who wandered in to make their wills. As one of them said, " To see the young man's heartening. He's like a geranium in the window, makes you nigh forget the wrench of ' I give and bequeath.' "

Mrs. Arkinstall was a small, pebbly woman of inexhaustible (and quite necessary) obstinacy. She wore a royal blue dress immensely trimmed with braid, and a high comb in her black, polished hair. Young Philip Arkinstall followed. Philip was innocent of Chinese moustaches and devious conversation. He was direct to bluntness. But he had his father's

changelessness of purpose. He went through life like
a hound on the scent. What he wanted, that he would
have. He would follow it until he or the desired object
expired of exhaustion. His philosophy was simple.
Men's respect was an aid to power ; respect was won
by money ; money was gained by chicanery and bullying. Woman was created because a monastic life was
not good for man. One special woman had been
created for him, and that woman was Catherine
Velindre. He had polished hair like his mother's, a
square head, a fighting mouth, and hot grey eyes.
He was the only person at Dormer from whom Catherine
had ever been known to hide. He sat down and
stared at the door where she would come in. Jasper
also stared at the door. He had presented the wreath
and had seen it starrily crowning the smooth auburn
hair. His face had been quite pale with adoration,
and he had snatched her hand and kissed it.

"Alice!" whispered Amber. "If I were you I
should run away with Charles."

Alice's face became faintly rosy.

"Where?"

"Anywhere!"

"But how could we live? Where could we live?"

"Under a haystack—anywhere."

"But the crochet, and the d'oyleys?"

"Burn them."

Alice sighed. What would be the good of life
without d'oyleys?

Amber thought, "She doesn't love him. If she
loved him she wouldn't care what sort of house she
had." If she herself loved—ah! but that would
never be. She was lonelier than ever to-night. Even
Ruby's infantile friendship was gone, monopolized by
Ernest. The man of her dreams, how different from
anyone here! The love of her life, how far removed

from the lukewarm, the mercenary, the lustful!
" That love is made in fairyland," she thought, " and
in fairyland it stays."

Then she forgot her own untold story in seeing
the stories of others unfold. The two men watching
the door stiffened, their eyes gathered intensity.
Catherine swept in. She had a boyish figure, except
for her breast, which was full and feminine. The
starry crown suited her. On her bare neck was Philip
Arkinstall's last Christmas present, a locket and
chain ; on her arm was Jasper's, a forget-me-not
bracelet. Her long eyes, her long fingers, her long,
elaborately bound hair were instinct with provocation,
self-esteem, hauteur.

" I shan't give that gel much more tether," said
Philip to himself.

" What can I do for her to show how much I love
her ? " thought Jasper.

Sarah, peering in from the door of the back hall,
whispered to Marigold that " if 's Catherine took on
like that, she'd know trouble." Marigold nodded with
the immense wisdom of partial experience.

Jasper and Philip got up at the same moment.

" Sit here," said Philip.

" Here ! " whispered Jasper.

His eyes were a prayer. But when he turned them
on young Arkinstall, they were positively ferocious.

Catherine took Jasper's chair. The two young men
stood beside her.

" Law ! " said Sarah. " She's the girl for lovers.
Young Arkinstall, Master Jasper, and Master Peter.
Fancy three lovers ! "

" Two," said Marigold.

" Many and many 'ud be glad of one and that one
as miserable and poor-spirited as you like, but 's
Catherine's got three as well set up as ever I see."

" Two," said Marigold.

" You strike two as regular as a clock," said Sarah.
The musicians began.

" Mr. Mallow plays like a saved soul in Paradise,"
said Sarah.

Mr. Mallow was much redder, much more inflated in
the cheeks than even the most rotund of cherubs.
He did not spare himself. He played loudly and with
regularity. Mr. Dank was explosive. Mr. Greenways
was plaintive. The dancing began.

" Here's bride and bridegroom," said Sarah. " She
looks down already. But what a couple! Well-
matched they are. The good beef that's gone into
them two bodies!" She was lost in admiration.
" Eh! There's the bell. That'll be the Rectory and
a drove of visitors."

Grandmother sat with her chin resting on the silver
knob of her stick, looking at the dancers with a mingling
of curiosity, displeasure and goblin mirth. She watched
Mrs. Cantlop gloomily.

" I knew she'd have a new one!" she thought,
watching the flamboyant rose-red bows with a wist-
fulness that turned to glee as the mass of silk and lace
alit like a large migratory bird on the Rector's shoulder,
and floated to the floor. Mrs. Cantlop was, in grandmother's phrase, roistering. Her white hair seemed
in half a mind to follow the cap; her plump face was
red and damp from hearty exercise; her purple dress
had been more than once caught by one of Solomon's
firmly-planted feet, and a long loop of the lavish
tatting on her petticoat trailed in her wake and threatened the venturesome Rector with headlong downfall.
The good man knew it was reckless to dance with Mrs.
Cantlop. The experience of years told him so. Ob-
servation of others told him so. It was like the
race in the fairy tale; defeat was sure, the penalty

immediate. Yet he did it, like the kind soul he was.
And while he gyrated under the continually falling
shadow of the cap he often wondered why it was that
Mrs. Cantlop kept her eternal juvenility. He came
to the conclusion that it must be because she loved
so much the personality she had created—the Keturah-
cum-Keturah's-father ghost on which she spent her
devotion. And sometimes the Rector's conventional
ideas, firmly planted by school and university—the
idea that a man's first duty is to maintain his wife
in physical (not psychical) comfort, that a woman is
admirable in proportion to the number of her progeny
—sometimes these ideas flickered in the wind of doubt.
Then he was almost tempted to think Mr. Cantlop
would have done better for his wife by giving her
what she wanted, his own company ; that Mrs. Cantlop
was perhaps doing more for humanity by simply
loving Keturah-cum-Keturah's-father than Mrs. Darke
had done by lovelessly producing four children.

Sarah, looking through the crack of the door, eating
raisins, whispered to Enoch (tip-toeing through the
hall) that the Rector was dancing to his doom. But
Enoch did not hear this, nor did he hear her subsequent
observations.

" Mr. Ernest's the lad at the sugar-plum shop to-
night ! The missus makes a funeral of every randy.
's Catherine goes well ! "

Catherine might have been a toy train by the way
Sarah spoke. " It was a pity I was obleeged to break
that fan Mr. Philip give her for her birthday," she
continued to Mrs. Gosling.

" Miss Amber ought to get a young chap to lug her
round," said Mrs. Gosling, already mellow with good
marriage wine. No miracle ever struck her as so
truly divine as that of Cana.

" Look at Mrs. Cantlop's cap ! " murmured Sarah.

" The old lady's grinding-mad with Mrs. Cantlop for getting it."

" Where's Master Peter ? " said Mrs. Gosling.

" The quieter that lad is," replied Sarah, " the further he's in mischief, like the cat in the cream jug." Enoch was also silently asking that question. He was wondering why Marigold, so sweet in her new spotted muslin apron and the cap with the little streamers, had vanished and left him in the cold. Being a practical person, he was at present engaged on a tour of investigation.

" Oh ! " said Sarah, suddenly, " look's the Rector ! I knew he'd meet trouble."

" It was to be," said Mrs. Gosling devoutly, looking compassionately at the prone figure of the gallant Rector.

The musicians, dumbfoundered at the cataclysm, wavered into silence. Grandmother laughed, and her laugh was like the sound of the winter wind in the old ivy of Dormer, like the sigh of freezing water lapping in the rustling reeds. Ernest came forward with proffered help, showing by his expression that he could have better upheld rectorial dignity. Solomon hoisted the unfortunate gentleman to his feet, ran a practised hand from knees to ankles and remarked : " Sound ! "

Mrs. Cantlop, breathlessly penitent, fanned everyone near her with a highly-scented handkerchief, and Sarah advanced with the hall clothes' brush and the instinctive motherliness which awakes in all but the most hardened men and women at the sight of prostrate misfortune.

Grandmother pondered complacently on the retributive punishment of vanity. She watched the dance begin again. There they were, slowly whirling, softly lighted, gliding in a perpetual-seeming June,

floating dreamily as the dandelion clocks under the
dreamy suns of her youth. Blown by soft winds now !
Lit by bright lamps now ! But she knew, ah ! she
knew well, that winds grow wild at summer's end ;
that the night turns cold and grey ; that the frost
settles. And the dandelion clocks, where are they ?
Rotting—rotting ! The hand of old age was heavy
on her, and she did not hear the plaintive flute, the
loud piano, the shrewdly blown clarionet. She heard
only, out of the dark forest, out of her dim heart, a
voice full of trouble, crying : " It is ended ! "

Perhaps it was something of this trouble reflected in
her face that brought Amber across the room to sit by
her. They watched the dance go by. Ruby passed,
pink as a tulip. Catherine came by, creamy as a
guelder rose. She was in the arms of young Arkinstall.
Jasper's eyes, brilliant as sunny brook water, followed
her as she floated by. His face, ardent and wistful
when it dwelt on her, grew tense with jealousy when it
turned to Philip. But his was the next dance ! It
seemed to Amber that they were all like creatures under
a spell, like the mist of midges that dances, whirling,
in a tiny vortex, beneath the humid, dusky branches
of the yew. They dance, but they remain in one place.
They whirl for a few moments as if enclosed in an
invisible cone. Then, in the midst of their dance,
they die as they have lived, beneath the humid, dusky
branches of the yew. So at Dormer they danced,
as it were, in prison. They were like the companies
of knights and ladies who wandered of old into the
airless halls of enchantment, and drinking nightshade
wine, and hearing a music full of poppies, drowsed into
an everlasting motion more deathly than death.
There was just this quality of airlessness about the
Dormer revels. Around them, below, above, like the
invisible air about the midges, pressed the faces of

their ancestors—earth-pale, unassuaged, as must be
the ghosts of the unhappy; merciless as must be the
unperceptive mind. They had lived by the laws of
others. They had danced in the slumbrous prison
of tradition. They would enforce these things. In
the dusky corners of the ceiling ashen faces seemed to
linger; beyond the dividing doorway, from the
twilight gloom of the drawing-room, mournful eyes
seemed to peer; through every note of the music
there seemed to murmur voices of denial. Like bees
on an interloper they pressed in on the small picture
of life, crowding silently, ceaselessly, till the very air
seemed ready to crack. Ruled by the dead, held by
the dead in eternal copyhold, filled by the dead until
there was no room for the living, the house seemed to
have gone mad with its own antiquity, and antiquity
is predatory.

Suddenly grandmother spoke, muttering to herself,
and Amber's curious vision faded.

" All young," said grandmother, " all froward, and
all damned ! "

Meanwhile, in the kitchen, Mrs. Gosling brooded
over cooking ducks, and Enoch brooded over Marigold.
Where was she ?

" Enoch, you look a dream ! " said Sarah, coming in.

Enoch wore a discarded coat of Solomon's, something between covert and frock, and a coloured waistcoat and a pair of check trousers (once belonging to
Mr. Gosling, who had been a publican). To crown
all, Marigold had tied round his neck (oh, the rapture
of that tying !) one of her own blue ribbons.

" Mumchancing again ! " cried Sarah, irate that
her homage was ignored. " When the angel Gabriel
calls out the name of Enoch, I believe you'll mum-
chance and lose your turn for Paradise ! " But Enoch
was gone.

He wandered along the stone passage until he came
to the dairy, and at the dairy door, in the shadows, he
stopped, stricken and forlorn.

For there, in the damp, sweet-smelling place, at the
far end, lighted by a flickering candle, he saw two
graceful shadows dancing along the whitewashed wall,
and one shadow had a cap with little streamers.   They
did not care for the music of flute or violin, for they
heard the voice of youth singing as he swayed in the
apple-tree—the tree laden with rosy fruit, where Eve
gathered—and his song came thrilling to them across
the pans of faintly crinkled cream, and made the rough
dairy floor as smooth as glass.

" Eh, Master Peter ! Master Peter ! " whispered
Enoch. His hands shook ; his legs trembled as he
turned and stole away. Tears were on his face as
he came back to the kitchen and sat down heavily.
He must think—and thinking was strange to
him.

" What, rainin' ? " asked Sarah, seeing his wet face.

" Ah ! Rainin' sore," said Enoch.

But Sarah, going to the door, said :

" Why, it's fine as May ! A lover's night if ever !
You're mooning, Enoch."

A lover's night—a lover's night ! Ah ! but it was
for other lovers, not for him, not for him.

In the dining-room, Mrs. Darke still looked on like
a queen watching the revels of an alien race. Grandmother still frowned at Mrs. Cantlop, and Mrs. Cantlop
still danced. Catherine still gave her eyes to Philip
Arkinstall, her thoughts to Peter's whereabouts and
her errands to Jasper.

" Cathy ! Cathy ! " said Jasper, at the end of a
dance. " Mine's the next."

" Did you find out where Peter was ? "

" Yes."

" Where ? "

" I can't give him away, Cathy."

" Very well.   I shall use your dance to find out."

She went away.   Returning with a gleam in her eyes, she whispered to grandmother :

" Cheesecakes in the dairy ! "

Now if there was a thing grandmother liked, it was cheesecakes.

Slipping off into the next dance, Catherine watched her departure with satisfaction.

Amber went across to Jasper.

" I suppose you wouldn't dance with me, dear ? "

" You aren't much good at it, are you ? " said Jasper, sullen with misery.

Amber sighed, feeling that tragic sense of her own incompetence which is peculiarly bitter when the desire to help is strong.

They sank into depression.

In the dairy the dance went on with giggling and laughter.   But upon the laughter and the dance and the fluting of youth broke suddenly, like the sound of doom, Mrs. Velindre's voice.

" Great-grandson ! " said Mrs. Velindre ; and the two culprits were stricken into stillness.

" Great-grandson, how dare you dance with a servant !   Woman—go ! "

Marigold went, and as she went grandmother's voice followed her.

" The abomination and the mouse ! " said Mrs. Velindre, and she hobbled away, leaving Peter still speechless with astonishment.   For why, in the name of all things malevolent, should grandmother have come to the dairy—a place to which she hardly came twice a year ?

" Now there'll be the devil of a row ! " he thought
with irritation.   " And all about nothing ! "

As a matter of fact, neither he nor Marigold had
had the slightest thought of harm. Grandmother's
stick came tapping across amid the dancers. Catherine's long eyes turned towards her over Philip
Arkinstall's shoulder, watched her go up to Mrs.
Darke, watched the two go away together. She
would teach Peter to ignore her, Catherine Velindre,
for a servant ! She would teach Marigold to aspire
where she, Catherine, might have set her eyes ! She
laughed softly.

" Stupid, people are ! " she said.

" Damn stupid ! " said Philip.

He thought, " She's scheming again. Well, let her
scheme ! Meanwhile, I bide my time."

In his thoughts he knew what he would do. He knew
Catherine better than she ever dreamt. He knew her
schemes, her determination never to marry him. He
knew her brain was worth ten of his, and that she was
powerful because she had no weak spot of love for
anyone. He knew that she used him only as a rod to
bring Jasper to his senses. Very well. He would
take the only course by which he could outwit her. He
would bide his time, and he would compromise her.

" They never see where they are being led," said
Catherine, who was still simple enough to take a
transparent delight in her own schemes.

" No," said Philip.

" Blind as bats ! "

" All but you, Cathy.   You see everything." He
permitted himself to laugh, and the laugh partook of
his father's.

XI

MARIGOLD'S WARNING

CATHERINE knocked at Mrs. Darke's door. There was an appreciable silence, then a curt, " Come in."

Mrs. Darke's room was large, tidy and cold. It was tidy with the inhuman neatness of an hotel bed-room and a conventional mind, a neatness that came from emptiness. A woman's life history is generally written in her room. But in Mrs. Darke's room nothing was written. All the world might have come and peered in without learning a single thing about her. There was nothing to show that she had a husband or children—no mementos, no gifts from Solomon—as a matter of fact, Solomon's gifts were infrequent. This was not from meanness, but because on his rare visits to the Keep there were always cartridges and dog biscuits and such things to buy. There was no picture of him either as a young man or a middle-aged one. Perhaps this did not matter very much, for Solomon's soul at the age of twenty had been exactly the same as Solomon's soul aged sixty, therefore no particular interest could attach to his face. His mother, in a fit of family pride, had once suggested his having his portrait done like the Squire of the next parish, in hunting pink. Mrs. Darke, caught between the precipice of a direct statement on one hand and the whirlpool of needless expense on the other, chose the precipice, and said : " However expensive it was, it would still be only Solomom, and I have Solomon."

There were none of those reassuring little indulgences and luxuries which, by proclaiming a person to be something of a sybarite, generally give security of a certain dependableness. From the sybarite you are more sure of mercy than from the ascetic, because he is a creature of the emotions, and desiring passionately the good things of life, he can guess the tragedy of being without them.

The furniture was severe and gloomy, for Solomon's mother, to whom the room had belonged, held Calvinistic views, and Mrs. Darke had not troubled to alter it. She went in and out like a stranger, leaving no impress on anything in the house, for the desire for artistic self-expression comes of a healthy individualism and not from the disease of egotism which is stunted development. Mrs. Darke was quite unindividual. She was a part of her class and creed, just as a bit of meteorological stone is part of a sun or a star. But it will never be a world unless it has movement. Nor would Mrs. Darke ever be an individual, because she had no living impulses. Her longing to be bowed down to, her greed of power, were also the results of this lack of growth. It was as if, very far away in the mists of the subconscious self, she heard a voice cry that she did not exist, never had existed, and in fear of being nothing had resolved to seem to be everything. The outer form was all in all to her. She was one of those for whom ceremonial is made. She had always done her duty by her husband and children. She had seen to it that Solomon's winter coat was put away with pepper in the summer, and that his frayed cuffs were mended by Marigold or her predecessors. Her offspring had all suffered vaccination, baptism, dentistry, and confirmation at the correct times. She ruled Solomon's house in the orthodox manner. She had a gift for autocratic rule,

and was a staunch believer in matriarchy. She disliked
her own mother, who bored her, but she would never
confess it even to herself. She had a certain dour
loyalty to the dour laws she obeyed. That she did
not love Mrs. Velindre was not astonishing, for in
nothing but physical fact was that lady her mother.
For the real mother is, first, a passionate lover of her
children, recklessly spending herself in the manner of
all lovers. The idea of either Mrs. Velindre or her
daughter in the guise of a reckless lover had in it more
of mirth than conviction. They had somehow missed
the gift, for it does not go inalienably with the pro-
duction of offspring, and it is sometimes found in
strange places—in the eyes of spinsters or invalids,
in the smile of some whom the world despises.

" Well, what is it now ? " asked Mrs. Darke as
Catherine entered with her usual circumspect softness.
If anyone had ever wanted to confide in Rachel Darke,
they must have found it an uphill road. She looked
at Catherine now very much as a Squire looks at a
poacher. But Catherine was quite undismayed. Like
a smoothly polished statue, she was impervious to
rough weather.

" Forgive me for intruding, dear aunt," she said
amiably, looking round for a comfortable chair. Not
finding one, she lay down on the bed, for she liked to
be as comfortable as possible. This was the first
time for some years that she had interviewed her aunt
in this room, but she had remembered the cold and had
put on her winter coat. She lay very blandly on the
ancestral birth and death bed, her fur collar well up,
setting off her rich hair.

Mrs. Darke looked more than ever like a squire
contemplating a poacher. She paced to and fro, hands
locked, tormenting one another. So might a lady
abbess walk, as she pondered on the penance of an

impenitent nun.   A lady abbess was what Mrs. Darke
should have been, since power was what she thirsted
after—power for its own sake, not necessarily over
many, but completely over a few. Having been
allowed no power in her youth, even over herself ;
no responsibility even for her own actions (for she had
been dominated by Mrs. Velindre and family opinion)
the desire had grown into a lust. To tyrannize was
metheglin to her, and things had come to such a pass that
she had the habitual drunkard's mad and cunning
craving, only what she wanted was the human soul.
On that she fed, on that she gloated as any cannibal
might. If it fled from her, she clutched at it ; if it
escaped, she used all her finesse to catch it again ;
having caught it, she tore it in bitter, silent rage.
Catherine was aware of this idiosyncrasy. She understood her aunt (for beneath their respective manners
of chillness and suavity they were both savages) and
she wielded a peculiar power over her by pretending
to offer herself as an unconscious sacrifice, like a
plump, gay-feathered bird. Innumerable times did
Mrs. Darke imagine that she had sent Catherine
quivering with mental pain to spend a night in tears,
and on all those occasions Catherine had nestled into bed
very happily, murmuring, as she opened her favourite
devotional book, " Fooled again, dear aunt ! "

" Are you ill ? " inquired Mrs. Darke, and her eye
told that she would give short shrift to malingering.

" Never better, Aunt Rachel."

" Who have you quarrelled with ? "

" I never quarrel, dear aunt."

" Are you in debt ? "

" Solvent, auntie."

" Then why come to me ? "

" For all you know, Aunt Rachel, I may want to
see more of you."

Mrs. Darke laughed—a short and cutting laugh. Who had ever wanted to see more of her, anything of her ? Certainly not Solomon, who in his loud and hearty way ignored her existence whenever it was possible. Not her mother, for she was in the position of abdicating monarch, and in an absolute monarchy that is an unpleasant position. She mingled, in her treatment of her daughter, pathetic echoes of autocracy with equally pathetic shivers of fear. When Mrs. Velindre irritated her, Mrs. Darke said, in her incisive voice.

" I shall lock you up ! "

To grandmother, who loved to hobble about with her tall, knobbed stick, and peer into everyone's affairs, going softly in list shoes, this threat had a creeping horror. She avoided her daughter whenever she could. For each member of the family, Mrs. Darke had an especial rod, except perhaps for Sarah. Sarah feared nothing, and had the courage of her convictions. There were times when she even lingered near Mrs. Darke, " singing for trouble," as Mrs. Gosling said, like one queen wasp meeting another. On one such memorable day Sarah broke a kitchen cup, thus laying herself open to her mistress's icy satire. Mrs. Darke had concluded her speech with :

" I think, as the old Derby jug is never in your hands but once a year, it may outlast you if you die soon."

Whereupon Sarah, in scarlet wrath, had seized the heirloom with a shriek of : " Outlast me, will you ? " and had dashed it on to the flags. Strangely enough she did not get notice for this. After all, who else would have done so much work in so short a time for so little money ? Later, dabbing bits of it on to her " world," she had been shamed into partial repentance by Enoch's reproachful gaze.

" Well, aunt," said Catherine, curling herself more comfortably, " it's about Mrs. Gosling's girl."

She never called Marigold by her name, thinking it foolish and knowing Marigold to be proud of it.

Mrs. Darke started. So Catherine knew ! The last person who should have known.

" What about her ? "

" Granny told me."

" I shall lock her up ! " muttered Mrs. Darke. " Told you she's in trouble ? " she asked Catherine, her mouth sneering, for she found these unruly emotions of youth contemptible.

" Yes. It's very sad, aunt."

" Did she name the man ? "

" Aha ! Aha ! " thought Catherine. " You didn't want me to know ! " Aloud she said : " I am sorry to say she did."

If Mrs. Darke cared for anyone it was Peter. He was superficially very like herself. She had planned his marriage with Catherine years ago. Catherine would live here under her rule, produce children, and uphold with her money the falling fortunes of Dormer. The way in which her controlled rage shook her was horrible to witness. Catherine watched, amused. Mrs. Darke was whelmed in class hatred—a futility of the human race even more devastating than the foolishness of national hatred. It was well for herself and for Marigold that the girl was not in the room at the moment. Mrs. Darke tore her handkerchief in two. Catherine winced, disliking the noise. Then, seeing that it was going to happen again, she said : " Dear aunt ? "

" Well ? "

" What will Peter do ? "

" It's a mistake—a mistake. It must be Jasper."

" I know it isn't Jasper."

" How ? "

" Jasper has proposed to me."

Mrs. Darke's face was again distorted. The one son wouldn't marry Catherine, and must. The other son must not, and would.

" Did you refuse him ? "

" Of course, aunt. How could I marry an infidel ? "
This at least was hopeful.

" Shall you send the girl away ? "

" Shall I ? Shall I ? She will go packing at once. Prostitute that she is ! "

" Oh, dear aunt ! "

" Nonsense. You are not so innocent as all that, Catherine."

" And will Peter go also ? "

" He will not. He will stay here as arranged. His father and Ernest are talking to him."

Catherine shook with silent laughter. She could so well imagine the conversation.

" Will Peter marry her ? "

" *Marry* her ? I'd sooner see him dead."

" Will he marry someone else ? "

" Of course. The family must go on."

A curious look tenanted Catherine's eyes for a moment. It had in it both anger and fear. At the back of her mind was always a lurking intuition that she was doomed to carry on some man's family. She emphatically did not want to. She wanted to be a queen in her own right, to rule men, to enslave, but never to be enslaved.

" Suppose the girl you have thought of won't take Peter at second-hand ? Who *is* the girl, auntie ? You always have plans. I'm sure you have decided."

Mrs. Darke walked across the room, flinging over her shoulder :

" That is not your affair ! "

" I think it is," said Catherine. " Behold the lamb for the burnt offering."

Once more Mrs. Darke's handkerchief suffered. Things were going worse and worse. She had not dreamed that Catherine guessed. And now she had not only guessed. She had found out about Marigold. Mrs. Darke almost raved.

Catherine enjoyed the upper hand for a while. Then she administered balm.

" If the girl went away—right away for good, and Peter was sorry, and turned from this low affection to a higher—well, it's a woman's duty to forgive."

" He's about as good as you'll get," muttered Mrs. Darke.

" A woman should help him to turn the new page and choose the new road."

Mrs. Darke's usually expressionless face, winter-pale and at the same time volcanic, expressed relief. She had planned this match, and her plans were her career.

But Catherine knew, in her heart, that she never would marry Peter, never forgive him. She would bring pressure to bear on Jasper, bend him to her will, marry him.

" Have you interviewed the girl, aunt ? "

" Not yet."

" Could you send for her now ? "

Mrs. Darke, for once, was obliged to submit. She would rather have seen Marigold alone, but she rang the bell.

" House afire, mum ? " queried Sarah, looking in. She wished to emphasize the undesirability and unusualness of ringing bedroom bells.

Mrs. Darke felt that the house *was* afire.

" Send Mrs. Gosling's girl up," she said.

" Almighty God take pity on 'er," said Sarah devoutly, as she went downstairs.

Marigold stood in the doorway—a washed-out Marigold, with crumpled apron and dejected little streamers. She was dazed by the storm that had descended on her. For the last two hours her mother had scolded, Sarah had looked askance, Rectory-Lucy had sniffed, even Enoch had been silent. Master Peter had " caught a holt of her " and pranced across the dairy, and she hadn't thought any harm. She had cried till she thought she could cry no more.

" That's warning ! " said Sarah when the bell rang, and sure enough it was. She stood shaking, wondering what they all thought she had done.

" Take a week's notice ! " said Mrs. Darke.

" Yes'm, thank you."

Marigold had something of her mother's apologetic manner.

" Go and hide your head away from respectable people."

" Please'm, I partly think I'm respectable."

" Don't bandy words, you bad woman ! You may be thankful to get off so lightly."

Marigold tried to avoid Catherine's pitiless eyes.

" Why do you tremble if you have not done wrong ? " said Catherine.

It was a hopeless question. It has been a hopeless question to the simple for many a long year. The sensitive and the timid always do tremble, being in the right, and by so doing put themselves in the wrong. Being accused of evil, they are crushed, and immediately this is taken for guilt.

" How long have you cohabited with my son ? " asked Mrs. Darke in a terrible voice, regardless of Catherine's expostulation.

" I don't rightly understand, mum ! " said Marigold.

" How long is it since you slept with my son first ? "

Marigold was suddenly faint, for all her robustness. Her face was scarlet, pulses beat all over her. She swayed as she stood and hid her face in her hands

" Ah ! that's clear to you, is it ? " said Mrs. Darke ;
" that finds the weak spot."

" The spot—the spot ! Wash out the spot of sin ! "
said grandmother, entering.

" Answer, girl ! " said Mrs. Darke.

" Yes, answer ! " said Catherine, curious. Life
interested her ; so did Peter.

" Answer ! Answer ! " piped grandmother.

But Marigold could find no voice. To think that of
her ! And she never so much as let a man kiss her—
not even Enoch under the mistletoe. Only Master
Peter had kissed her that once unbeknown.

" She daren't answer ! " was the verdict.

Marigold raised her head, and out of the confusion
and terror looked pride, the simple pride of a country
girl to whom her good name is all.

" I didn't never do such a thing," she said on a
shocked sob. " Master Peter wouldn't lower 'isself
to ask it, nor me to say yes to it."

They laughed. They did not believe her. Rectory-Lucy
did not either, nor her mother. She began to cry again.

" If you're a respectable girl, why do you cry ? "
inquired Catherine.

" Weeping and gnashing of teeth ! You'll go to
hell ! " said grandmother.

" I'll goo away from this place ! " said Marigold,
with a flash of spirit. " And I won't never come back.
I'll goo to my auntie ! "

" I wish her joy ! " said Catherine.

" And when the brat's born, don't bring it here,"
said Mrs. Darke. " To the workhouse with it ! "

" There wunna never be no brat, and there inna no
wrong, and there wunna—never, never ! " cried Marigold
again. " And what for you should all think ill of me as
never done you no wrong——" she sobbed. " Ask Master
Peter ! " she cried suddenly. Again the three laughed.

Ask Peter ! How indecent ! How like a common
girl to suggest it ! Besides, of course, Peter would deny
it, like any other young man.

" Do not dare to speak my son's name ! " said Mrs.
Darke. " We know the truth. Be grateful I don't
send you off to-night. It is not for your sake I keep
up appearances, but for the family's. Your wages
are here. Take them and go."

" I dunna want 'em, mum."

" The stick ! The stick ! " said grandmother. " In
the old days it would have been the stick across your
shoulders ! "

Marigold turned to go. Her plump figure, supple
and strong, annoyed Mrs. Darke by its independence
even in the midst of the confusion.

" Your dress is tight already ! " she said. " You
know what that means ! "

Catherine was horrified. She had never thought
her aunt could be so coarse. In fact, Mrs. Darke never
was, but in her rage and hate she had forgotten herself. Catherine went out of the room in expostulatory
silence, brushing past Marigold in pale, derisive purity.

Marigold, as she went downstairs, came slowly and
by gradual steps to the conclusion that being good
did not pay. And a faint, fluttering regret was born
in the depths of her heart—regret that she had
suffered the penalty without having tasted one crumb
of the joy.

Peter, in the deserted dancing room, was feeling
much the same thing. There sat his father and
Ernest, the judges. There stood he, the culprit.

" Here's a splother," said Solomon.

" Pity—pity ! " said Ernest.

" What have you got to say for yourself ? " asked
Solomon.

" Nothing," replied his son.

"An illicit connection with one of the servants ! I'm damned ! " said Solomon.

" A hallowed love—a sacred love," continued Ernest. " Ah ! how different from this ! "

" I don't love anybody ! " said Peter.

" Then there is no excuse."

" There's no need of excuse ; I've done nothing."

" Lies—lies ! I know young men ! " Solomon spoke with a kind of gruff tolerance.

" The human heart is desperately wicked," added Ernest. " All we like sheep——"

" I tell you I've done nothing. I've not gone astray so far. But I will ! I will ! " Peter added.

" A love that society can countenance," Ernest remarked, " is safe because it is sanctioned, and sanctioned because it is safe."

" You make my head ache," said Peter.

" Give the girl up," ordered Solomon.

" I can't."

" Don't say ' can't ' to me ! "

" I can't give up what I haven't got."

" If Catherine knew, she wouldn't marry you."
Peter laughed.

" She needn't. I don't want her. Pale thing ! "

" If she knew you had danced with a servant in the dairy——"

" I don't care who knows. There was no harm."

" If there'd been no harm, would you have wanted to dance ? " said Solomon.

" Well, I'll go to bed, father. It's no good arguing. Good-night."

He was gone, a tumult of new ideas and personalized emotions in his mind. As he and Jasper were going to bed, he said :

" Marigold's pretty, isn't she ? "

" Passable," said Jasper with a yawn.

" If you were me, should you marry Catherine ? "

Jasper sat up in bed with a bounce.

" If you say that again I'll knock your head off,"
he remarked.

Peter sighed. Everyone was very combative to-day.
But as he fell asleep, he thought again of Marigold.
Decidedly she was pretty, very sweet to kiss. And he
had only kissed her once ! They all blamed him. Very
well. He would have a few more—a good many more.

The house settled down. The night sounds began.
Death-watches, creakings of furniture, the ticking of
clocks like the falling of water-drops.

Suddenly in the comparative silence a door opened
and a figure rushed across the landing to Amber's
room. But the door was locked. Another figure,
stout and clad in pyjamas, followed.

" I'm going to Amber ! " said a voice, low but determined.

" You shall not make me look ridiculous," said
another voice, low but very angry.

Another door opened silently, to the width of an inch.

" I don't like being married. I don't like you,"
said the first voice.

The second voice tried persuasion.

" All that marriage means—companionship, love,
children."

" I hate children ! "

" A little replica of me ! "

At that the first voice dissolved in laughter. A third
door opened.

" What is this noise ? " said Mrs. Darke. She stood
there in a bar of moonlight in a grey dressing-gown,
grey of hair and face. And it seemed as if a mental
greyness gave a deeper tone to all the rest.

" She is hysterical, hysterical," said Ernest. " We
must be patient."

He stood there in his new pyjama suit, dignified and
with a consciousness of being in the right.

" Patient ! " said Mrs. Darke, who had no more
patience after the troubles of the day. " Don't be a fool,
Ernest. Loose that door, Ruby, and go back to your
room. You have made the bargain. You must keep it."

" I won't ! I won't ! He looks so fat in pyjamas ! "
answered Ruby in a sibilant and infuriated whisper.

Catherine, watching through her inch-wide opening,
shook with laughter at the scene.

As Mrs. Darke and Ernest, taking each an arm, pro-
pelled Ruby across the landing, she gently shut her
door, chronicling the scene in her mind as a useful
rod for Ernest in the future.

The long day was done. The house watched over
its sleeping children, careless, it seemed, as to whether
they dreamed happily or sadly. If the house stood,
what mattered the single soul ? Let Ruby be bound
to a hated bargain, let Marigold be cast out, Peter
marry without love, Jasper be broken in spirit, Amber
lonely, and the rest malformed in soul. What matter,
if the house went on ? The house must go on, just
as it was, just as it had been for so long. It would
go on surely, for ever. It lay under the dim forest,
regarding the flashing stars with its many eyes. And
all around it through the night the forest whispered,
muttered, fir and spruce and pine with their dark
creative music, and with harsher voices the bare trees
that had forgotten leaves with summer. They sang,
and the lipping ivy on the house sang with them, of
things that had been before the earliest wattle hut.
They sang of lichens and mosses and elm samaras
and rosy seed of pines already preparing for the day
when Dormer should be taken back into the earth,
curtained in green. For nothing that is built by man
for the subjugation of the single soul can stand.

XII

THE GROTTO

On the day after the wedding Catherine went to tea at the Rectory. She liked to look her best, even for a middle-aged man and woman, which was one of her pleasanter qualities. Sometimes also, young Arkinstall would vault over a stile as she came home, and walk with her. She despised him, but he enlivened the tedium of a walk. To Catherine a lonely walk was intolerable. She had no kinship with the wild, and if there was one thing she disliked more than walking alone, it was walking with Amber, for Amber insisted on talking about trees and birds.

To-day Catherine did not, as usual, ask Marigold to wave her hair. She went down to Sarah in the kitchen. Marigold knew how great a slight this was, for she knew Catherine disliked Sarah.

" Aunt," said Catherine before she started, " they will wonder at the Rectory what the fuss was about. Can I tell them ? "

" Tell that hurdy-gurdy of a woman ! Not a word ! "

Catherine smiled. She liked to " draw " her aunt. Then she departed, looking her best. And her best, as poor Jasper knew, was very good indeed. Mrs. Darke went to call on Mrs. Arkinstall in order to comfort herself for the tiresomeness of her married daughter by reminding Mrs. Arkinstall that her daughter was still unmarried. An unhappy, sullen

Ruby had been taken for a drive by a hurt and dignified Ernest.

Marigold sat in the old school-room, where she sewed every afternoon, and the November sun lingered on her bright head. As she sewed, she cried, and as she cried, she pricked her finger, so that the shirt she was mending was bedewed with little points of red. Everything was very quiet. Grandmother was in the dining-room, asleep, and Amber in her own room, reading. Sarah was clearing up the kitchen and singing : " There is a fountain . . ."

Marigold sewed and sobbed, for she had " warning " to go in a week, and her heart was here.

Suddenly the French window was opened cautiously, and in walked Peter.

" I knew you'd be crying," he said.   " They told me —the governor told me—you were going. So I just walked off from the Wallows to see you. I'm damned sorry, Marigold."

" Oh, Master Peter, I misdoubt someone'll come ! "

" They're all safe. Marigold ? "

" Master Peter ? "

" Since they started on me, talking and that, I've thought about you a lot. I didn't before."

" No, Master Peter."

" You're pretty when you cry. Ruby looks like a great pæony."

" Oh I Master Peter I "

" Don't ' Master Peter ' me I Say Peter."

" I couldna I No, never could I."

" You must."

He knelt in front of her and took away the sewing.

" What's this you're doing ? "

" The cuffs on your blue and white shirt, Master——"

He put a hand on her mouth.

" Peter ! The last I'll mend for you."   She sobbed.

" Do you love me, Marigold ? Say ' Yes, Peter ! ' "
He had both hands now. The pretty head drooped.

Peter kissed her. He was not in love with her, but
his father's talk of an illicit connection and Ernest's
talk of unholy love had kindled in him a curiosity and
awakened in him a kind of emotionless and almost
impersonal passion. He was aroused and inspired by
their groundless suspicions to make the suspicions true.

" Say ' I love you, Peter ' ! "

With trembling lips and swimming blue eyes she said it.
In the midst of his kisses she suddenly stiffened.

" Hushee ! Hushee ! There was a door slammed.
You mun goo."

Her voice was like a pigeon's.

" Meet me in the wood when you've washed up
tea ! " said Peter.

He was gone, but by the entrance to the woods he
was waiting for her in the evening, and every evening
until her last. In the last sweet moment of the last
sweet hour, when Sarah could be heard down by the
gun-dog's kennel crying, " Marigol' ! Marigol' ! "
Peter spoke with the cruelty that can dwell with
passion (for in the last week he had learnt a young
passion, not the love-rayed gift of the great gods, but
the woodland passion of a faun).

" You are going to-morrow," he said.

" To-morrowday ! Oh, I wish I met be dead afore
to-morrowday ! " cried Marigold suddenly, in a voice
broken with love. " If it 'ud thunder now, and a bolt
fa-al, or a wind come out o' the sky, and this wold
yew-tree fa-al ! "

" Silly ! What d'you want to die for ? I don't
want to die."

" Master Peter ! Oh, my darlin', what'n you done
to be more than the world an' all ? "

" I dunno ! " Peter laughed shortly and rather shyly.

" I'd as lief be under the daisies if I canna bide in Dormer valley ! And that new girl mindin' your things and all ! "

She cried again heartbrokenly.

" Well, you've got to go, so there's an end," said Peter. " But perhaps I'll come and see you."

The sun came out in Marigold's face.

" And if you're sorry to leave me, and if you're as fond of me as you say——"

" What, Master Peter ? "

" You won't say good-bye now."

" Oh, but I mun—I'm agoing at five and it's prayers after supper and then bed—and there's Sarah hollering agen."

Peter whispered.

" Oh, I couldna ! Not in the black o' night ! Not all up to the grotto ! "

" Good-bye, then."

" Oh, no, no ! "

" Then come ! I'll make a fire."

" What'd Sarah and Rectory-Lucy say ? "

" They won't know. Besides, they all thought harm of us when there wasn't any harm. Let's give 'em something to cry for."

" Oh, Master Peter, the things you say ! "

" You and me, Marigold, you and me in the grotto as if it was our house ! " He conjured a picture of terror and fascination.

" P'raps you'll never see me again after to-morrow."

" Dunna say that, oh, dunna ! There's Sarah all of a hoost, skriking, I mun goo."

" Come then, as soon as Sarah's asleep. Say ! "

" Maybe I wunna," said Marigold, turning to run down the wood, " and maybe I 'ool."

Going to bed in Sarah's scintillating attic, Marigold

felt lost in the thought of to-morrow. Sarah eyed her
tears in no unfriendly spirit. Before, Marigold had
been a powerful and permanent rival. Now, since
the fateful hour of the dance, she was obliterated.
Her "intended" was now hers only. She always
spoke of Enoch as her intended, thus attaining that
to which fine literature aspires—the expression of the
precise truth. When asked whether she was Enoch's
intended also, she replied : "Oh, he treasures up his
dark designs ! " Now all was well. Mere resistance
on the part of Enoch was, she felt, unimportant. In
a lavish mood she had lighted two tallow dips, and
in their wavering light she surveyed her room with
complaisance. It was a scene of almost barbaric
splendour. The multiple-tinted crockery-work glit-
tered savagely ; the patchwork quilt was bewildering
in its variety ; the scarlet rug, made from the scraps
of numerous flannel petticoats, defied the pink glazed
calico that draped the dressing-table. A good room,
Sarah felt, and good ornaments, very suitable for
setting up house.

Marigold sat with her head leaning against the whitewashed wall beneath a huge text worked in wool.
She was feeling the burden of the fact that, when one is
very miserable, somebody always lights two tallow dips.

"Ah, you cry ! " said Sarah. "It'll do you good.
So you're away to your auntie's. Well, 's Catherine'll
be glad. If Sarah Jowel's got eyes, 's Catherine's had
more to do with it than she'd care to say. She gets
to what she wants cross-lookards, does 's Catherine,
like a bird to crumbs."

"Somebody's made right wrong," sobbed Marigold.
" I wish I was dead."

"Ah ! I'm that-a-way myself, times," said Sarah.
"Love's so lungeous ! It churns up your innards
summat cruel ! "

She began to sing in her resounding voice, " There is a fountain filled with blood." This chirurgic hymn was a favourite of hers.

Marigold went on crying. The lungeousness of love had become very apparent to her. Everyone was angry. Miss Catherine blazed at her with eyes of haughty virtue. The old lady had a text for every meeting, and did not mince her words. The mistress —Marigold shivered at the thought of Mrs. Darke's glacial regard. And the angrier they were, the more furiously did Peter make love. He snatched her hand as she went in to prayers. He waylaid her at every dim turn of the stairs. He was strange and wild. And now she had practically promised to go to the grotto. She was trepidant, jubilant ; but chiefly she was afraid. When Sarah breathed deeply and the house had sunk into silence, and night had flung her purple curtain over the forest, she must steal out and meet Peter at the grotto.

" If you'd give your word to do a thing, would you do it if it wunna right according to catechism ? " she asked.

" Well," said Sarah judicially, " I met, if I bettered myself by it, and if it was respectable." She was arranging the cottonwool in her ears for the night.

" When true lovers part, it's a bad day for 'em," she said. " Put out the candles, if you're only crying. Tears want no tallow. But if I was you, I'd come to bed, Christian. And see, Marigol', I'll give you one of those jars. No, seeing I'm sorry for you, I'll give you the pair. A bit of property's a grand medicine for all ills." She clapped in the last piece of cotton-wool and got into bed.

Marigold also got into bed and lay there inertly. The lover, faced with parting, becomes a dumb creature beneath a heavy mallet. She listened to the rats gnawing and scurrying within the walls. They were

like the unholy things that harbour in outworn forms—
the petty hates, the tyrannies, the deceit and fear.
The attics were alive with their stealthy goblin noise ;
it was as if they knew the night was theirs and that
none would gainsay them. There they were, and
there they would stay. Only if Dormer fell would
they depart. Their shrill squeaking and quarrelling,
their occasional falls when they dislodged a quantity
of loose mortar, the perpetual fear that they would gnaw
through into the room kept Marigold in a fidget. At
last she heard, through the half-open door, very faint,
coming along the echoing passages, the voice of the
dictatorial clock announcing twelve. She must go.
In spite of her dread of the dark woods, of the judgment of her fellows, the sorrowful to-morrow had
receded, and there flowered in the lightless room the
wild rose of love's ecstasy. Sarah heard Marigold
stirring, for her sleep was what she called " a dog-
sleep." She guessed where Marigold was going, and
as the faint creakings of the attic stairs were hushed,
she turned over restlessly, as if to shuffle off responsibility, and murmured : " I've got 'ool in my ears,
hanna I ? For all I'm supposed to know, the girl's
in bed and asleep."

Marigold, passing the door of Ernest and Ruby,
wondered why it was right for them to be together, not
loving each other (for she was sure they did not care for
each other), and why it was wrong for Peter and herself to be together, when they did love each other.
For Marigold, in common with other lovers, quite forgot to find out whether her gift was returned. She
envied the sleeping house, which was foolish of her,
for sleep is only a shadow. Those who go out of the
dreaming house into the forest are at least awake,
however dark the forest may be.

The solid pilasters of the stone porch looked ghostly

in the moonlight, and from each one, as she opened the door, sprang a rod, lying darkly on the floor of the hall. In the cold air her breath stood up, white, small and palpable, as men have imagined the soul to stand at its passing.

She went swiftly down to the bridge and along by the water, and as she went, accompanied by her vagrant shadow, another shadow, taller and less vacillating, followed under the lee of the bare woods. The black silhouettes of the lower trees lay, spectral and large, half on land and half on the water. Marigold's shadow and the shadow that followed her threaded them. The wind made a snake-like, hissing sound in all the yews of the hillside as Marigold sped upwards. As she neared the grotto, a voice, low but imperative, called her from beside the water :

" Marigold !   Marigold ! "

And the echoes that haunted the cup where Dormer lay took up the music of the word and played with it, sending it like a ball from slope to slope.

" Marigold—gold—gold ! "

But the broken echoes were flung back with a mocking sound into the silver water, for she did not hear. Already Peter had stepped from the grotto, already she was in his arms. " You are late ! " he said crossly. Then in the sweetness of kissing her he forgave her, and they went into the grotto. A red fire of logs blazed on the rough hearth that used to warm the Dormer ladies when, in a day long gone, they spent their maiden leisure in lining the grotto with shells. On the table was such a repast as Peter deemed suitable. Marigold eyed the collation, recognizing the contents of the larder. Her breathless pallor gave way before her laughter.

" There'll be nought for dinner to-morrowday ! They'll all be clemmed ! "

And a peal of laughter startled the stony grotto as she saw, beside to-morrow's pudding and the ham, Mrs. Velindre's beloved quince marmalade and the potted meat without which Ernest could not breakfast. Peter shouted, tossing back his head with his wild faun air, snapping his fingers. To-night the wood-god was predominant in him. It was in his cheeks; in the straight, eager profile in which he resembled Jasper; in the wave of his hair that was flung back like a crest, as if to cool an over-hot forehead. It was in his loose-knit figure, which had, in spite of the gaucherie of youth, the grace that is given even to the clumsy by primal impulse. He had the touch of princeliness which passion, even the callowest, the crudest, gives to the young.

"Apron!" he cried. "Cap! What do we want with them? Off with 'em! Ho! I like you better without a cap!"

He held the plait of hair, coloured like sunburnt bracken, in both hands. The logs blazed, and every pale shell flushed in the red light. Had the staid ladies, who set them one by one in place, known for what festival they built that beauty of mother-of-pearl, had they heard echoes of that laughter which now leapt with the leaping flames, maybe they would have stayed their hands. Little would be done in this life if men knew for what they built. So a great king may set forth to build a palace of black basalt for the god of war. And behold! When he has finished it, Fate says: "This is not what I wanted. Come, you tendrilled things, you blossomy things, wreathe this basalt into beauty! Come, you white and golden doves, make a nest here, make a music here! For this is a bower for the peaceful spirit of brother-hood."

Here was a place meant for the tame revellings of

conventional ladyhood, and behold ! that rough, wild thing, young passion, took possession. Marigold's head, outlined by the iridescent wall ; her face, thrown into relief by the dancing light, faintly rose-tinted ; her eyes, dark with present joy and future sorrow, made a picture so sweet that the last remnants of caution left Peter. He would forget that he was to marry pale Catherine and consolidate Dormer. All that would come in time. But now, here was Marigold and here was he, and the red light surged over shells of saffron, of salmon pink, of veined purple and scarlet.

Peter stooped to a great conch that was the central ornament above the fireplace, and shouted into its sounding hollow, " Marigold ! "

The confident music seemed to defy that other music without, the music that had fallen into the water.

" Oh, hushee now," said Marigold. But she smiled, for she too refused to parley with the morrow, and who should hear them, safe in their magical house in the dim lost centre of night ?

Outside, climbing with slow and heavy steps, a great knobbed stick in his hand, Enoch heard the laughter —very faint and maddening, like the provocative voice of an unkind love who has betaken herself to the submerged halls of faery.

He stood still, and the attentive trees stood about him on this side and on that, surveying him as though they questioned. His face was dark and drawn with rage, and the fierceness of a creature defrauded. That he was of so quiet a nature made this volcanic fire more terrible. So wild a fury shook his massive body, that it seemed to conjure a visible picture on the dim screen of night—a picture of two lovers dead amid broken shells and scattered fire. But even as his hand was stretched towards the door, he paused. Far down, in startled silver, out of startled mist, a cock crowed.

The sound was a key that opened within his mind the
great door of nature. He paused, and the trees
seemed to question him. They summoned his soul,
his deepest, most mysterious self ; and when it came
at their call they communed with it, creating with its
help a better thing than the desire of killing which had
grown up like a dark fungus in his mind. He had
watched, knowing this hour would come. He had
waited in the garden, sure that one night she would
steal forth. To be up all night was nothing to him.
He was always out before the light. He could not
have borne to miss the intoxicating secrecy of those
hours when who knows what strange things are out
and about—hours haunted by inexplicable sounds,
significant happenings. Those are the hours when
sheep and cattle do as they list, and look upon the
world with eyes different from those that humans
know ; for at this time they have not yet called in
their souls for the day—their timid souls that must be
barred in the shippen of silence, where they sleep
behind eyes shuttered with sullen or wistful inexpres-
siveness. In dew-dark summer mornings Enoch loved
to be among them as one kin to them, and at the first
shrilling of the sunrise chorus, when each beast was
startled (walking at ease with its soul) by its sudden
shadow flung blue before it by the early ray, Enoch
also went as three—his broad and sturdy body, his
half-tamed soul, and his pansy-tinted shadow.

An hour less or more mattered little to him. He
had meant to save Marigold from the obloquy that in
the House of Dormer falls on a generous lover. He
had intended to follow her and threaten them both
with discovery and drag her from the very arms of
passion, carry her if need be to her mother's house.

And now here he was, foiled by his own personality,
tied hand and foot by his own rage. For he knew

that if he put his hand on the door he would kill Peter
Darke. He would strike from those black eyes the
glow of triumph, trample in the pine-needles that
haughty figure, that hawklike air.

He gazed round him at the multitudinous witness
of his temptation, at the secret yews peering over one
another with their great stooping shoulders and their
appearance of having their heads hidden. Yews are
the owls of the tree-world ; they have the same curious
look of having drawn down their heads into their
bodies. Beyond the yews he saw a dead holly, stark
and pale, with arms flung up as before an inevitable,
incurable horror. A little fir tree kept up a low
descant, caressing with its finger-tips the side of the
grotto. It was well for those within that they did not
laugh at that moment. A laugh would have meant three
lives. But Peter was drinking deep in the grey wells
of Marigold's eyes, and no sound disturbed the night.

" Killing's allus untimely," muttered Enoch, and
it seemed to his soul that the unheard echoes were
crying with a sweet chiding : " Untimely, untimely ! "
But it was not on the sandstone that their silver
voices struck ; it was on the cliffs and crannies of his
deep and unknown self.

The heavy stick shook with the grip of his hands,
his hands that hated Peter. Marigold, his little girl,
about whose life every root of his being turned, Marigold was stolen from him. He had loved her as unconsciously as the willow-wren loves Africa when winter
winds are in the sedges. His slow mind had not
known it. His slow tongue had not spoken it. But
now, too late, he understood. His quarrel with Peter
was not that, being of " the gentry " with " money in
pocket and money to come," he had used his superiority
to dazzle Marigold. Nor was it that Peter was antici-
pating marriage. It was that he intuitively knew

Peter's intention of marrying Catherine in the future.
This secret and others were known to him and to the
rest of the dependents at Dormer. Men are the toys
of their underlings, who feed them and clothe them,
wake them and put them to bed, knowing beneath the
outer manner of subservience the autocracy of a child
with its dolls. For he that supplies the stark human
need, whether of body or spirit, is king of the world.
Peter would marry Catherine and be well thought of.
And what of Marigold? This was the core of his
rage, but it was not the innermost core. Deeper than
that lay the knowledge that Peter, in pushing him
aside, had denied Marigold the best love. For he knew
that Peter's affection for her was now, whatever it
might be some day, a thing flimsy as a cobweb;
and that his own love was genuine and solid as the
heart of a young tree. Love which is only strong
enough to increase the lover's happiness is a poor
thing. The love that is worth giving is fire in the
giver's hand, a thing of woe and insufferable ecstasy.

"Kill and swing for it, Enoch Gale! Kill and
swing!" So cried a voice that came he knew not
whence. The night wind stirred in the black tree,
but it was not the night wind spoke. Was it the
ancient mutter of the herd pasturing in the dead ages
before it found a soul?

Suddenly Enoch flung the stick as far as his strength
could send it. It fell crashing into the undergrowth.

Within, Marigold stirred.

"Hushee!" she whispered. "I mun goo! There's
summat bad in the 'ood!"

"Go? You shall never go."

"Didna you hear the crackling? That was the
ghosses breaking through from underground."

"Silly! I'll take care of you."

Enoch was running with clumsy haste away from the

grotto, uphill, eyes shut to escape the red glow from
the slit of a window. He plunged through the spinny
of dead hollies, where the livid boles shone like unlit
corpse candles. At last he came to the place called
by Amber the Birds' Orchard. There in a grassy
hollow beneath a crab-tree he flung himself upon his
knees. The black, complex traceries of branch and
twig came and went upon his upturned moonlit face
with the flowing motion of water. All things below
in the valley grew small, shrank to nothing. The
voices of the owls, echoing among the glades, came up
thinly ; the song of the water sank to a low humming
Dormer lay far below ; he could see its dim blur through
the traceries of the mist-beaded woods like a sleeping
creature curtained with dew-spangled cobwebs. Deep
in mist was Dormer valley. Even the grotto was half
obliterated. But here upon the open hill were no
mists, no sounds, nothing to distract the spirit waiting
attent and eager for what would come upon it out of
the unfathomable.

Enoch spoke, and his voice with its tree music
seemed to possess the air long after he had spoken.

" Dunna leave me stray in the dark night ! " he
said. " I bin nought but a poor beast in a big
pasture."

Whether the comfort for which he waited was to
come from beyond the stars, or from the mysterious
hillside or from within himself, he did not trouble to
ask. He simply waited in the silence, while the keen
air fingered his face. It was one of those winter
nights that mourn for Bethlehem—a night on which
the spirit longs to traverse low green hills, strewn
with sheep, under shaken gusts of music ; a night on
which to meet what is rarer to-day than a miracle—
a few simple men caught in a spell of wonder ; a night
on which to reach at last a place low and small, full

of sweet breath and the trampling of clear-eyed cattle, and holding, as the seed holds the tree, the very core of life. Alas, alas for us who in these latter days find the wan hills all silent and deserted, with none to beckon us to certain peace, with no noise of angels in the silver clouds. Yet, when the solemn wind begins to move along the mountain, walking in the heavy trees ; when every dewy leaf has a gleam of recognition for the wet-eyed stars, does there not come upon us a sweetness greater than the fragrance of flowers, a desire—passionate and vague—for a beauty that is not less real because its revelations are subtle and its essence beyond the reach of the senses ?

It was for this that Enoch, all unconsciously, waited with upturned face caressed by shadows. It was on account of these hours of ecstasy that he was called " simple." It was by virtue of this strange sacrament of which he partook—a fruit that never appletree bore nor sun ripened—that he turned to go downhill again in the dim morning with a light in his face. He was not in aspect a likely candidate for saintship. He shambled, and he wore, as usual in damp weather, an old potato sack draped over his shoulders. His eyes were full of grief, for he had seen joy go singing past, and he knew that it was lost to him. He was no more an ascetic than is any primitive creature. He was not of those whose spirits, cadaverous with long exile in material things, sit mournfully in the garden of earthly beauty, laying no finger on the rose and gold, waking the hollow echoes with the cry : " All these shall perish ! "

He wandered down towards the water. " It'll be sobbin' wet to-morrowday ! " he said.

A laugh rang out in the forest, falling into the stream like a flower thrown from the tree-tops. The gibing echoes laughed lightly, elfishly.

" Eh, Marigol' ! " muttered Enoch, the sweat standing on his forehead so that the chill fingers of the breezes pricked him like electric needles.

They came, the two young lawless creatures, one loveless, down the quiet sloping path where the red elder leaves still hung. They came in the panoply of early physical beauty. But it was on Enoch, cloaked in his sack, leaden-eyed, dank with grief, that the greatest light of beauty rested.

When she saw him standing there, Marigold screamed, and the echoes screamed like frightened fairies. But it did not matter ; if anyone heard they would not heed, for the woods were said to be haunted by shrieks. Not only were the voices of the hedgehog and the bat heard here, and that of the Death's-head moth—a bewitched whisper—but legend said that here the mandrake cried, and that in this hollow of ancient greenery the voices of creatures trampled by the multitude lived within the echoes.

" Well ? " said Peter, red and awkward and therefore blustering. " What are you doing, spying here ? "

" Sir, you best know what I'm here for."

" Well ? "

" To see our Marigol' righted."

" Righted ? " queried Peter with a forced laugh. Marigold had crept into the shadow of the elder tree where Enoch stood.

" I've yeard tell as you're set to marry Miss Catherine one fine day," said Enoch. " No offence, Master Peter."

" Well, what if I do ? "

" Miss Catherine's posy-ring wunna be bought with *your* gold," said Enoch, with a flash in his brown eyes. " If you come to Miss Catherine's chamber it'll be lover, not 'usband she'll call you."

" What do you mean ? "

" I mean this-a-way, Master Peter. You'll wed our Marigol' to-morrowday."

" I won't."

" Master Peter ! " Enoch spoke sadly, reasonably, but with a latent anger. " Master Peter ! You've took my Marigol' off me. For you *was* my Marigol', my dear "—he turned to the weeping girl—" and that you know. You've brought her low, Master Peter— ah ! she'll be low in the eyes of men when this night's doings come to light."

" Dunna say it, Enoch ! Dunna say it ! " cried Marigold.

" I mun say it to-night, my dear, and then never no more," said Enoch. " If so be you was fond of me, I'd marry you to-day in spite of all—marry you and love you true."

She clung to his sleeve in a passion of grief.

" But seeing she dunna, and seeing as any bit of love she's got to give (for she is but young, Master Peter) is for you and no other, it 'ud be no manner use. So you'll marry our Marigol' to-morrowday."

" I tell you I can't ! "

Peter thought of his parents, of Catherine, of Ernest and the neighbours, of the wrath and laughter. Why, life would not be livable at Dormer. And all for a servant—a very pretty servant, of course, but still only a servant. Marigold had now ceased to be wildly exciting. She was no longer forbidden fruit. The fire in him was slaked. But Catherine was still forbidden fruit. Catherine could send a rarefied excitement through his veins. There was something alluring in those long eyes of hers. No—he could not tie himself for life to this pretty little thing, so shrinking and so yielding. He had won her ; she would soon bore him.

But Enoch's unmoved, equable voice broke in on him.

" You'll marry her to-morrowday, Master Peter. If pocket-money's short, I've got a bit saved for the licence and that."

Peter stamped with rage.

" I won't !   You can't make me ! "

" Oh !   I thought you was fond of me ! " sobbed Marigold.

" If you dunna," said Enoch stilly, " you'll not see to-morrow's sun."

Marigold screamed again, and again the echoes bandied the sound from one to another.

Peter looked dazed.

" It's this-a-way," said Enoch.   " I dunna care for life now, not a farden.   If you wunna do my bidding and right my girl, I'll drown you like a kitten in Dormer brook, and hang for it."

" Oh, God !   Oh, God ! " cried Marigold.

Peter's eyes looked dangerous.

" Dunna make un do it, Enoch, if he dunna want to ! " pleaded Marigold.

" I be stronger than you," said Enoch.   " I could break you in two, easy.   And I'd do it."

Suddenly Peter sprang at him, for his temper was up and meekness was not in him.   But a grip of iron was on his arms in a moment ; he was helpless in the grasp of muscles hardened by years of toil.

He realized defeat.   He understood that Enoch was that invincible creature, a man who does not care whether he lives or dies.   He made terms.

" Well, look here !   If I do it, nobody's to know. She must go away——"

" Ah !   I'll goo to my auntie's."

Enoch looked at Peter with mingled scorn, envy and anger.

"Go away! You've a chance to be near Marigold and you say go away!" he murmured.

"Yes. She must go," said Peter. "Nobody must know."

"Till when?"

"Never."

"You'll come to a better mind. But still, if you'll go and see her now and again?"

"All right."

"So be it!" said Enoch with a great sigh. "But mind you, Master Peter, no randies. No goings on with Miss Catherine, or——" he gave a significant sideways nod towards the water.

Peter was aghast. That Enoch, of all people, should develop these murderous tendencies! Then he suddenly felt sorry for Enoch. He remembered the dancing firelight in the grotto, and the hawthorn freshness of Marigold. He turned to go. Then he came impulsively and boyishly back. "Wish it hadn't happened," he said gruffly.

"It inna your fault so much, lad, as the fault of the bitter old house," said Enoch.

His voice rang over the water as they went across the bridge, and the house loomed up in the first sombre daylight. The mists, herded by a rising wind, passed before it like strange creatures with an uncertain wandering motion. Almost it seemed that the solid walls trembled, so that the watcher might expect at any moment a sliding collapse inevitably fated. For the falling of houses and cities and empires—all the solidities of man's invention—is not with a crash of masonry in the hour when all men flee. Years, centuries, before the crowded humanity inhabiting them feels a flicker of disquiet, with less sound than a midge makes, they have fallen in the echoing soul under the owl-light of dreams.

XIII

THE BEAST WALK

WHEN something dramatic happens, people are usually too busy to notice it. On the morning after Enoch's vigil by the grotto, two dramatic things happened. Jasper went to purgatory for Catherine's and the truth's sake, for it was his first day at Mr. Arkinstall's; and Marigold set forth on the journey which was to make her the bride of Dormer's heir.

Ernest reasoned with Jasper at breakfast—the denuded meal with no potted meat—for he was really a kind-hearted man, and Jasper's miserable face worried him. Catherine pointed out how much easier was the life of a country curate than the life of a farm-hand. But Jasper " hardened his face," to use a quotation of Sarah's, and turning to Peter said : " Coming ? "

" In a minute." Peter was cross and absent-minded. He was wondering how the day off to-morrow was to be managed, and he wanted to say good-bye to Marigold.

" Well, I'll go on," said Jasper. He strode off down the drive, his shoulders bent like those of a man carrying a heavy burden.

" Lord ! " said Solomon, " I'm sorry for Arkinstall. Not but what he deserves it."

" Deserves what, uncle ? " asked Catherine.

" The worst farm-hand ever man had," said Solomon. " And he's got it."

Peter pushed back his chair. " Can I ask off to-morrow, father ? " he said.

" What for ? "

" I thought I'd get some new leggin's."

" They're quite good," said his mother.

" And a few cartridges."

" Plenty in the house," said his father.

" And I want to see about Christmas presents."

" Too early ! " said his grandmother.

" Damn ! " said Peter.

" What's that ? What's that ? " Solomon was particular as to swearing.

" Swearing is an ugly habit," Catherine swept from the room.

" There, now you've offended the girl ? "

" Let me have a day off, and I'll buy her a present."

This extreme cunning won his point. He departed, but not to the Arkinstall's. He went down the lane towards the Four Waters, and there he awaited the cart.

Meanwhile, Marigold was seen off by Sarah and her mother. She slipped away like dew from a flower, and the house seemed to take no cognisance of her going. Only the forest sang its old, low song, and the water murmured of mountains and the sea—of things greater than Dormer.

" Well," said Sarah, " I shall miss you, Marigol'. Her that's coming is but a poor thing. Gowk's her name and sullen's her ways. I'll miss you proper."

Her protestations were the more genuine as she knew the departure to be inevitable.

" When you've raught back, Enoch, you can lug up the new girl's box," she said. " And to-morrow you met as well churn, seeing I'll be drove for time."

" To-morrow'll be a day off."

" A day off ! " When had Enoch ever wanted a day off ?

"Ay. That's the colour of it," said Enoch. To himself he said : " I'll miss you proper, Marigol' ! Ay, I'll miss you proper ! "

" I partly think you'd better be a quieter girl at your auntie's than what you've been at this 'ouse," said Mrs. Gosling.

" Scrat on ! " Enoch remarked to Jenny, feeling that things were getting strained. They drove away, and the house was unaware that any dissolution had begun within it. Enoch was glad to remember the five pounds in silver which he had given to Marigold as a wedding present, and the bunch of violets that reposed inside his hat, to be presented at the station. Thinking of these things, he smiled his queer melodic smile. At a turn of the road, there was Peter.

" Good-bye, Goldie ! " he cried. " Give us a kiss ! " In the manner of young lovers they forgot the feelings of Enoch. " I'm coming to-morrow, you know where," said Peter.

" I know you be," replied Enoch, with a grim mouth. While Marigold journeyed on in hope and Enoch journeyed back in despair, things grew very strained at the Wallows. Mr. Arkinstall became more and more devious, more and more subtle as the day wore on and as he realized Jasper's incompetence. Philip, for his part, had determined to drive Jasper away. A pretender to the hand of Catherine should not receive anything of encouragement at the Wallows. So if a dirty job had to be done, Jasper did it. If anything fell, it fell on Jasper. If a young horse had to be harnessed, Jasper harnessed it. Sometimes he looked up towards Dormer and thought how near heaven was to hell—for Dormer would be heaven, he felt, if Catherine would only love him. If he might have her and his books and a chance of success in life what a glory there would be on the days ! As it was, there

seemed no chance of anything but a choice of two evils.
Either he must go (" and go he shall ! " said Philip),
or he must stay and bear it. He gritted his teeth and
decided to stay.

He came home from his first day with worn nerves
and in a state of black depression. Like many
commonplace men of his type, Mr. Arkinstall had a
hatred for anyone in the least unusual or above the
ordinary standard. He kept Jasper loading turnips
till he was almost sick with exhaustion. When Jasper
flagged, he wove sarcasms of an amazing circuitousness,
indulging in an orgy of insults to which his oriental
expression gave a subtlety not their own.

All day Jasper promised himself that he would go up
to his room after tea and work. He could pass exams.
even if he worked alone. If he passed the exams.,
Catherine would surely see the foolishness of his working at the Wallows. Then perhaps she would come
with him into the world. So he comforted himself
with lonely enthusiasm. After tea he fetched a candle
and lit it. Grandmother eyed him over the top of the
Lion. Then, as he was going out unseen by the
others, she announced with startling suddenness :

" He's gotten another wax candle ! "

Mrs. Darke looked up.

" Why do you burn so many candles ? " she asked.

" To do my work."

" What work ? "

" Books."

" You don't want to work at books. You are learning farming. You are not to be a scholar."

" Not a scholar ! Never a scholar now ! " Grandmother harped, in the manner of the insensitive, on the
one unendurable thing.

" I can't spare you candles," said Mrs. Darke.

Jasper turned and went out. He would buy the

candles himself. But he had no money. He went to
look for his father and found him feeding the " gun-
dogs." They received their supper with imperturb-
able pessimism, as if they had been soured by their
life-work of putting others in the way of getting what
they themselves wanted, and as if they knew that
Solomon liked them not for what they were, but for
what they did. And as they trailed after Solomon
on their leads, day by day, they had an air of being two
very old people playing with a small boy. It was evi-
dent that when his back was turned glances of amused
tolerance were exchanged.

"Father!" said Jasper with a mighty effort,
" could you let me have some pocket money?"

Solomon was ruffled by Peter's affair and by the pro-
spective inconvenience of Enoch's holiday.

"I'll find the cash," he said, " when you find
God."

At this moment Ernest loomed above the kennel
wall. He had a way of appearing above Jasper's
horizons like a round red sun, persisting in shining on
the evil and on the good. He breathed forgiveness on
Jasper at every turn. He insisted on loving him. He
said :

" One cannot do much for the poor fellow, but one
can at least give him companionship."

Jasper, finding this unbearable, tried hints, silence,
finally rudeness. But they had no more effect than
paper darts flung at an elephant. At the present
moment Ernest made things worse by saying :

" Right, sir! Right! That's cricket! First
things first."

" If fools held their tongues——" exploded Jasper.

" Though I can't forgive an insult to my cloth,
said Ernest, " I can forgive an insult to myself, freely
—freely."

" In the devil's name," shouted Jasper, " stop this damnable forgiving."

" If you want to quarrel," remarked Solomon, " quarrel elsewhere. You're disturbing the dogs."

Jasper went back to the house. As he flung the door open Ernest, following, said :

" I want to be friends, Jasper."

" Well, I don't ! "

" Refuse a friend ! "

" I don't want friends just now. I want myself. I want to be let alone and have room to breathe."

Ernest expanded his immense chest. The chain on which dangled his Maltese cross was tried to the uttermost.

" *I* am always able to breathe," he said. " *I* am never conscious of stifling. It is life—the true life—that you want. *Mens sana in corpore sano.* ' 'Tis Life, more life, for which we pant.' Come to the Captain."

Jasper looked at him, and his expression verged on the murderous. He was reminded of a frog which Peter (who had been cruel as a small boy from lack of imagination) had inflated by putting a straw into its mouth and blowing. He felt that Ernest would like to put a straw into his (Jasper's) mind and blow until he was inflated with all the orthodox views that Ernest held. Ernest was quite unconscious of any criticism.

" I am only trying to cheer you, my dear fellow—to cheer you and draw you out of your gloom," he said.

" If you cheer me any more, I shall go melancholy mad."

" What you want, my dear Jasper, is to be more robust—less morbid ; to be less (if I may say so, as your spiritual pastor) less conceited and more obedient. Obedient to the Captain, to myself and to the Rector."

" Obedience is a vice," snapped Jasper. " It is a

pet vice of stunted personalities who can't act for themselves, having no ideas, and who claim merit for copying the ideas and actions of others."

He went into the dining-room, comforted by the knowledge that he had turned his sentence quite passably. The epigram has never been given its due as a tonic against the ills of life ; but a tonic it certainly is, or why are so many books written ?

In the dining-room no one had moved since Jasper went out. Catherine looked up with disapproving raised eyebrows. Jasper sat down and turned over the leaves of an old magazine which had lived on the side table with the family Bible since a chance visitor left it there. Sitting thus, humped in his chair, sullen as a winter bird, and feckless with the lack of spiritual food, he glowered round at the others. Not one of them, he thought, understood or wanted to understand his primal needs. He had not the faintest idea that Amber followed his weary road step by step, footsore when he was footsore, hungry when he was hungry Catherine he regarded as too far above him to be able to sympathize with his troubles. They could not, he thought, glimpse in the mistiest way the kind of life that was home to him. He was different, as a freak bird is different ; so they disliked him. As he sat there, he felt, below the desultory conversation and the fixed expressions of their faces, their spirits stalking his spirit in the silence of semi-consciousness ; snapping at him ; coiling like snakes ; peering out from the ambush of their creed and from the stronghold of received opinion at him, walking defenceless through the night.

In this cellar of being, where he sometimes came he felt them all to be totally different from the everyday people he knew. Even Catherine, when he descended into this crepuscular chamber, lit so startlingly by flashes of insight, seemed alien to herself. Once even, he had glimpsed on that angelic profile a sneer. As for grandmother, she was a fierce adversary tilting at him with the armed, exuberant hate of a knight of the middle ages, and with the face of an angry wasp. He chuckled when he thus envisaged grandmother. But at the thought of his mother he did not laugh. His face grew wan with the tormented expression of neuralgia. Only his was a neuralgia of the soul.

" You fidget a good deal, Jasper," said Catherine.

" Fidget ! Fidget ! Fidget ! " said grandmother.

Jasper threw the magazine into the fire and went into the kitchen.

" A bad-tempered boy—a very bad-tempered boy," muttered grandmother.

" Sarah," said Jasper coaxingly, " give us two or three candles ! "

But Sarah was in no mood to bestow candles.

" Don't talk of candles to a woman tormented, Master Jasper ! " said she. " I've no mind to give you candles. And what's the use of this wilful nonsense of book-learning ? If you've got a big print Bible for duty and the death and birth column every week for pleasure, what more is there ? "

Jasper was beginning an argument, but at that moment Enoch came in and Sarah's wrath fell on him. She had found the rough draft of the letter Enoch had written for presentation with the violets.

" Love you, you says ! And darling, you says ! Parting for evermore, you says ! Who are you to say love and darling, as knows no more of love than a calf new-born ? And you sitting and looking at Jemima Onions day in, day out, mum as a mouse in cheese. To go and write the like of this all unbeknownst, and to a girl as canna do crockerywork and makes pastry as hard as a lawyer ! "

Jasper felt that others besides himself were incompletely happy.

" I'll go to the Beast Walk," he thought. " At least they're not alive."

He was falling back upon a habit of his childhood. When people misunderstood him, refused to reply to his questions, insisted upon conforming to their standards, then he went to the Beast Walk—the place he loathed more than any place on earth. To climb this path harrowed his soul, made his face even at ten years look quite wizened. But now, in his young manhood, the dark spell was infinitely stronger. He drank here of a charm thick as black honey made from purple poison flowers by bees in hell. This curious psychic state was mysterious to him as are the instincts of all animals—man and brute. No one else felt it, though the place was certainly not cheerful. It was one of those admixtures of man and nature which has somehow gone sour in the making. To reach it you crossed the wooden bridge at the back of the house, turning to the left under the trees in the shadowy path that led towards the Four Waters. Halfway between the bridge and Mrs. Gosling's cottage the Beast Walk went straight uphill from the water. There was something significant in the way in which this broad and rather pompous walk ended in the soft, thick stream without reason or explanation.

Nobody knew when the Beast Walk was first thought of. Only grandmother could remember, as a little girl, being told by her grandmother that it had been finished in her own archaic childhood. The walk, during the whole of its ascent, was bordered on each side by strange beasts and birds cut out of gigantic yew trees. It ended at the grotto, which dominated it. Just here, the wood was composed of yews and hollies so old that they gave the impression of having

existed in the primeval forest. The upper woods
were equally old, and much more lovely ; for there, in
sheltered dingles of the hillside, oak and beech, the
silver flickering birch, the true-service tree and the
scarlet-fruited spindle stood in an elfin age that tran-
scended youth, because the age of trees does not imply
loss of beauty. But down near the water the hosts of
the yews spread their black tents, like the dwellings of
gnomes.

In each generation the regnant Darke had cut one
or two of these into such shapes as pleased him. Swans,
horses, fowls, peacocks, cattle and sheep crowded the
walk, and there was one very malevolent-looking
monkey. But the Darke idea of an animal's body
seemed almost as wide of the mark as their idea of its
soul. Some were almost indistinguishable. All had
a nightmare touch. This was accentuated by the fact
that they had not been trimmed for a long time, so
beak and claw were exaggerated, and the outlines of
head and wing and udder became vague and ominous.
They were like a herd of prehistoric beasts trooping
down to drink at the stream. Jasper thought, as he
looked at their lowering ranks, that it was as if each
ancestor had breathed such ferocities as were in his
soul into his especial creation. So the walk had come
to symbolize in his mind the Lares and Penates of
Dormer, and the beasts were pictures of hoary tradition, prescription, decrepit and unwieldy laws, custom
grown senile, a predatory collectivism. It was this
predatory atmosphere that most impressed him at
Dormer. He felt sometimes as if he had come into a
wild beast show and found all the beasts loose. He
was realizing that there are depths of savagery in the
human heart deeper than that of killing ; that when
law is put before love and the material before the
spiritual there is nothing left wherewith to combat

evil ; that the commonplace is the soul's peril ; that
a person with low aims, paltry pleasures and an in-
ability to love or hate passionately is more dangerous
than any beast of prey ; that his righteous and respectable relations and neighbours were going to be lions and
tigers in his path.

The walk was always impressive—on a lurid evening
of thunder when the heavy air pressed upon the woods
and the beasts were tinged with reddish light ; on a
foggy December day when they loomed through
yellow curtains ; in snow, when each lumpish shape
wore with ironic mirth a white chlamys ; in windy
weather, when they were like creatures silently reaching out for a victim, having in them something of the
horrific and the obscene. The grotto, built of grey
stone and flat as a tortoise, might have been a sacri-
ficial altar. But it was on a moonlit night such as
this that Jasper most detested them, and most nearly
attained through their sorcery creative expression.
As he turned up the walk, leaving the silver water
behind him, the grass seemed to be strewn with broken
idols. But it was only the inky shadows, even more
grotesque than the trees, prone upon the greenish
moonlight. He thought of his grandmother, as he
generally did in this place. He also thought how
strange it is that man can so easily create that which
becomes a god of terror to him, and with what eager
celerity he sets to work to make nightmares for his
fellows. Those at Dormer now, those at Dormer in
the past, had made and were still making springes
for the souls of people like himself. Because his soul
was alive and would fly they wished to cage it. Because it sang its own song they wanted to kill it.
Spiritually they were cannibals. Jasper had a particular passion for freedom, a wild, bird-like need of
personal liberty. If he could not grow as he would,

live as he willed, something told him that he would
cease to grow, cease to exist.

" I'd go away to-night," he thought, " if it wasn't
for Cathy. If she wasn't what she is—beautiful in
soul and body—I shouldn't care what became of me,
but she is—she is ! "

The mis-shapen monkey, its eye a hole through which
shone the greenish sky, mopped and mowed before the
moon and seemed to contemplate him with ironic
humour. Suddenly it came to him that here he was, a
single, friendless soul, in the wide, worn spoor of his
ancestors—of the herd that gallops because its neighbour gallops, is afraid with its neighbour's panic,
rushes on, flank to heaving flank, each goring its
neighbour in the agony of its own terror at the spectres
of its own imagining.

Jasper shivered, feeling the woods cold and ghastly
and companionless without the retinue of summer.
Already the autumn tree-music had dwindled to the
thin, eerie murmur of winter. With a shrug at his
own expense, Jasper walked on moodily between the
crouching forms, and sitting down on the stone bench
outside the grotto, took out his treasure, a photograph
Catherine had had taken of herself in her confirmation
veil. She had turned up her eyes and drooped her
mouth, knowing with her unfailing sense for artistic
effect that what would in Amber have seemed a grimace
would in herself merely look devout. And, as Jasper
was gazing at this with passionate intentness, suddenly
Catherine herself was there in a long white cloak.

" Like a moth," said Jasper quietly, " like a beautiful moth, you came."

She smiled, sitting beside him.

" Oh, come with me, Cathy, out into the world ! "
he cried. " You don't know, you wouldn't dream, how
well I can do in the things I want to do. Hated

labour is bad labour. I can do no good here. Marry
me, Cathy ! "

" When you become a Christian again."

Jasper was kneeling beside her, his right arm along
the back of the seat, touching her shoulders.

" God, whoever He is, wherever He is, must be
greater than you make Him, Cathy—too great to be a
bone of contention between lovers."

" If you become a Christian again, you could kneel
by me like this every night ; you could put your arms
round me ; you——"

" Take care, Cathy. I'm not a boy now."

" You could kiss me."

She gleamed palely on him. She would win, though
it cost her a blush. But Jasper had no more patience
—his arms were round her ; he kissed her hands, her
forehead, her mouth, with a kind of wrathful
reverence. She remained still and silent in a cold
rage.

" Well ? " she said. " Have you done ? "

Jasper came to himself. But he still knelt there
like a penitent awaiting the lash.

" You are not even a gentleman," said Catherine.
" I shall not speak to you again for a month—not till
Christmas."

He received the sentence in silence, absorbed in
wonder at his own temerity, letting his impenitent
eyes dwell on the lips he had kissed.

Catherine rose and drew her cloak about her, leaving
him kneeling there. Then suddenly she came back,
her hands outstretched : " If you'll become a Christian,
I'll marry you at Christmas."

She waited.

" If you asked me to change from one religion to
another," said Jasper, " if you asked me to steal for
you, perhaps even to murder for you, I'd do it. But I

can't invent a God for you, Cathy. I can't make the truth in myself a lie—even for you."

She went with a scornful smile. Long after she had gone he watched the space between the trees where she had disappeared.

" It's a long way to Christmas," he thought. And a long way it was. Peter, whose room he now shared, was very moody. Sometimes he whistled till Jasper threw a book at him, sometimes he was gloomy. Night after night, Jasper woke up to hear the door close softly. With a brother's loyalty he never gave the slightest hint of this to anyone, nor did he question Peter. If Peter forgot to make his bed look as if it had been slept in, Jasper did it. He tried to be as incurious as he could, but privately he glimpsed a romance. And when he heard Jenny's soft footfalls on the sandy drive and her staccato gallop far off on the road, he felt lonelier than ever. He spent his time in avoiding Ernest and trying not to let the family find out that Catherine was not speaking to him. Only Amber was left to him, and even of her he was rather afraid, for to the sensitive open sympathy is often painful.

Then one day even Amber's comradeship was taken away. She and Catherine were going to tea at the Wallows. They always went early because Alice liked chat. They had to leave a note at the Rectory, and so did not go by the most direct road, but skirted the Dormer and Wallows land. They noticed the cattle bunching, and coming up to them saw that their heads were down, and all turned inwards towards something on the ground. Low moanings and angry snortings made the scene more alarming. Suddenly Amber cried :

" It's Hetty ! They're goring Hetty ! "

Hetty was a new acquisition at Dormer—a little

Jersey cow, timid and wild. She had evidently
strayed into the Wallows land, and as she was
different from the big Herefords they had gored
her.

"Help me to drive them off, Cathy, quick!"

"I shouldn't go too near," said Catherine.

"Oh, she's hurt to death," murmured Amber.
"She must be shot. Run, Cathy, and fetch one of the
boys. I'll keep them off."

Catherine thought this preferable to staying.
Amber, confronted with the groaning animal, its eyes
dimly appealing, was full of wild pity. She wrung
her hands.

"Oh, be quick, Cathy! Be quick!" she whispered. She ran to the brook and fetched water in her
hat to moisten the poor dry tongue. But it was too
late. She stood on the bank and watched for Catherine.
How long she was! Oh, why could she not run faster!
Half an hour went by, an hour. Sixty minutes of
watching helpless agony is not pleasant. At last
after an hour and a quarter she saw Catherine with
Jasper and Philip coming leisurely along. Philip had
a gun. She beckoned. She ran to meet them.

"What a long time!" she cried.

"What a fuss!" said Philip.

"Hurry up, now you are here."

"My dear Amber, you're quite excited," Philip
spoke banteringly.

"Oh, don't talk. Shoot her quickly. What has
she ever done that she should suffer so?"

"First let's see if there's more money in her patched
up than there is in her dead," said Philip.

"You shan't, you shan't," Amber sobbed. "Shoot
her *now*, I say. She shall not suffer so."

Amber in this mood was new to them. Philip
sniggered. Catherine looked haughty.

"Best get on with it." said Jasper. "It's our cow anyway."

"Yes, but your governor'll want damages."

"Give me the gun," said Jasper. It was enough that Philip wanted delay ; immediately Jasper wanted haste. Also his natural instincts were the same as Amber's.

He took the gun and shot Hetty, and she laid down her tormented head and forgot life and its sorrows.

"And now," said Amber, "I should like to know what you were thinking of, Catherine, not to hurry as I asked you."

"I felt faint."

"Faint ! What business had you to feel faint ? There was a creature in agony, and you, a perfectly strong, healthy woman, felt faint. Nonsense ! I don't believe it."

Catherine looked pathetic. The two young men looked at Amber as if she were inhuman.

"You have no sympathy, Amber," said Catherine plaintively. "You think more about a soulless creature than you do about me."

"You are too selfish for any words," said Amber, turning away and walking on alone. In a few minutes Jasper caught her up.

"You mustn't say such things to Cathy," he said.

"They are true."

"Cathy is an angel."

"I know Catherine very well, dear."

"If you want me to be your pal, you mustn't criticize Cathy either to me or to herself or to anyone. Cathy is as far above you and me as——"

"Never mind the illustration, old boy !"

Amber laughed, but her laugh was rueful.

"Well, said Jasper irritably, "you've changed. That's all I can say. I can't feel to you as I did."

He turned and waited for the others.   Amber, with a bitter sense of frustration, went on alone, while the two young men eyed one another across Catherine's hat with flashes of hostility, veiled on the part of Philip, unveiled on the part of Jasper.

So it was that Jasper became doubly lonely.   He felt this most at Christmas.   As Amber said, Christmas was the time when they gave each other all the things they had bought at the bazaar at the Keep, which things would be convenient for the summer sale at the Rectory.   But Jasper had no presents to give, for he not having yet found a God, money had not been forthcoming from his father.   Ernest, Catherine and Mrs. Velindre all gave him devotional books which he put up on his mantelpiece and contemplated with dismay.   But neither this nor the fact that he had no gifts to bestow was what chiefly troubled him.   What grieved him was that on account of a philosophical difference of opinion he was tacitly shut out from all share in the sweet humanities of Christmas.   It was understood that he would not care for carol singers, would not care to go with Peter as of old to help the ringers.   The idea was that he was a sinner wilfully neglecting God.   He knew in his own heart that he was homesick for God and could not find Him.

It was the time of a winter day when the lonely heart aches ; when dusk has fallen, but the lights are not yet lit ; when the last sounds of day come sadly across the meadows with a forlorn, lost music, already becoming muted under the outspread hand of night.

Jasper felt bitterly alone when the family went off to church at half-past three.   He had felt it when they went to the choral celebration in the morning, for that service had been one of his greatest joys.   He

felt the irony of the fact that he, who could appreciate
these things, was shut away from them by his desire
to do right. Another irony was that they all took it
for granted that laziness was at the root of his absence.
He had tried to find comfort on Sundays in lighting a
fire in the grotto and getting Enoch to come and sit
with him, for Enoch was another absentee. He was
firm against all reasoning, from the Rector's mild :
" What have you against us, Enoch ? " to Mrs. Gosling's " Well, what I say is, on a cold morning a sup of
wine *is* a sup of wine ! " But Enoch had been less
companionable lately. So Jasper surreptitiously
followed the others down the drive, along the few yards
of lane, into the churchyard. The yews were piled
with sugary white ; Mrs. Cantlop's wreaths were
buried ; the negro boy had a warm snow vest all down
one side. The church windows glowed warmly and
invitingly, and Charles Dank was playing, " Oh, come,
all ye faithful ! " with an explosiveness never attained
except at Christmas. It was all very human, very
peaceful, Jasper thought—peaceful, that is, for those
who believed in it. As the voices rose within, he could
distinguish Catherine's clear, metallic soprano.
He thought how lovely she had looked as she came to
him in the hall in her winter coat and the cap with
violets that showed her hair to such advantage. " Put
away your pride and come ! " she smiled. " Come
with me ! "

As if he had any pride !

And then Ernest had come up behind him and
whispered : " Only come ! Only have faith ! "

Ruby said nothing ; she spoke very little now.

" Faith ? What is faith ? " said Jasper to himself.
And it seemed to him that his friend Hallowes was
right when he said that faith was generally an effer
vescent froth rising out of the bubbling contentment

of the more comfortable classes of humanity ; rendered
to an essence ; bottled, and offered peremptorily to
the less fortunate.

Jasper looked up at the angry reds and purples of
Death and Hell which stained the passing snow. It
was too eerie here, so he went round to the porch.
Sitting there, a little sheltered from the wind, he could
be more intimately in touch with the service. Ernest
was intoning prayers now ; Jasper could hear Mrs.
Cantlop's voice in the responses, very slow and hearty,
and Mr. Arkinstall's, turning the simplicity of the
service into subtlety. He smiled when Sarah set about
the creed as she would about a day's washing. Finally,
the Rector gave out his text : " When He maketh
up His jewels."

When who made up what jewels ? Jasper wondered.
For, to some minds, the more concrete religion is the
less they can take hold of it. What did all these people
want ? he wondered. What did they really expect ?
Was their reward that they would die with the crea-
tions of their own minds so thick about them that they
would not hear the snow-wind mourning : " It is the
end ? " Would the Rector close his eyes for the last
time to see within himself multitudinous jewels of
rayed splendour ? Would the woman whom no man
had loved die with the kiss of passion on her grey
lips ? Would trees whisper in Enoch's failing consciousness, and mountains of dressed poultry cheer
his aunt across the dark river, and gold mines set their
allure for Mr. Cantlop ? Or was there something real,
though vague and inexpressible, awaiting them ? If
so, it seemed to him a pity that they should cumber
the window of vision with all this stuff of their
imagining.

There was no comfort here. He went back to the
house, fetched his flute, and played himself up the

Beast Walk. And as he went, he smiled wryly at his
own expense, thinking how Sarah had said : " It's
wail, wail, wail with you, Master Jasper, like the Willy-
peewits weep-weeping in the moonshine, wanting
summat to cry for."

Jasper felt that he had a good deal to cry for. His
music fell like tears on the waters. He had learnt the
rudiments of the flute years ago from Mr. Greenways,
but had outstripped him by virtue of a greater
capacity for misery. Mr. Greenways was of so cheerful
a disposition that it was doubtful whether the heights
and depths of music would ever be completely unveiled to him. But, as Sarah said, " with these
whistles, what you want is a tune, summat as goes
with a hop, skip and jump, and not shuffle, shuffle,
like a tramp's wedding."

" I wish," said Jasper aloud, as he looked down the
vista of beasts from the grotto, and down the vista of
his own life, " I wish to God Hallowes would come ! "

BOOK II
THE FOREST

XIV

THE UPPER WOODS

WHEN the atmosphere of the house became too thunderous and Amber's nerves were strained to breaking-point, she crept away to the upper woods. This she had learnt from Enoch, for she noticed that when the kitchen rang with battle, when the butter did not " come," or some of his daily jobs went wrong, then, at the first leisure moment, he went to the woods. He had unconsciously fostered a love of nature in her, for he would bring her the rarely beautiful treasures of earth—a primrose plant all a-blossom in a nest of moss, a branch of grape-like buckthorn fruit, a young robin for her to set free from a cage of rushes. He never kept birds in cages, and his only pets were two tame hedgehogs that wandered about after him in a blind sort of devotion, and were fed like cats with saucers of milk.

Amber loved to think in winter of the life that ran in the dark tree trunks, of the muffled laughter in every grass-root and crocus bulb ; to hear the thrush chanting his prophetic vision of spring far-off in the southern valleys. She loved to watch for the purple, and gold and green marvels of elf-land that blossomed out of the dead-black branches ; to kneel by the rockery and slip her finger into a corolla of the blue gentian, where it was warmer than the outer air. She

waited eagerly to see, every year, the blackthorns
float like clouds along the copper-coloured slopes ;
to hear on a spring evening, singing in the bare ash
tree against a sky of dewy purple, the first blackbird.
It seemed to her that while Dormer lived by law, the
forest lived by impulse. Through a gradual awaken-
ing to natural beauty, she reached a perception of
beauty peculiar to herself. She began to perceive
analogies. Nature became for her, not a fortuitous
assemblage of pretty things, but a harmony, a poem
solemn and austere. It was for her no longer a flat
painting on the wall of life. Beauty breathed there,
light shone there that was not of the flower or the
star. A tremor, mysterious and thrilling, seemed to
run with the light through all matter, through a
single open blosson of the wild gean tree and through
the whispering forest.

Something watched there ; something waited ; on
this side or on that, always a little above her, a little
beyond. Was it there, where the quicken burned,
or there where the yellow snapdragon crowded—
every small mouth half open, as if about to tell her
the secret ? Young and fugitive it seemed, as the
baby thrush that hopped in callow dignity across her
path, yet darkling and terrific as the core of a thunder-
storm. When she turned quickly, it was gone, like
the shy emmet, slipping under the layers of the leafy,
ferny wood ; it was fled like the night-wandering
moth into the topmost, heavy platform of the pine,
fused in fierce moonlight. So her going out into the
green world had in it something of a religious rite.

On a still morning of early June she went up to the
Birds' Orchard. She often did this before the day
of petty irritation began. For everything was still
the same at Dormer. Its inhabitants rasped on one
another like rocks grinding beneath the tides. Ruby

lay on the ancestral sofa most of the day now, and
she had become almost as tearful as Mrs. Cantlop.
The family was much exercised about Peter, who did
not show the eagerness for Catherine's hand, which
they expected. Jasper, very tiresomely, did. He
and Amber had drifted further apart. Amber was
now in the unfortunate predicament of having no one
to laugh with, but she found some comfort in the
inconsequences of the bird people.

She did not care for the lower woods ; they were
so near the house, so much under its influence. The
huge fissured boles of the yews, dull red, each one a
scheme of clustered columns, upheld the massive
black-green foliage, so that the wood seemed like a
low chamber with a heavy carven roof, under which
twilight always brooded. The floor of this place was
deep with the leaves of many centuries, which had
gathered with the thickening years till they muffled
the footsteps. When Amber thought how the contemporaries of Harold Hardrada had probably walked
in this very wood, under trees which now were jagged
stumps, and considered their fragile joys, their tiny
griefs, so huge to them, she shivered, feeling antiquity
to be fearful—almost cynical. The hollies, the boles
livid, grotesquely twisted and writhing, were old but
dwarfish. Their leaves, with the hard, light-refracting
polish (breaking the light as granite breaks water)
were sparse. They were in flower, but the thin grey
froth of blossom hardly seemed to belong to spring,
though it possessed, like everything in nature, its
own individual beauty. This wood, in its silence and
stillness, with its massive yew foliage, like wrought
iron, might have been part of a petrified forest.
Through arcades that seemed like the recesses of time
Amber hurried upwards, avoiding the Beast Walk.
Through a company of fir trees set with points of bright

green flame she came at last to the upper wood, and
was instantly at grips with beauty. There was for
her literally something of wrestling, of the mood
which says : " I will not let thee go until thou bless
me," in her communings with nature.

Suddenly a blackbird fluted, and the notes, liquid
and glassy, made room for themselves and their silver
echoes, seeming to need all space in which to expand,
to rise in full tide, submerging everything. The
bracken, still unopened, stood ranked in bright green
slender pillars, and Amber thought that the troops of
hyacinths that marched in and out among them were
like the procession of a Lord Mayor's Show in faery.
It was very early, and the wood was in a charmed
stillness. The blackbird fell into a long meditation,
and Amber shut her eyes, listening, not with the ear,
but with the soul. Here, where the sounds of the
world died away like a lapsing tide, she heard the sad
rumour that life makes, stirring and murmuring in the
silver hush of nonentity. She heard the moth-flicker
of worlds slipping out into their age-long life, and
their return—faint as the hum of a spent bee—to
their everlastingly mysterious cause. Leaning against
a wild pear tree, she was aware, by her inward hearing, of the tidal wave of sap that rose so full and strong
that she could almost imagine it roaring like the sea.
Then a tremor of wind shook the flowering tree-tops,
and she awoke again to the senses, to the strangeness
of these utterances of the leaves. For the forest tree
keeps in her heart secrets of days long gone—days
when the little bruit of man was drowned by the
infinite grave forest murmur ; when the trees spoke
aloud the things that now they only whisper. Every
tassel and streamer, every rosette, and cluster and
catkin, all the minute, unnoticed bloom of the woodland, seemed to envelop her in scent and rustling

music. Close about her she had the bloom of the wild
fruit trees in the Birds' Orchard. It was steep and
green as the hills in a dream, and up the slope, poised
in attitudes of wind-blown grace, climbed a company
of crab trees. Their brown and fissured trunks were
lichened and mossy ; their tops were broad, and low
and rosy. Standing on the slope, Amber could see
them, mushroom-like, spread with pink tapestry.
She could see the burnished bees, tethered by desire,
hovering in thousands, falling in and out of the rose-
coloured cups. She was drenched in the scent which,
although more delicate than that of an orchard tree,
is not less heady—the scent of wild apple in the early
sun. The pale flowers and the bright, close-fisted
buds were packed layer upon layer in the exquisite
freshness of romance. From the middle of a cup-
shaped hollow rose a wild pear tree, forty feet high,
flowering late on its windy hillside. It was white as
a summer cloud, with its cymes of large, rose-like
blossoms. Its scent, more unearthly than the apple,
wandered down with the breezes that stole along the
dazzling terraces. Amber loved pear blossom ; she
delighted in the creamy, nut-like buds, each with its
cross of soft rose-colour, a little paler than the velvety
stamens of the open flower, and contrasting delicately
with the silver calyx. She listened to the bees, crazed
with the high tide of honey, sounding up and down
the pillared whiteness their effortless monotone. But
she could not linger by the pear tree ; there were so
many other things to see. She had the feeling, almost
of greed, that such days bring—days with something
glistening in them, a touch of the eternal. She felt
like a child on the sea beach, loaded with shells veined
with rainbow tints, pearly, fiery, and all with the sea
in them—all remembering the deep water. Every
petal, every leaf, seemed to be conning some memory

of profundities whence it had come. Every curving
flower seemed full of echoes too majestic for its
fragility. She climbed to the buckthorn grove.
There they stood, creating their own atmosphere, as
do all groups of trees. They dwelt in green fire, for
their leaves—thin as those of beeches—were young
and fresh. Their stems were of regal purple. Their
creamy flowers, long-stalked, five-petalled, sweet,
starred the bases of the leaf clusters. Near by were
the spindles, gracious with shining leaves and mysterious fourfold flowers. At the top of the inclosure
was an old hedge of white beams, that had ceased to
be a hedge and become trees. The upward, springing
boughs, the soft and downy leaves, were drifted over
by flowers, so that each tree seemed to stand amazed
at its own whiteness, like a young bride in an ample
veil. A breath of scented air came from the hill tops
and stole among the branches. That which had form,
and knew the mortality which is in form, trembled
before that which passed, formless and immortal.
It seemed content to linger here for a little while,
before the momentary existence of this visible beauty
slipped into nothingness ; but it did not commit its
whole self to any creature of matter, neither to dew-
dark petal nor gold-eyed bird. It passed in the wood,
as sunlight passes, or as the wind goes by, lifting the
leaves with indifferent fingers, or like the rain, stroking
the flowers in childlike carelessness. Because of it
the place became no mere congregation of trees, but
a thing fierce as stellar space. Yet in the wood it
never nested, never came homing to the spangled
meadow. For it possesses itself for ever in a vitality
withheld, immutable. It was this that drew Amber
with breathless curiosity into the secret haunts of
nature. It was this that struck her now into a kind
of ecstasy, so that she neither saw nor heard the

stranger who came down the hill and stood watching her beneath the blossom.

So it came to pass that he surprised the very self of Amber Darke abroad in the blue day, hovering like a bee in the foam of flowers. Who knows where the spirit lodges, in what grey cell or dawn-cold turret of the mind ? Wherever her lodging, Amber was playing truant, wearing, for all her thirty years, a loveliness to which her physical self did not entitle her, and to which Catherine would have denied her right. But beneath Catherine's critical eyes it would have folded like the evening pimpernel.

The stranger came nearer, in a kind of eagerness, as though impelled. He snapped a stick, and she turned with a little cry. They looked at one another, and their look was that of friends who have met a long while since, in other lands, to the sound of wilder music, but with the same remembered ecstasy. Dim thoughts came to them of primeval forests which it seemed that they two, wandering hand in hand, had traversed ; of antique seas far away on whose loud shores they had, as childish playmates, slept ; of huge, serrated mountains where they had climbed— mountains now worn to low green hills. Where were those forests and those roaring seas ? They could not tell. In this world ages since ; in other worlds ; in the strange Saharas of their own secret souls—it did not concern them to know. What they cared for was the knowledge that they had always known each other. Amber knew that all her thirty years at Dormer had been a holding of the breath in expecta- tion of this moment. Michael Hallowes knew that his harsh and chequered career had been one long search for this woman who now stood before him, tremulous and alight. To him she seemed as lovely as a sun-drenched petal, in which neither colour nor texture can be seen, all being steeped in radiance.

She, looking up at him, saw only his eyes, in which dwelt an energy of vitality not of physical origin. His mind had the qualities of flame. He was one of those men who, passing through filthy places, burn up evil as they go. His face had the strong sweetness that belongs to a man who has been through the mire of human sin, and has come through with his spirit intact. All the trees, metal-green, jewel-green, dawn-green, splashed and flecked with rose, and mooned over with patines of cream-colour, regarded them benignantly over each other's shoulders. They seemed to crowd together, even to nudge one another, for all their tall dignity, that they might look upon a marvel. The bird-cherries sent down peace in pale flakes. The little crofts, the bays of half-cultivated grass land bounded by lavish hawthorns, the steep vivid slopes where cool, chicory-coloured shadows blossomed, were all swimming in ox-eye daisies, white as the wake of a ship. Across them swallows flashed, very low, and their sharp wings seemed to churn up foam from the daisies. A scent came up, so keen that it made the heart ache, as did the fresh, amazing colours—the flushed flowers, the blanched flowers, the empurpled swallows, tinted like the thunder-clouds that haunted the horizons of Dormer.

" Tell me your name ! " said Michael, in a voice at once commanding and caressing.

" Amber Darke."

" Jasper's sister."

" Then you are Jasper's friend ? "

Her heart sang. For if he was Jasper's friend, he would come to Dormer. He would sit in those shadowy rooms, she would rest in the protection of his voice, his smile, in the aura of his presence. All that the house meant—the iron barriers between one and another, Catherine's lacerating personality, Mrs. Darke's arctic eyes—faded and became unimportant.

Michael stretched out his hand in a sudden impulse towards her, then caught himself back into immobility, and said only :

" He never told me."

" What ? "

" That you lived at Dormer."

At the idea of Jasper thinking her so wonderful, Amber laughed her clear and merry laugh that was like a child's. Michael was not offended. Already he held the essence of her personality within his own, and when one human soul does that with another, misunderstanding is impossible.

" If I had known, I should have come sooner," he said.

Amber neither flushed nor trembled. She was not the queen-woman receiving homage, nor the slave-woman awaiting subjugation. She was not consciously a thing of sex or of physical existence at that moment. That Michael should come to Dormer and find her, was to Amber as inevitable as the fusion of colours or the pull of stars one upon another.

" Why should you have come ? "

" You know."

" Tell me ! "

" To find you and fetch you away."

" Ah ! "

" As children find the first primrose. Why do they look for the first primrose, Amber Darke ? "

A smile curved her mouth mischievously. She was not going to be led down that road.

" Why do they look for it ? Very well, I'll tell you. Because it is beautiful."

" But I am not beautiful."

" Not beautiful ! "

He stepped back with half-closed eyes.

" I suppose, if one could get past your soul and look at your features, you might even be plain," he said. " But your soul sheds such a light, Amber. I shall never be able to see your features."

Amber sighed in utter content, and her sigh was like the soft lifting of young sycamore leaves. Here was a man, strong, sane, cognisant of the world—one that must have seen many beautiful women—telling her that she was beautiful, proclaiming himself by every glance her lover. Her lover ! The tints of the apple blossom deepened in her cheeks. She looked round her at the old familiar nooks of the Birds' Orchard, and her eyes were full of tears. She stopped and gathered an ox-eye daisy, for Michael's long gaze began to make her shy.

" Give me that daisy ! " said he.

She gave it, and picked another.

" And that ! "

Their eyes met, and they broke into laughter. A rabbit that had washed its face several times in an endeavour to decide whether they were harmless, decided in the negative, and was gone. From below, the descant of many birds ascended, and far down amid the maze of fluty voices the stable clock struck eight. Amber started at the didactic whisper of sound.

" I must go ! " she said.

" May I come ? "

Might he come ? Might he have the keys of her life, of her heaven and hell ? Might he take her and all she was or hoped to be ? Oh, yes ! Oh, yes ! But might he know all this now ? Oh, no ! Amber's Quaker spirit primmed its mouth, and Amber's little goblin of humour shook its head. And what Michael

Hallowes received in lieu of the outspoken passion of a lifetime, was :

" We shall be pleased if you will come to breakfast, Mr. Hallowes."

But possibly Michael was not deceived. For he, too, possessed a goblin of humour.

Amber did not see the expression of his eyes as he replied, following her retreating figure :

" I shall be pleased to accept ! "

Nor did she know that two brown and rather possessive hands were stretched towards her muslin shoulders, and as suddenly taken away again.

" I won't startle her," he resolved.

" But I shall not call you Miss Darke," he added.

" No ? "

" No, ma'am.   I shall call you Amber."

" Very well, Mr. Hallowes."

Michael smiled across Amber's hat, as if the hawthorns understood his mind, and could appreciate the quizzical situation.

As they neared the house, faces appeared at the lower windows and watched their advent.

" Amber with a man ! " said Catherine, as if she stated an impossibility.

" A nice one, too," said Ruby wistfully.

" An untidy fellow," remarked Ernest.

" Too thin ! " judged grandmother.   " Now, you're too fat, great-nephew."

Ernest ignored this.

" He looks like chapel," he said.

Pressed to the kitchen window were the faces of Mrs. Gosling, Sarah, and she of the sullen temper. Said Mrs. Gosling :

" Miss Amber's met her fatal.   Hark at 'em laughing ! "

But at this moment Jasper saw them.   Amber,

watching his tempestuous welcome, thought : " If anyone can save Jasper, here is the man to do it."

They went in to find Solomon preparing to read prayers.

"No prayers ! " said Michael, and disappeared with Jasper. Amber, hearing about Abimelech, began to realize that there were going to be clouds even in this extraordinarily blue and sunny day.

" That gentleman's eyes," said Sarah, as she sternly fried the bacon, " probes your innards. If I'd ever took so much as a button, I wouldn't dare meet 'em."

" Did you see the fray on his shirt cuffs ? " asked the sullen one.

"Ah ! but 's Amber's a good one at the needle," replied Sarah, and even the sullen one was able to see the connection.

In the dining-room conversation flourished more than it usually did. Amber was silent, for she was conscious of Catherine's vivisecting eye, and she was still tremulous from the sense of Michael's presence beside her, and aware of his long, eager gaze, demanding that her spirit should reveal itself to his completely, and without any shadow of reserve. The finding of such a gaze on herself is, to a plain woman, both disquieting and delicious—disquieting because she knows her limitations ; more delicious than a woman of many lovers can ever guess. The woman of many lovers seldom experiences it, for passion— pure, crude and vital—is a gift that comes to very few. As the meal went on in the usual way, Peter sulking, Solomon saying the same things, her mother looking the same things, grandmother eyeing Michael and flinging at his head ever and anon extracts from the *Lion*, Amber found it more and more difficult to believe in Michael's reality. She told herself that she must be imagining the different tone in which he spoke to her. It surely could not be true that, while to everyone else he spoke coolly and indifferently, to her he spoke with the caressing command of the Birds' Orchard. Then Amber realized that Catherine intended Michael for her own. Catherine's face was becomingly flushed ; her pointed lips had pricked two dimples in her cheeks ; her eyes turned—leisurely, green, speaking an etiolated sex— towards Michael's sombre ones. Sombre Michael's were, but in their depths laughter lurked.

" Are they laughing at Catherine ? " Amber wondered, adding characteristically : " Are they laughing at me ? "

It was obvious that Catherine liked his curt voice, his downright way of expressing himself. Ernest had just remarked that he believed in the greatest good of the greatest number, to which Michael, without any ceremony, replied :

" Bosh ! If each individual is allowed to be himself, he'll attain his own good ; and you can't co-ordinate individuals until you've got individuals to co-ordinate."

" That doesn't sound right," said Solomon. " I dunno what's wrong, but it doesn't sound right."

They pondered on that.

" Why are you so foolish as to go out early, Amber, when you are always ailing ? " asked Catherine, and received a full, ruminative glance from Michael.

" Don't encourage her, Mr. Hallowes ! " she finished.

" If she wants to go to the Birds' Orchard, it is not our business," said Michael.

Catherine frowned. She would show him whether he could contradict Catherine Velindre ! She would lure him, she would bind him. She would lull him —and then ? Ah, well ! Maybe she would reward him.

A strange man. A queer, wild, seamy, passion-stirring being. Those eyes could be kind, but they could also be merciless. They could express passion —a devastating love for one woman.

"And I will be that woman!" said Catherine Velindre.

"When people are over thirty, they should be a little careful, Amber," she said.

Amber's eyes grew hot with tears. What man would look at a girl again, even with passing interest, when he had been told she was over thirty, and when he could see that she was plain? That look, which had rested upon her in the forest, would not rest on her again. She did not look up when Michael spoke :

"Dear me," he said, with speculative interest, "I should not have thought you were more than twenty-nine, Miss Velindre."

If ever a face looked vengeance, hers did. He should suffer for that—when she had bound him.

But instead of replying angrily, she dissolved into melting femininity. She leaned on the table, so that her well-moulded arm and shoulder were shown to advantage. Her head drooped submissively. Her eyes—secret, with the expression of the courtesan vaguely lingering about them—looked up at Michael under their thick lids and lashes with such an expression that he was reminded of a picture of an Egyptian slave-market. As she had laid snares for Jasper, so she laid them for Michael ; but she had a very different man to deal with now. Michael looked at her coolly, with a purposely irritating air of appraising and depreciating goods, and a faint dismay was born in Catherine's mind.

He turned to Amber, and immediately the thrilled and thrilling look was there. She thought, as she shyly glanced at him, that it was the look a little boy might wear if he was suddenly set down outside a faery town—heard the bells ringing, saw the golden minarets within, the nodding poppies on the walls, the shadowy people passing inside the fretted gates —and was told, " Soon, in a little while, perhaps you shall have the key."

" Can it be I myself—Amber—that has aroused this passion ? " she thought.   She could not believe it.

Suddenly on this hidden, tumultuous joy came Solomon's voice :

" What's your trade or profession, any way ? "

" None."

" But what d'you do ? "

" I'm learning to look after sheep."

" But you're an educated man."

" Looking after sheep gives me time to think."

" Time ?   What d'you want time for ? "

" To explore myself and look for God."

" Look for gold, did he say ? " cried grandmother.

" No, God."

" But He's in church.   You needn't put yourself out looking for Him."

" I never found Him in church."

" Young man ! "—grandmother eyed him with dis-favour—" you've got a devil ! "

" So have we all, ma'am ! "

" What was your father ? " asked Solomon.   He had become very suspicious of Michael, and was determined to sift him, host or no host.

" He was a good many things," replied Michael

" But what did he make his money at ? "

" Well," said Michael judicially, " sometimes I think he made most as a chimney sweep, and some-times I think he did best at the fried potato business."

His eyes, for all their quiet sombreness, could not conceal their gleeful laughter, as he glanced from one face to another. There was a silence so deep and so long that Amber wanted to scream. She felt that the ancestors on the walls would, if it lasted much longer, begin to talk from very nervousness. There was not a sound except the distant voice of Sarah singing to an obbligato of tinny crashes :

" Foolish sheep, why will you scatter ? "

Ernest was the first to recover ; he came to the surface with a long sigh and an " Interesting !— interesting ! "

Ruby giggled She could always be relied on for that.

" Jolly good trades, both," said Peter, feeling that he himself had made a speciality of the working classes.

Without a word Solomon got up and went to the gun-dogs. He always did this under strong excitement. Catherine's eyes dwelt upon Michael. Was he telling the truth or was he not ? It was difficult to know. If it were the truth—what then ? She who had dreamed of bishops—was she to fall so low as fried potatoes ? It spoke something for Catherine Velindre's strength of character that she swallowed the fried potatoes. It also said a good deal for Michael's personal magnetism that a woman of her stamp could continue, after such harsh treatment, to smile provocatively on him. Jasper pushed his chair back.

" I'm off now ; coming, Hallowes ? " he asked. He was bitterly disappointed that Michael had so soon offended Dormer. He had hoped to see so much of him. Now he would not be asked.

In the general movement Michael leaned down, and said :

" You'll come with Jasper to see me, Amber ? "

" Yes."

" I live at the Shepherd's Hut at Forest Gate. You know ? "

" Yes."

" You'll like coming ? "

" Yes."

He was gone. As she ran up to her own room she
reflected that she had said yes to everything—would
have said yes, she feared, to anything he had asked
her. He was, it seemed, a person who dealt in affirma-
tives. He was also a person, she knew, as she looked
at her burning cheeks in her little mirror, to whom
Amber Darke could not say no.

She flung herself upon the bed and hid her face in
the pillow.

" Oh, yes—yes—yes, Michael Hallowes ! " she
whispered. " Yes, and yes a hundred times. Yes
and yes for all the years of my life. Yes—yes—yes—
to anything—to everything— " she burrowed deeper
in the pillow—" to everything you ask of me, for
ever and ever."

She stayed there, still and silent, for a long while.
Then she sat up, and said with decision : " But you
shall not know that, Mr. Michael Hallowes. Aha !
You shall think it is no and no ! Yes, you shall think
it is no for a long time. When will he ask us to go ?
Will it be to-morrow ? Will he say ' Amber ' again ?
Will he look down at me and smile again ? "

" What ails you, 's Amber ? " queried Sarah, entering, intent on bed-making.

" Nothing, Sarah."

But when Sarah got down to the kitchen again,
she nodded to Jemima's grave.

" *We* know what ails her, girl ! " she said con-
fidentially. " Love's so lungeous."

And Amber, feverishly sewing new frills into her
best blouse, thought so also. But it was a very
different kind of lungeousness from that which Marigold
had felt.

XV

MR. CANTLOP COMES HOME

IT was on Saint Swithin's day that Amber received her first love-letter. Since the June morning when her real life began she had only seen Michael once. Jasper had refused to go and see his friend oftener. This puzzled Amber. It also struck her as suicidal. If there was one person to whom Jasper, drowning in the tides of intolerance and misunderstanding, spiritual despair and fear, could look for help, it was Michael. And now he refused to see Michael. Amber could not know that Catherine, white and regal in her favourite frock, had come on Jasper in the Beast Walk, and had penalized any intimacy with Michael.

" If you love me," said Catherine, " you do not want him. If you want him, you do not love me." Catherine was aware that Jasper's going to tea with Michael meant Amber's going to tea also.

" If I don't go and see Michael, will you be—as I want you to be ? " asked Jasper. He had grown thinner, browner, a good deal sterner. He bargained where he had pleaded.

" As you want me to be ? " Catherine pondered.

" You know what I want you to be."

" Do I ? "

" Now, look here, Catherine, you shall not say you don't know."

He grasped her hands, and she was aware that

the Wallows had at least given him some very service-
able muscles.

" I want you to be my wife, now—next week—to-
morrow. I want you to put aside everything, your
religion, your old-maidish point of view (it is old-
maidish, Cathy !), everything, and give yourself to
me. Now you know."

He laughed ruefully, but he did not loose her hands.

" I have given up a good deal for your, Cathy. No,
it's no use trying to get your hands away. I am sorry
if I am hurting you, but you have hurt me. You say
you love me. You say you want my good. I tell
you the only way you can compass my good is by
giving yourself to me. Will you, Cathy ? Will
you ? "

Perhaps if Catherine had not met Michael, the
young manhood of Jasper would have won her, struck
from her all her poses. But she had become aware of
a harder metal, tasted a stronger meat. She was
afraid of Michael Hallowes, and of all the strange
blossoms in the garden of woman's love for man, this
purple blossom of fear is the most fascinating to a
nature such as Catherine's.

" If I give up Michael—though God knows why I
should—will you fix a limit to this hell ? "

Catherine pondered again. She must keep Amber
away from Forest Gate. Therefore, she must keep
Jasper away.

" I will tell you, yes or no, in two months," said
Catherine."

" Say six weeks—that's too long."

" Very well."

" And you do love me ? If you don't, I won't go
on with this. Do you ? "

It was necessary to say yes.

" Loose my hands now, Jasper."

He kissed them and let them go.

"I shall count the days. It will be the last Sunday in August."

"Yes."

"And as you do really love me, and it's only a matter of conflicting ideas, I shall hope for the best. Say you love me!"

Catherine flushed. Jasper was becoming an intolerable difficulty. Well, it must be said.

"I love you!" said Catherine Velindre.

But as she fled across the water she saw sombre eyes with mocking laughter in their depths; heard a voice deeper than Jasper's and more inflexible; glimpsed a character of which the main fabric was wrought in iron.

That had happened yesterday, and to-day Amber received her letter, unofficially, through Enoch.

"Jasper is not coming to see me for six weeks, God knows why. Will you come to-day? I will meet you at the gate of the Forest at ten o'clock."

As she read those words, so few and simple, her heart grew turbulent as the silver passion of July wheat-fields under the wind.

At ten o'clock. So early! She stole away over the silken water, under the summer lapping of the leaves. What would Dormer say to her? Let it say what it would when the grave, beautiful day was over. But now—Michael awaited her—herself and not another. As she went, all beautiful things seemed to run to meet her. Already there had come the faint dusking-over of the wheat-fields with the soft, rosy fawn which steals away the green of summer; which glows and flushes through hot days and yellow-moon nights until at last, through every phase of saffron, tawny, almost salmon-colour, they have reached the time when they can hold no more beauty. The ripples that swept over them, water-green and pale, when the first clover flowered, now flowed in a slower rhythm, each wave longer and stiffer, less like water than honey. She thought, as her gaze lingered on the plain, that there a shadow wavered which was not painted by any tree, slipping away before the eye of man like dew from a lifted leaf. It seemed, as she looked ahead at some green-veiled arch of the forest, that the curtain might be twitched aside at any moment, and some revelation of the divine peer out upon her. But when she passed the archway there was only the leafy, mazy pattern of summer green. As she listened to the low breathing of the forest, she half thought she heard an echo fall—like the striking of a wing on soft resistant air, or the music of wild swans passing above the roof of cloud, sounding upon their muffled golden gongs.

But Amber's meditations did not last long. A very long time before she reached the gate of the Forest, there was Michael lying on his elbow across the path, gazing up into the blue crevices between the leaves, smoking an enormous briar.

" Come and sit by me," said Michael. She spread her white skirts among the beech mast and the pine needles.

" Have you ever had a love letter, Amber ? " he asked.

She reflected that unexpectedness was one of his great charms.

" No."

" One ?   Surely ? "

His smiling eyes dwelt on her so long that she turned away with a shy laugh.

" One ? " persisted Michael. " A short, sharp, practical thing—but surely one ? "

" Perhaps one," she assented.

It was then that the doves began their fairy mischief-making. Not the wood-pigeons ; this was not a haunt of theirs ; but the little fawn-coloured doves that purr with a continual velvet softness, an iteration which expresses everything for the lover.

Michael sat up and threw his pipe into the pine needles.

" Say—' I had a love letter this morning, Michael, and though it said nothing, it brought a man's life with it.' "

Amber smiled to herself. Those hours with her own passionate heart in her little room at Dormer must be concealed.

It was yes—inevitably and gloriously—but not yet.

" I had a letter from a very authoritative man this morning, Mr. Hallowes," said she. " But it was not a love letter—I hope."

" You hope it was ! " said Michael. " You do ! It is no use looking prim, Amber, and you may say Mr. Hallowes a hundred times, but it won't defend you."

Amber was examining a wild rose.

" This attack is unmerited, Mr. Hallowes," she remarked, after a long silence.

The wood pigeons purred, the wind ran lightly like an aerial squirrel in and out of the tree-tops.

Michael took away the wild rose.

" I have been patient," he said.

" Patient ! "

" But now it's time for that gnome of mischief to which you give house-room to go to sleep. I want to talk to you."

" Yes."

It was the vaguest whisper of sound.

" You know you and I are one, don't you ? "

Silence.

" Don't be demure, Amber ; you know it. You knew it in the Birds' Orchard."

" Perhaps."

" How soon can you come to me ? "

" Oh, Michael ! "

" Well, how soon ? "

" Do you mean, marry you ? "

" Yes. If marriage is what you approve of. We are tied faster than marriage. I am not prejudiced either way."

He leaned on his elbow and regarded her.

" Yes. I should like you to marry me, please, Amber."

" I will think about it."

Michael smiled. He found her reserves almost more fascinating than any other quality.

" And now home ! " he said. " I've cooked the dinner."

It is true that the happy have no history. And as Michael and Amber could not have said how the day passed, what they said or thought, neither can the reader expect to know. Instead, he must be content to return to Dormer, where, at three o'clock on this same Sunday afternoon, the Rectory surveyed its glebe in drowsy peace. Into the silence fell at long intervals the croaking caw of a rook, intensifying the quiet. In the garden the rambler roses blazed, the lilies stood each in an aura of stillness that was about the flowers like light round the moon. Nothing stirred except the Rector's bees, who seemed to think of taking an unfair advantage of his siesta by swarming. The Rector, in his cool, green-lit drawing-room, was having his usual conscientious Sabbath slumber over Paley's " Evidences." The good man always did violence to his wishes on Sunday, putting away all his books on gems, not so much as cutting the leaves of the latest brochure on diamonds, though it had only arrived on Saturday. Paley was dutifully opened after dinner, but the house was so quiet (Rectory-Lucy being out and even the cat sleeping the sleep of repletion) that a bland complacency came over his thoughts. He pondered on his good fortune in having avoided matrimony, and a great peace overwhelmed him, so that Paley remained where Paley had been opened at half-past two. This weakness of the Rector's was bitter to Ernest, who was unable to see what a much better parish priest the Rector made simply because he could not read Paley. When the Rector sat in his armchair and slept rosily, the veriest sinner must have confided in him; and while his intellectual light gave an uncertain ray, his humanity shone like a lighthouse upon all who came near him.

Mrs. Cantlop—who was not equal even to looking at an unread Paley—was asleep upstairs with her windows tightly shut and curtained.

The afternoon wore on very pleasantly. It was at about half-past four that the Rector with a little start opened his blue eyes on a sight so surprising that he polished his glasses for several minutes.

Seated in the corner of the sofa, in the shadow of the Japanese screen, was Mr. Cantlop, with a bundle in a red handkerchief beside him, and the expression of a Buddhist seeking to be absorbed into the One. It seemed that if Mr. Cantlop could have transformed his small, spare self into one of the buttons of the upholstery, he would have done so and been thankful. He sat so quiet that the Rector was reminded of ghosts, and he had an air of not having come from anywhere.

" Is that you, Cantlop ? " asked the Rector.

" Yes, it's me," said Mr. Cantlop.

" My dear man !   I'm delighted ! "

The Rector discarded Paley and shook hands violently.

" Well, well ! This is delightful ! I'll go and tell your wife."

" I'll go," said Mr. Cantlop faintly.

But the Rector felt that if Mrs. Cantlop woke to find her husband materializing in the room—materializing was the only word for his entrance—she would have a heart attack from sheer joy. So he left Mr. Cantlop in the drawing-room, which seemed emptier for his presence. After warning Mrs. Cantlop—warning seemed to him the right word—the Rector went into the kitchen, murmuring—" All across the Atlantic, poor little man ! Tea ! "—as if some kind fairy would procure it.

Then he poked the fire till the lower part of the grate fell out with all it upheld. " Now, now ! " said the Rector with tolerant reproof. He found an oil stove and boiled the kettle on that. Then he fetched all the eatables out of the larder and conveyed them, the cat proudly serving as acolyte, into the dining-room. Finally, Mrs. Cantlop came down in tears, brooches, her best cap and a great deal of lace, and utterly overwhelmed Mr. Cantlop. When the Rector, perspiring, slightly sooty, and with a new and deep respect for Lucy, triumphantly announced tea, he found Mrs. Cantlop and the red bundle in possession of the sofa, and a crushed Mr. Cantlop just existing between them.

" A remarkable man ! " thought the Rector, who was something of a psychologist, and who found Mr. Cantlop's consistent self-annihilation more remarkable than other people's self-assertion.

They went in to tea, Mrs. Cantlop sugaring the Rector's cup lavishly, and the Rector, who hated sugar, drinking it uncomplainingly. Mr. Cantlop enjoyed his meal furtively. He could, in eating a dinner for which he had not only paid, but overpaid, look as stealthy as a fox that has robbed the hen-roost ; and no burglar, meditating the acquisition of another's gold, could have looked as sly as did Mr. Cantlop in lawful possession of his own.

Not that he was in possession of his own, unfortunately ; for when the Rector said : " Well, Cantlop, I suppose you've brought a sack of nuggets ? " Mr. Cantlop was heard to whisper : " Lost ! "

And lost it apparently was—the whole gleaning of his twenty years.

The Rector sighed, reflected that his means must be stretched to include the three of them, and murmured something about treasure in heaven. For this Mr. Cantlop seemed very eligible, for he certainly would never have any on earth.

After tea they went to Dormer House, for the Rector had news to give Ernest. There had come this very day at lunch a note from a neighbouring vicar with a hint that a distant relation of his own thought of presenting a living to Ernest. This meant an immediate move for Ernest and Ruby, and though Ruby would rather not have moved just now, she was so pleased to be leaving Dormer that she made no complaint.

Ernest's success and Mr. Cantlop's future career were discussed at length.

" Why not sexton ? " asked grandmother, and everyone knew that this was Mr. Cantlop's true vocation. It was tacitly understood that Mr. Cantlop would perform his duties in so secretive a manner that no one would guess his occupation, the village presumably thinking that it was done by gnomes in the night.

" You're no bigger than when you went ! " said grandmother.

Mr. Cantlop writhed under a sense of incurable insufficiency.

" Where's the gold ? " she continued. " You've gotten none, I do believe, William ! "

" No, ma'am."

" Then what good are you ? "

To Mr. Cantlop, who thought nothing of his own good qualities and had always been ready to acquiesce in public opinion, this dictum that money was the end-all and be-all seemed unanswerable.

It was not until Amber came in, looking almost pretty, and so full of happiness that she infected all she came near, that Mr. Cantlop really felt his home-coming to be a festival.

" You have come back to her ! " she said. " That's better than gold, isn't it, Mrs. Cantlop ? "

" It is, it is, my dear ! " She wept again for joy, adding, " And dear William might have got entangled with those foreign ladies ! "

Amber's silent delight in this picture was cut short by Catherine's voice, asking :

" Where have you been ? "

Then the storm broke, and Amber began to disbelieve in her own happiness. It was borne in upon her that she was plain, that she was not young, that no man would want to marry her. It was pointed out that the son of a chimney-sweep without money or influence was not the husband for a daughter of Dormer. Catherine summed it all up.

" But, of course, it is just dear Amber's imagination. She is too much alone."

No one believed in it. Did she believe in it herself ? Amber wondered when she leant into the purple mid-night from her window, and looked up towards the forest. No ! In this house she could not believe in it. This dull, tired, insignificant woman that looked back at her from the eyes of those at Dormer was not the same creature that had wandered, free, happy, beauti-

ful, with Michael Hallowes in the golden sunlight.
And as she heard the stealthy noises of the house, she
began to wonder whether she would ever see Michael
Hallowes alone again.   Intuitively she knew that they
would watch her, that misunderstanding would be
fostered, that Catherine would spread her charms.   A
terror of Catherine grew up in her mind. Alas!
Alas! Catherine was so beautiful. Remorseless and
lovely, the pale face floated before her mind ; lovely
and cold, the green eyes looked into hers.

" She is stronger than I ! " was Amber's thought
as she fell into a restless sleep.

And Catherine, watching the stars ride up from
beyond the forest, strengthened herself for the binding
of Michael Hallowes.

Hour by hour the clocks uplifted their voices,
preaching of mortality, of striving, of busy anxieties.
And hour by hour Amber lay awake rejoicing that,
whatever came to her, she was no longer their bonds-
woman.   For to-day, in the large silence of the forest,
coming home softly over the dewy moss, to-day, for
the first time, Michael had kissed her.   It was not the
selfish kiss of the faun, nor the bluebottle kiss of marital
duty.   It was the kiss of a lover.   Before his hands
were laid gently on her shoulders, before his eyes took
their fill of hers, she had been a plain dull woman in a
plain dull world.   He kissed her, and she stood in the
rose-light of immortality.

XVI

PETER'S LETTER

It was mid-August, and hot, thunderous weather, when the storm centre at Dormer began to whirl with some activity. Michael and Amber had only seen each other once, but Enoch had acted as letter carrier. Ernest and Ruby had gone. Jasper welcomed the beginning of corn harvest as a means of killing time by hard work. Peter, urged by his elders to make some advances to Catherine, led a harried life, avoiding Mrs. Gosling, Enoch, Catherine and his parents.

On this blazing August day at breakfast, after the girls had gone, Solomon said :

"My lad, you ought to marry."

"Marry or burn!" said grandmother.

"I don't want to marry," said Peter with sincerity. He felt already too much married.

"You're young for your age," said Solomon, "a young innocent."

Peter smiled as he went off to work. But he would not have smiled, if he had known the surprise fate had prepared for him.

It began when Mr. Greenways gave Enoch the letters. As a rule he sorted the letters in almost unbroken silence. Sometimes on a Saturday he would say, as he flung the *Golden Chance* across to Enoch :

"Another three ha'pence thrown away. He never wins anything."

But as a rule Enoch watched him in silence. He admired the arbitrary way in which Mr. Greenways allocated the letters. But to-day there was one over which Mr. Greenways pondered long, and which he finally handed to Enoch with raised eyebrows. As his face was of the kind that expresses surprise very readily, looking amazed even in sleep, the impression Enoch now received was that Mr. Greenways was going to have a fit.

" Look ! " said Mr. Greenways.

Enoch looked, and his face was dismayed.

" That's Mrs. Gosling's Marigol'," said Mr. Greenways. Then he read the address very slowly :

" Peter Darke, Esq."

There was no mistaking Marigold's large round letters, which ran across the envelope like fat boys playing leapfrog. " If this roof opened out into the kingdom of heaven," said Mr. Greenways, " or if my missus spoke me fair, I couldna be more struck of a heap. It beats all ! "

" It's a good thing you're one for keeping counsel, Mr. Greenways," said Enoch.

" Mum ! " said Mr. Greenways. " Mum as a mum-ruffin ! " He still looked like a startled gnome. All the way to the house, with the summer-faint song of the Four Waters in his ears, Enoch puzzled. What ailed Marigold to forget herself like that ? But now that she had forgotten herself, what should he do ? Peter might be gone to the Wallows when he got back. He went early in harvest-time. He had better keep the letter and slip down to the Wallows with it. It was a thing he had never done—to keep back a letter. He had the translucent honesty of the majority of country people who work for their bread, and he had a sense of responsibility. He duly delivered the Dormer letters at the Dormer front door, and if anybody ever wanted their letters in any other way, they had to go to Mr. Greenways for them. But this was an occasion of extreme urgency, for someone would recognize the postmark, even if they did not know the writing.

Enoch delivered the letters without it, and put it into the breast pocket of his coat, carefully wrapped in his handkerchief. There were generally a few odd jobs to do before his day's work, and while he did them he hung his coat in the kitchen.

Now it was Sarah's daily practice to go through the pockets of this coat with a view to finding out any secrets Enoch might have. Whom she loved, she chastened. Enoch was her intended, and she regarded his pockets as potentially hers. No sooner, therefore, had Enoch gone across the yard than Marigold's letter was in her hands. She saw with relief that it was not addressed to Enoch.

" What a brazen piece ! " she murmured to the kettle as she put it on the hottest part of the fire. " Now boil, you ! and look sharp, or Enoch'll be back."

The kettle having complied, she began to steam the letter open. But first she ousted the cats, for there was something about the opening of letters which made her dislike those four lucently amused eyes.

" I'll learn you to outface your betters ! " she said. Then she read the letter.

" My Dear Husband,

" I write to say as there is a little Girl. Nine pounds and eyes your colour. Sunday was a month since you came. Please to come. It's a very nice little Girl.

" Your dutiful wife,
" Marigold."

Sarah turned her pebble-coloured eyes up to Jemima Onions' grave.

" You could blow me to Paradise with a puff," she said, " if you'd a mind."

She did not see Catherine glance in as she passed the kitchen door.

Suddenly Solomon shouted for the gun-dogs' breakfast. Sarah jumped " like something scalted " and put the letter into the top dresser drawer. It was unfortunate that Enoch called for the " fowls' meat " at the moment, so that Sarah was absent for some time. It was also unfortunate that Catherine knew of Sarah's drawer. In a moment the letter was in her hand. In another moment she had realized that Peter, who had preferred a working-girl to herself, was in her hands. Let him pay for his impertinence ! She was bored with Jasper, but Jasper had not swerved in his allegiance. Let Jasper have Dormer ! Certainly Peter would not get it if this were known. She did not care what they did with Dormer. She wanted nothing more of it nor of the Wallows. She wanted (oh, strange fate for Catherine Velindre) a hard life on a lonely hill-top with a penniless man who proudly owned for father a seller of chip potatoes. As she stood in the kitchen with Marigold's letter in her hand, a fierce jealousy overcame her. For Marigold had given a child to the man she loved. To live in that bare hut on the hilltop—with Michael ; to experience passion—with Michael—such was the desire of Catherine Velindre, the proud, the ambitious. She struggled against it ; she despised herself for it ; but there it was, unalterable.

She put the letter down on the table and went to the dining-room.

" Grandmamma ! " she said, " did you give Sarah any copies of the *Lion ?* "

It was a vexed question between Mrs. Velindre and

Sarah—the status of the *Lion*. Sarah refused to
regard it as literature, and treated it merely as paper.
Out went Mrs. Velindre, and Catherine smiled one of
her long, secret smiles.

Very soon grandmother came tapping back.

" Fetch my daughter ! " she said.

" What for, grandmamma ? "

" Do as you're bid ! " said the old lady.

She remained, while Catherine was away, murmuring
to herself :

" Pounds ! Nine pounds ! Little girl ! Gideon !
Marigold Gosling ! Hell fire ! "

It was characteristic of Mrs. Darke that when Mrs.
Velindre took the letter from her beaded reticule and
placed it before her, she only said :

" Ring for Sarah, Catherine."

When Sarah came, she ordered breakfast, deciding to
discard prayers for to-day.

" Fetch the master," she said, " and tell Gale to
fetch Master Peter and Mrs. Gosling."

She began to eat an egg, but it was less like a meal
than an execution. Mrs. Velindre drowned her lumps
of sugar one by one, as if they were both Marigolds.

Sarah returned to the kitchen and sat down heavily.

" There's only one thing as there's a God's plenty
of for Sarah Jowel," she remarked. " And that's
trouble. It must be 's Catherine. She's as deep as
Dormer pond. She'll lose a brother when the devil
dies, no danger ! There they'll all be, ravening and
roaring, and Enoch'll ne'er overlook it. I may plead and
better plead, but he'll be as sullen as a daylight owl."

She rocked in her chair, until the cuckoo clock,
striking in loud and ribald tones, reminded her of her
errands. " You're wanting in the room, sir," she said
to Solomon, awaking him from a long, bland siesta
on the wall of the gun-dogs' kennel.

" Read that ! " said Mrs. Darke, when Solomon went in.

" Well, the lad's got himself in a pretty fix," said Solomon. " But what's to be done ? "

" Done—done—done ! " said grandmother, like a bell tolling.

" I dunno."

" Tch !" said Mrs. Darke, and tore the letter across and across.

" Tch ! Tch ! Tch ! " echoed grandmother, till the room seemed full of elfin sneezes.

And now, as if they had not enough to think of, in walked Ernest, announcing weightily :

" I have a child."

" So has Peter, confound him ! " said Solomon.

" I am a great grandmother ! " said Mrs. Velindre.

It was left to Amber to ask :

" How is Ruby ? "

" Physically well," said Ernest. " But mentally, strange—strange. She does not like the child."

" Why not ? "

" Her reason is the most curious thing about it. She says it is because the child is like me. A strange aberration—it will pass."

Amber was thankful that Michael was not there. She was also glad that Solomon returned to Peter's affairs.

" Uncle," said Ernest smoothly, " hush it up ! Hush it up ! "

He spoke so mellifluously, that it was like a lullaby. The scandal seemed already asleep, like a cross but persuaded baby.

" Hush it up, eh ? But how ? "

" Money, sir. Give the girl money and let her go away."

" Let her look for gold, like Mr. Cantlop ! " said grandmother.

" But suppose she loves Peter ? " cried Amber.

" Oh, love ! Sentiment ! " said Solomon.

" Suppose she won't go. She seems to be legally married," suggested Catherine.

" Money ! A great deal of money ! " reiterated Ernest.

There was a deprecating tap, and Mrs. Gosling crept in.

" Well, Gosling, what have you to say ? " asked Mrs. Darke.

" What about, mum, please ? "

" You know quite well. Your girl and Master Peter."

" It wunna my fault, mum ! I'd neither part nor lot in it. I says to Marigold : ' Dunna you take on soft with Master Peter ! You'll look very old-fashioned,' I says, ' when that 'appens as will 'appen ! ' And I partly think it was Enoch's doing as Master Peter married Marigold."

" Whoever was to blame, you go."

" Go ? "

" Go."

" But you wouldna make me leave my cottage, mum and sir ! I never thought to leave it till I went in every-man's carriage. Some like moving. It inna Lady Day with them unless they move. But I canna-abear it. And all them lickle gooseberry bushes I put in ! " She wept into her blue and white check apron. " I partly think the old maister wouldna have given me warning, with no fault of mine."

" Well, well, missus, I'll see you don't lose by it," said Solomon gruffly.

He fetched his cheque book and wrote under Ernest's tutelary eye.

" 'Nough ? " he queried, pushing it towards Ernest.

" More than enough ! " murmured Ernest reverentially. Money always made him feel devout. He took his share in the contemplated betrayal of a soul without a qualm. To do him justice, it never occurred to him that Marigold might prefer Peter to money, nor that it was as great an honour for Peter to be loved by Marigold as to be loved by any lady in the county. His comment on the match was : " Preposterous, my dear sir, preposterous ! "

He thought Solomon's cheque wildly generous. After all, it was a great deal more than what was paid for another betrayal of love a long while since, in Jerusalem, the account of which Ernest always read with such fine elocution.

" There, Mrs. Gosling ! " said Solomon. " Now you can both start afresh somewhere."

" Well, I'm sure, sir ! " Mrs. Gosling was quite dazzled by the vast sum, even though it was only " picture money." She thought how she would convert it into real, convincing half-crowns and shillings, and make wash-leather bags to hold it. " And thank you kindly, sir ! " she said. " I mun stir myself to move for Marigold's sake. I partly think I needna be idle. For there's a time for each and every when they want fettling for the Lord. And maybe I met take the gooseberry trees along of me ? "

She came out from her apron. Her attitude had completely changed.

" If Marigold's willing, Anne Gosling's willing," she said. " So long as you can make it all right about ' let no man put asunder.' "

" Here's Mr. Ernest. He's a parson."

" Quite all right, Mrs. Gosling," said Ernest. " Circumstances alter cases."

Mrs. Gosling retired, comforted and " ticking for gossip," as Amber said. She was in the condition of the clock in the hall, which when it had gurgled must speak at once all that was in its mind. No sooner was she gone than Peter came in, handsome, flushed and sullen. He leant against the door, aware of storm and —as Sarah said—smelling trouble. Most of the faces in the room took the expression of a cat at a mouse-hole when a whisker appears.

" Well, you, sir ! " shouted Solomon. " What have you got to say ? "

Apparently the happy father had nothing to say.

" A pretty pickle ! "

" Nine pounds ! Gideon ! "

" Nonsense ! "

" How old is it ? "

" Husband of a servant ! "

So the chorus ran.

" My dear fellow ! Unwise ! Unwise ! " soothed Ernest. " What possessed you to do such a thing ? "

" They did it in the Bible," said Peter.

" Hold your tongue, sir ! " stormed Solomon.

" I meant, why did you marry her ? " amended Ernest, apparently unaware of the deductions to be drawn from the remark.

Amber laughed, and Peter, perhaps for the first time in his life, became aware of her as an individual, and not as a mere part of the furniture of women that garnished Dormer. He looked across at her with a whimsical smile. Something in his comely nonchalance annoyed Catherine.

" Marigold has eyes like bluebottles and cheeks like raw meat," she said, with pale and pensive satire.

" If you were a man, I'd knock you down," said Peter, beginning to appreciate Marigold.

Catherine laughed disdainfully.

" Now, good people," said Ernest, " let us be calm. Let us ask ourselves—' What would the Captain do ? ' "

Whenever Ernest was confronted by a problem, he said this. When people were restive and inquired how they could find out what the Captain would do, he simply said : " Ask the Captain."

" The long and the short of it is," said Solomon, " that you must separate."

Immediately Peter decided that he wanted to live with Marigold and no one else.

" She's going. It's settled," said Mrs. Darke.

" It must be unsettled then," replied Peter.

" No one will know," said Ernest. " There will be no scandal. All will be well."

He felt that he would not be able to breathe again with comfort till all was really well and Marigold on the sea. In all his professions of willingness to bear crosses, it had not occurred to him that the Captain could invent anything so horrible as this.

" You all talk as if I'd done wrong," said Peter. " I've not done wrong. I've acted honourably. She's my wife. I suppose I can marry whom I please."

He happily forgot, at the moment, that he had married to please Enoch. Mrs. Darke looked at him, and around her seemed to boil the thunderclouds of class hatred and matriarchy.

" Never," she said, " will I have the woman here ! "

Had she known that her hatred of Marigold was weaving Marigold's future happiness she would have died rather than say it.

" Then out I go ! " said Peter. " I'll go to Marigold."

" If you go, you'll never come back, mind that ! " said Mrs. Darke.

" Very well. I'll go to-day."

" But are we, am I, never to see your little girl ? " asked Amber.

" Bless me ! " Peter gave an amused chuckle. " I haven't seen the little beggar myself yet ! "

He turned towards the window as the swiftest means of exit.

" How will you get your living ? " asked Solomon.

" You've no money. You will have to stay here," said Mrs. Darke in a tone of triumph under which ran, like a creature in the grass, something of foreboding, something even of fear. What was it, she wondered, this unbidden stirring in her stony heart ? Was this what they called love ? oh, no ! no ! Let it not be love. Could it be that Rachel Darke, in this late hour, was to be tormented by this feckless, unreasoning, routine-destroying phantom ?

" You are dependent on us," she said again.

" Don't go, Peter ! " Amber spoke anxiously. " Surely something can be done ? "

" You've no profession and no money," said Catherine. " You can't go."

" Money ! Money ! " chanted grandmother " Money rules the world."

" I'll go to the West and sell knives !·" said Peter.

" Knives ? What for ? " cried everyone.

" To cut loose with—to get free with. Yes, that's what I'll do—go to the West and sell knives."

He vaulted out of the window. As he went across the blazing lawn with his young, defiant shadow, the house seemed to fling its own shadow after him, standing like a moated grange eyeing with its unsunned western windows the first of its children to burst from its prisoning shelter. It seemed to gaze after him when he had long disappeared. As the day grew hotter, the walls began, ever so slightly, to shake in the haze.

Inside the house all was still, until the clocks began to stir and murmur on the silent air, that was full of the hot scents of thunder weather. Their clamour seemed to arouse those in the dining-room.

" A child of Sattan," said grandmother.

" Satan," corrected Ernest.

There was a rubbing on the door, and Enoch walked in. He held his purse, made by Sarah of corduroy bound with black tape and fastened with a large linen button.

" I've druv plough for you, sir, from a lad," he said, " and my feyther for yourn. I wish you well, and the family well. But I wunna take your money—not a farden piece of it." He drew the cheque out and gave it to Solomon. " What me and mine needs, we can yearn," he said.

In his eyes was an angry sparkle seldom seen there.

" And though you've given ours warning to go from Dormer Valley, I wunna go from the village."

" But, surely, my good man, you'll not refuse money ? " said Ernest.

" You'll listen to reason, Enoch ? " added Solomon.

" It wunna be able to be done," said Enoch, answering both together.

He turned and went out into the kitchen, where Mrs. Gosling and Sarah sat crying on either side of the kitchen fire under the shadow of Jemima Onions.

As Enoch's steps died away across the yard, Sarah said :

" Enoch's worse than 'im above when he's roused ; for you can plead pardon of 'im above through a third party, and say you never meant it. But Enoch knows you meant it, and there inna no third party. I feel so bad, you'll be bound to fetch the doctor to me—only I feel too bad for the doctor. Fetch me the beast-leech ! "

XVII

THE GODS ASSEMBLE

THE last Sunday in August came, and still Dormer
lay under the burning and airless heat. It was the
weather that wakes in all animals a strange restless-
ness, when the young ponies on the mountains fear
they know not what, galloping furiously hither and
thither, without aim or destination ; when the sheep
cry all night long ; when in the sullen evenings the
young gnats mind them of their wings and volley
upwards to their mating ; when the woodpecker's
laugh grows hysterical ; when it has even been known,
in the hot, moonwhite midnights, for a hive to seethe
with such unrest, and for the late-hatched queen to
wake with such a wildness in her blood, that a swarm
has gone raging up into the molten, silver sky.

For many days there had loomed, around and above
Dormer Valley, gigantic clouds which grouped themselves beyond the circle of darkly wooded, rooky hills,
like people in an amphitheatre. Some towered like
gods in white mantles, with folded arms ; others
seemed to lean forwards upon the woods, as on a
granite balustrade, brooding on the house of Dormer.
Some appeared to rest, chin on hand ; some were
hump-backed, ponderous ; others, like stealthy little
gods of mischievous intent, crept and climbed, peeping
over the shoulders of the giants. They were mostly
of that terrific pink peculiar to thunderclouds, and

fiercer than grey or black—a very pale brick-colour tinged with yellow—which seems like a caricature of all the rosy and firelit and flesh-tinted pinks, which is at once awful and ghoulish. With these, rooted in the tempestuous navy-blue low on the horizon, grew up clouds of a blanched ash-colour, very melancholy and wan. Sometimes the colours varied as in lime-light. Violet, stark silver, leaden grey-green—these passed over them like changing tints over a group of statuary. Occasionally at night they would move slowly round the horizon, and Jasper would think with relief that they were gone. But in the morning they were back again, taller and more majestic, more intent, with the same air of patient waiting for a drama in which—so his feverish fancy told him —he was destined to enact a tragic part. On this Sunday the sun rose coppery above the stifling valley, and sometimes there came a hot gust from the east more oppressive than stillness. The swallows felt this oppression and flew seldom, languorously and low, over the water. The warblers hid themselves. The silent pigeons made no stir amid the leaves. It was one of those days when dry places are full of acrid scents, and damp places are fœtid ; when the fresh fragrances of spring seem to have been changed into scents unhealthy and oppressive ; when summer curdles, and the year turns rancid from very richness.

Jasper was thankful that to-day he need not go into Mr. Arkinstall's molten harvest fields. He felt utterly exhausted under the pressure of a doubt which, even at its vaguest, is torture—doubt of the beloved. He had watched Catherine's face when Michael's name was mentioned and when she had not been on her guard.

He wandered out into the yard and met Enoch taking the pigs to consume windfalls in the orchard.

Jasper paused, hesitant, wanting sympathy, but not knowing how to ask for it. Enoch, characteristically, gave it without being asked, and by talking of something else.

Having given a long ruminative look at Jasper's face he turned squarely round with his back to him. This was his custom when people were in trouble. He would not have thought it delicate to " outface " them. Thus posed, with a bit of half-ripe wheat to chew, and a wary eye on the heavy eastern sky—as one who expected some demon to materialize there— he said :

" The sun's dealing straitly with us, Master Jasper. Very straitly, he be."

" Yes."

" It makes the beasts mortal fratchety. They wunna stop where they're put. Ours broke pasture last night, and her at the World's End public got out, and she hanna raught back yet."

The person referred to was not the landlady, but a much more important person in Enoch's eyes—her cow.

" And Wallows broke out, and Rectory," he went on. " Pond's dry at Rectory, but I canna see what for they wanted to break out at the Wallows. It's the weather goes to their yeads. No beast can stand it."

He turned sideways and indicated one of the sows.

" Now that un," he said, " what d'you think she'd done when I came to the pigsty but now, Master Jasper ? Clomb right over the door, and there she was, bompassing and boasting, and the rest screaming ' housen afire ! ' I never heard such a belownder. But she allus was a restless piece."

" D'you think it'll rain soon, Enoch ? I hate this weather."

The tenseness behind the commonplace remark made it almost electrical.

" Well, Master Jasper, it met, and agen it metna. But the more of a frizzle now, the more of a souse after. And the more things go callywessen now, the more they'll drive a straight furrow after."

With this he finally swallowed the much enduring bit of corn, removed his eye from the east, turned round, and perceived that the " piece " had set off for the Wallows, leading with her the rest of the pigsty population.

If Jasper had not been so miserable, he would have shouted with laughter at the picture of svelt bodies, thin perky tails and willing little feet vanishing down the lane, while Nemesis with a long bean stick followed with obstinate, unhasting tread.

Jasper went into the dim drawing-room, where only the motes stirred in narrow shafts of sunlight that struck across the dust-coloured carpet through defective slats in the Venetian blinds. It was airless, for all the windows were shut, but it was shady, and the shrouded piano with its tidy sheaf of sacred music seemed to promise a reassuring muteness. A blue-bottle that had caught its wing in the web of a spider so old and crafty that it had even managed to elude Sarah, made an intermittent, forlorn buzzing, as if it saw and did not like the ghostly company of departed bluebottles to which it was to be gathered. Jasper got up and released it. Then he lay down on the sofa. It was Uncle Thomas Hilary's bequest, and it still bore the marks of Uncle Thomas's occupation, for being a ponderous gentleman he had " sat through " the springs, as the Darkes of several generations knew. Jasper curled himself into the attitude which best avoided the springs, and tried to read. But even that anæsthetic failed him. Catherine's face, oval and

almost faultless, so clear in complexion that it seemed
to imply clarity of soul, floated across his vision with
the floating motes. He shut his eyes and saw her
as she had looked at the dance—the graceful head,
the gentle outlines of shoulder and breast, the softly
lifted frill of her dress. He remembered how his
hands had been full of an ungovernable desire to
touch her ; how he had fought with the desire and
conquered it. What good had it been ? Did she love
him any better for it ? She said so. Did she understand him ? He doubted it. He had kissed her that
day at the grotto, he had outsoared Peter's scornful
—" I wouldn't take up with a girl I daren't kiss."
Catherine had not kept her supremacy without some
cost to herself. But her eyes remained coldly clear
and untroubled when they dwelt on him, unchanged
in their liquid greenness, through his most impassioned
moments. And those same eyes had lighted at the
name of Michael Hallowes. He had seen the chill
mermaid glance quiver and warm to a green flame.
He had seen the vexed, confused, red flush in her pale
cheeks. Or was it his imagination ? " Oh, God ! "
he thought, " let it be imagination ! "

He pulled out Catherine's portrait and kissed it
many times.

" Who's eating lozenges ? " said grandmother from
the inner room, whence she emerged, feather-brush
in hand, nodding inquiringly like a Chinese queen
with a gaudy fan.

" I see you, great-grandson ! " she remarked, tapping
her way to the sofa. " You've gotten a touch of the
sun."

She nodded again, and a little stone idol of missionary
extraction (made with a detached head strung on wire)
which nodded all day in the empty, silent room in
perpetual affirmation of a negation, gravely returned

her bow. The two round, hard faces, the two hard, curiously decorated heads, greeted one another across Jasper's body with an air of affinity. Jasper thought as he looked at them that grandmother was old enough and grotesque enough to have shared a temple with the idol somewhere in the bat-haunted past.

Grandmother began to dust the piano, saying : " Our God is a jealous God ! " And the four chandeliers of Aunt Charlotte-Lucy (deceased) which flanked the idol, seemed to echo her with an elfin, accusing clash.

Jasper got up and went out. He wandered along the stream, dreaming upon the deep, interfusing shadow beneath the twisted thorn, where lay within the water, in a kind of tragic beauty, cross on brown cross and multiple thorny crowns. He wished that he could see there the reflection of the Man of Sorrows passing by across the world. Ah ! if only that fair and fiercely vital story were true, could he not follow with bleeding feet—anywhere, anywhere ! But with a fated beauty, even as he looked, the reflections quivered and were gone, as the may-tree felt the furtive electric wind that roams the world before thunder ; the crosses were softly shivered ; the crowns melted and failed upon the water.

Nothing was left but the marginal swords of the rushes ; the faint motions of water insects ; the shadowy head of a swimming rat.

Slipping into a hypnotic dream, Jasper imagined that he saw within the water, moving with the weird dignity with which a herd of cattle pass in a pool, the people of Dormer. But their faces were not the faces of daily life ; some necromancy had brought them out of their hiding. A wild and changeling company they seemed ; but he scarcely noticed any face except Catherine's. Her eyes looked chill and crafty as the eyes of a sea-queen, dwelling cold in the cold green ocean, never winning through to a soul.

The water wearied Jasper almost as much as the house. There were too many people in the house ; there were too many minnows in the water, the warm stream was alive with them. There was no rest here. And above, under the branches of the dark green, heavy trees, already tinged with edges of yellow, danced in languid mazes the multitudes of midges. The air was so heavy, the water ran so oily-thick, that Jasper felt stifled. He decided to go to the grotto. It would be cool there. He would take a jug of tea and stay there all day, until blessed evening brought Catherine and her long-waited answer.

As he went up the Beast Walk, the strange shapes seemed silently to jest and jape at him, alternately stirless and whispering. A vacillating air wavered over them in the heat, stirred them to multiple sibilations and fell to a calm that held in it, like a narcotic solution, the scent of the green yew and of the deep layers of dead yew beneath. Jasper liked it better when the trees were still ; for to the derided soul even the voice of the forest is derision. Lugubrious and hollow-sounding, it roars upon him in winter like the voice of a ghoul, hounding him from glade to glade under the complex traceries of grey coral. And in summer, when the green tongues lisp and murmur as they did to-day, so that the curtained woodland is full of a volume of soft noise, he is even more keenly reminded, if he is inclined to be introspective, of the ridicule of his fellows—as if each one laughed softly behind his hand. Now, as he thought of his own life, of the way he had been fooled by fate and was being, so he imagined, fooled by everyone, his face grew wild and bitter. When darting doubts of Catherine flashed like lizards in and out of the

crevices of consciousness, the stark holly trunks
seemed to him like the pillars of a torture chamber. What was his life? A round of drudgery
among people some of whom he detested. What was
his future? Instinct began to tell him that it was to
be either a long wrestle of wills between himself and
Catherine, or blank despair. He saw life without
glamour, without romance; and to see it thus is like
living in rocky and barren deserts. He heard the
shrilling of age in its wintry skeleton tree. He heard
the weak crying of infancy in its bleak, windy nest.
He saw the callow fledglings a-row, earnest, incompetent, doomed to innumerable downfalls and un-
thinkable labours to attain—what? Simply to attain
the anxious, restless preoccupation of parenthood.
The songs of maturity, so sweet, so compelling to the
hearer, what were they to the singer? "They are
what my love for Catherine is to me," he thought,
" terror and ecstasy, and very little ecstasy." Fools!
these poets, who imagined the blackbird singing in
April because he was happy. He was not happy.
He was full of a passion he did not understand and
never wanted. He shouted in a wild desperation,
hoping to get rid of his unrest by the outcry of his
soul. If he won his mate, he was triumphant; but
was he happy? Jasper doubted it. Where did
all the labour of home-building lead—the carrying of
heavy burdens—the feeding of unsatisfied young?
In his present mood he felt that Nature worked her
creatures like slaves, and, with her ironic smile—so
suave and so secret—fooled them into believing that
they were masters of the world. (Unconsciously
Jasper endowed Nature with the very smile of
Catherine.) And when the play was done, summer
over, fruits gone and song faded—what then? Nothing.
Only the shrilling of age in its wintry, skeleton tree.

"Curse it!" said Jasper furiously, "curse it!"
There was in his voice the agony of a straying creature
benighted in the wilderness.

The forest remained aloof, not taciturn, but indifferent. Only the echoes, in tones light and cold as the
voices of gibing fairies, faintly cried from the rocks
and the walls of woodland, "Curse! Curse!"

He knew that, if he stayed at Dormer, he could not
resist the sleepy poison of the place, where they were
so full of material preoccupations; where they destroyed the impalpable; where, for him, madness
lurked like a snake in the egg. Jasper, as he looked
with loathing at the leprous trunks of the dead hollies,
thought: "It's all the joke of a goblin jester, without
sense, without mercy, without even humour. And
he's got us in his clutches, body and soul!"

By which it will be seen that Mrs. Cantlop was right
when she said, "Jasper needs a tonic."

He did, but it was not the kind that is sold in bottles.
He had the misfortune—it is sometimes a misfortune
—to love wildly and yet steadfastly. Therefore,
Catherine being what she was, he moved in a circle,
and his struggles were fruitless. He saw life as a dark
ravine, a place where the bitter-berried juniper tangled
the feet; where the streams made a wintry clamour
of wrath and sadness; where the crying of the flock
echoed from the white water to the crag, fell, broken,
from the cold night sky, shivered into silence in the
hollows where gleamed the white bones of sheep.
This crevasse of the mind Jasper knew well. Thither,
at a chance word of any callous temperament, he was
driven, lamenting and lost. It is strange that those
who speak such words never dream that they have
sent a fellow creature forth into a place so wild, so
deathly. Jasper sat down on the stone bench outside
the grotto, and looked towards the house. He won-

dered why so many of the people down there were
warped by the very things that should have made
them weathered timber. Yet, in a way, he loved
them. One side of him loved them, the other was
irritated by them almost to frenzy.

He went into the grotto to avoid the intense heat
and to be out of sight of the contemplative, witnessing
clouds. For the human mind, when it nears the day
of despair, can only think with equanimity of the
mysterious creatures of space—stars, cloud, light—
when it imagines a personal God behind them.

Jasper went through into the tiny inner room where
no one ever came, fetched the rug and lay down,
utterly weary. The green light that filtered in through
the small ivied window was soothing, and after an
hour or two the book dropped from his hand, and he
fell into the dreamless sleep of those who are super-
latively wretched.

XVIII

JASPER BREAKS PASTURE

CATHERINE stood, wrapped in a long cloak of white which she affected, just outside the small, unglazed window of the grotto, in the wild, tempestuous evening light. She had just seen Amber come from the outer room of the little stone house, now dark and uncanny ; so she did not trouble to look inside, as was usually her prudent habit before sitting down on the bench. She looked after Amber's retreating figure from which even the shadows could not take the look of dowdiness, or, as Catherine thought, of dumpiness. Amber wore her usual summer afternoon dress— spotted muslin, with flounces, made by herself, and not very well made.

" What a Mother Bunch ! " thought Catherine, suppressing a titter.

She guessed where Amber was going. She was going further into the wood, so that Michael Hallowes should come out and look for her. Amber did this because the sweetness of being looked for was heady as faery wine to her, and because she needed its re-assurance—for she was subject to the swift darts of self-depreciation which make a plain woman withdraw from her love in a pride rooted in humility.

To-night Catherine had other views for Michael. She stood, swaying a little on her daintily shod feet, in the centre of a small circle of yew trees. This was, in its turn, ringed by the immense amphitheatre of statuesque cloud, very intent now, giving to Michael, as he came down through the Birds' Orchard, a sense of oppressively courteous attention. What were they waiting for up there, in that sad, pale, red light of theirs, like people expectant before the curtain as it rises on the chief scene of a play ? Catherine, seeing that Amber had quite disappeared in the dark yews, whispered :

" You can wait, and wait, and wait, my dear ! He shall not come ! "

She clicked her white teeth with finality, and sat down on the bench, looking up the path down which Michael would come.

He came.

She clasped her hands in the intensity of her passion for him.

" Oh, he is a man—a man ! " she thought.

" How he is glooming on the grotto ! I can see he is not pleased. Is it I he is not pleased with ? Oh ! I would rather have his anger than other people's praise ! I would rather be his mistress than the wife of a duke."

Michael paused by the grotto, and glanced in at the ivied window, for an intuition told him that Jasper would be there. Jasper lay in a half-waking state. Surely, he thought, Catherine could not be harsh to him. He remembered the feminine droop in the graceful figure. Surely she must lay aside cold theory for love—the womanly, the warm, the starry ! Then the long conflict would be over. She should keep her Christ. He would never lay a finger on her creed. She should keep that ; he would keep his honesty ; all would be well. He did not see Michael.

The hush that lay on the world thickened round

the grotto, as Michael stood and looked at Catherine ;
bats began to appear, uttering, amid their half-cynical
activity, soulless cries.   They were so eerie that even
Catherine, who had too glassy a mind to be, as a rule,
affected by nature, shivered and felt the place lonely.

" It is the only way," thought Michael.   " Cruel ;
but the only way.   It must be the knife."

The stone walls seemed to grow greyer with the
shadows of disillusionment.   Old lost dreams and
hopes came flocking, cold as snowflakes, stealthy
as bats, and clung dankly in the corners.   Down
below, the water made its continual plaint ; and once,
from the outskirts of the wood, there rang out the
high, nervous cry of one of the strayed animals.

" You have been a long time coming," said Catherine
softly.

Jasper stirred, rolled over, got up.   There she was,
his guardian angel, come at last to comfort him.   How
sweet she was, with her dimly coiled hair softly resting
on the large cavalier collar !

He peered out, and was just going to speak when
he saw Michael.   He sat down, holding on to the
table with both hands in a rush of jealousy so savage
that he could not move.   He did not hear Michael
ask briskly : " Where is she ? "

He only heard the reply, which was not a reply,
in the unmistakable voice of a woman speaking to the
man whom she passionately loves.   Horrible ages
of suffering rolled over Jasper as he heard those few
words :

" Why didn't you come sooner ? "

" Why did you want me to come sooner ? " asked
Michael.

Catherine's head drooped.   Dared she be frank ?
She looked swiftly at Michael.   No !   She must hint ;
she dared not be outspoken.

She slipped from the white cloak and stood before him in her green dress, made of silk and closely fitting. He thought as he watched her that she had the conciliatory air of a new wife in a harem. She trembled as she stood, for she who had laid snares for Jasper was snared herself.

" I have been told," she said diffidently, " that I am beautiful."

Michael said nothing.

She laughed nervously.

" Do you think so ? " she said, glad that the shadows hid her burning blush.

" Well, as you are now, looking less cold than ordinarily, I think you are," he said.

" Really beautiful ? "

" Quite."

" Am I," said Catherine, " the kind of woman a man would like to see in his house ? "

" I should think so."

" And would want to see with his children round her ? "

(" Oh, he is cruel—cruel ! " thought Catherine. " He will not help me. He makes me give myself to him ! ")

Then, as Michael did not answer, she said :

" Amber is not strong. Perhaps she will never have children."

" I did not come here to discuss Amber."

" Poor Amber ! She is cut out for an old maid."

" She has the qualities which make old maids, as a rule, the Madonnas of the world."

" Marriage with any but the right woman must be so dull."

" Damnably."

" I'm afraid dear Amber is growing too fond of you."

" You're a witch, Catherine Velindre."

" But witches were ugly ! "

" You're not a witch, then."

Catherine sat down on the bench. " What am I ? "

" Jasper will tell you that you are his future wife."

Catherine sprang up in rage and dismay. " What, *that* fool ? " she cried.

" What was that sound," asked Michael, " like a moan ? "

" I hear nothing—nothing but you ! I see nothing —nothing but you ! "

Catherine spoke with still intensity.

From the uttermost darkness beyond the serried gods of cloud there darted, yellow and silent as a lizard, the first forked lightning flash. It seemed to lick Catherine's passionate pale face before it slid into the dark grotto.

From far down the woods, near the house, came Sarah's voice, sharp and miniature, keeping on two nerve-wracking notes, the echo repeating the second syllable of each word.

" Enoch—noch ! Enoch—noch ! You're wanted— wanted."

" *You* are wanted, Michael," burst from Catherine's tremulous lips, " you are wanted by——"

" It is Enoch that's wanted, not me," corrected Michael. " And now tell me about Jasper. He is very fond of you, is old Jasper. And you ? "

" And I," said Catherine, " if I saw him burning on a slow fire, and knew that a word of love could save him, would give that word to——"

Again Michael saved her.

" Would give that word, of course," he said. " It's only a matter of principle that has gone wrong between you and Jasper. It will come right, because love is a primitive thing."

" I only said it was his views to get rid of him."

" If he had given up his honesty, his soul, for you, would you have spoilt his life ? "

" His life ? What's his life ? I don't care *that* for his life ! Foolish boy—with his empty face, and his ' Cathy this ' and ' Cathy that ! ' "

Thunder had muttered round the horizon for a long time. Now the first rattling peal fell from heaven.

Jasper burst from the grotto.

There are times, especially under moonlight, when the human face takes the look of white flowers, and when the personality is effaced, leaving simply human pathos. So Jasper looked, as he came from the low dark house into the immense, tenebrous night—as though his whole self had become transparent, and were being washed away on some roaring flood.

Catherine's face also, blanched and tragic as she looked after Michael, had this quality of helplessness. She had risked all and lost. For the moment she was beaten. She, the passionless, had been stricken, as the weak never are, by this overwhelming love which ruled her—who had always ruled herself and others —until she was terrified. Instinct had said—" Win this man ! Make him love you ! " She had failed, and her love had turned to a predatory beast, con- suming her vitality. She never took her eyes from Michael's retreating figure. Thunder crashed and echoed above ; but she was not afraid of the thunder. Jasper's eyes burnt upon her from his ravaged face ; but she was not afraid of Jasper. She had seen with awful clearness exactly what Michael thought of her, felt for her, in the one long look he had given her before he turned on his heel and left her with Jasper. She was a haughty woman, and she writhed as she saw again (she would see it all her life) the expression of scorn in Michael's eyes—worse, the expression of amusement. She could have killed him as she realized that he found her laughable. She had offered him herself, and he had waved away the gift as one might discourage a persistent beggar. She knew that if she could have won Michael's love, she might have become, by virtue of it, a simple direct creature, living sweetly in the sunlight. Though she had been, in the house of Dormer, a cold and cynical egoist, love could have awakened her, persuading, commanding, dragging her into happiness through pain. The lover must suffer infinitely, the egoist not at all.

She looked up at the tormented trees, where ran the furious, electric wind, like a hunting leopard. She looked at the dark sky, where only a central clarity of dim air was left as the cloud-gods crowded inwards, their moon-silvered heads almost meeting. From the bases of their thrones, where night was thickest, came the continuous, terrific peals ; and flashes coruscated there like electric sparks struck by their feet from the granite hills.

At last she was obliged to look at Jasper, whose long stare, full of curiosity, wonder, disgust and horror, had never left her.

So might one of the cave-dwelling hermits have looked if, after opening his low door to a purple-winged seraph, he had turned and beheld, where the seraph had stood, an ape. His soul was sick ; his face had a hollow look—the look of winter, of withering and decay.

A small thing to make shipwreck on, perhaps, a woman's ridicule. But it was enough, she had revealed herself.

So they stood for a moment, alone among the sounding shadows. Unbearably, from far below, came Sarah's call :

" Eenoch—noch ! Eenoch ! "

Jasper took a step towards her.

" Liar ! " he said, and brought his open hand down
in a stinging blow upon her mouth.

Then with a sob he turned and went down the
Beast Walk. As he flung himself onward in the mopping and mowing of the shadows, he saw beneath
him a kindly velvet greyness, heard the soft " lap-
lap-lap " of Dormer brook, swollen by thunder rain
that had fallen on the hills early in the day. The
voice of the Four Waters, bee-like still, and still saying
what it had said before the beginning of man, had
grown loud and commanding. What with its imperious
summons and the cajoling murmur of the little waves
below, it seemed that the water was rising like a silver
wraith and softly enclosing him. Liquid sounds were
all about him—drippings and gurglings, plashes,
the rush of little eddies. His soul seemed to be
globed in water, like a tiny insect in a rain drop. As
he went, he did not think of Catherine, with her predatory purity ; nor of Dormer, with its vault-like
air ; nor of his love, trampled and dead. He thought
of water—green, saffron, blue, brown, white, every
colour. His mind became for those moments the mind
of a water-creature. He dreamed the dreams of the
long-rooted lily, the darting trout, the caddis, moving
on its secret enterprises, clad in its brook-finery of
little stones and nestling in the sand. The coot and
the vole, the water scorpion, and the bull-head that
hides under the stones—these were his intimates.
He knew them in a flash of time—their desires, their
passion. They lived for the silver water ; in the water
they died. He also was impassioned for water—since
it gave a velvet-soft wound, opened a green, easy
corridor down into death. Yes ! That was where

he would go, down where the water-buttercup rooted,
and the rosy-budded milfoil swayed, and that strange,
sorcery-breathing bloom, the buckbean, planted its
feet in the mud. Peace was there—golden peace,
where the great clumps of tansy and figwort made
all day long a brown and yellow blur upon the sheet
of steel; dark blue and silver peace, where a rift of
night sky slashed the grey current and held far within
it the sad, clear eye of a star; black, stirless peace,
where a yew tree laid its great bulk upon the pale
water, like a weary giant on his bed. Weary? Ah,
but Jasper was weary! He was so infinitely tired of
trying to make people understand that he was not
either an idiot or a villain, but just a plain, simple
youth wanting to make his own destiny in his own
way. Why wouldn't they see that? But, even as
he thought of it, the indomitable faces rose before
him, hard with the inevitable hardness of spiritual
ignorance, as unable to get out of their superstitions
as he was to get back into them. He saw that, and
he was sorry for them, realizing that they were the
victims of their own Juggernaut. But for Catherine
he was not sorry. He wished he had killed her.

" If she had gone on the streets," he thought, " and
I had found her plying her trade in some filthy den,
I could have forgiven her, brought her home, worshipped her still. But this—there is no cure for this.
Her very soul is putrid. There is no cure for me
but the water. She will never follow me into the
water."

He stood beneath the yew tree that was shaped like
a monkey, and let his eyes dwell on the murmuring
flood, while he tried, with youth's bepuzzled frown,
to visualize Dormer without himself in it. There
they would all be, busy, absorbed in outward observ-
ance, and Catherine would buy a becoming black

dress. Suddenly he realized that, instead of his personality being fainter because of his death, it would for the first time be really ponderable.

He laughed at that—the wild laugh of a soul unmoored by some great shock from the safe and homely things of life.

Then he heard Sarah, back in the garden, calling : " Eenoch ! "

It brought the world in, and the fear of being afraid, of being once more tied down to the daily life he hated.

The water closed over him with a soft, assenting lisp.

XIX

WHILE these things were happening, Ernest had arrived. He had come to say that " something must be done " about Ruby. She was " queer."

" Great-aunt," said Ernest, " she said she did not like the child. I said that in her husband a woman sees the ideal to which her child will attain, and she laughed—laughed immoderately. Ruby seems insane ; she *is* insane. She has delusions ; she thinks I am not a nice man."

He felt hurt. He had done his duty by God and his fellows in giving them a living likeness of himself, and this was his reward !

" She must be shut up," said Mrs. Darke.

" I fear so, I deeply fear it," said Ernest. Then, as conversation flagged, he went out to find the younger members of the family.

He could walk as softly as a cat, and had often, while living at Dormer, " beaten " the woods for lovers, in the cause of morality. He had approached Mr. Mallow about this, but Mr. Mallow said :

" I've no instructions as to lovers, sir. If they like to go daggling about in the nasty, muddy 'ood when they met be comfortable by the fire, I says, let 'em go dagglin' ! "

Catherine, as she saw Ernest looming over her, almost before Jasper had disappeared, began to cry.

It was the last intolerable insult of fate that Ernest should witness her humiliation. Ernest, who had never thought of Catherine as one who could cry, became very much interested.

" Confide in me," he said. " I may say I make a speciality of grief."

Catherine was prevented from replying by sobs of rage.

Ernest, feeling that he must be broadly human, tried facetiousness. " Suppose I guess ? " he suggested.

" Suppose," said Catherine, springing up in a vortex of wrath and silken gleams, " suppose you mind your own business, Ernest, instead of coming purring over me ! "

" You *are* my business," said Ernest, " all in one, you know."

He acted as a tonic. She stopped crying and came out of her inertia.

" If you worry me," she said, " I shall tell everybody what I saw on the night of your wedding, and what I heard."

" Heard ? Saw ? "

" Between twelve and one, on the landing," said Catherine incisively.

Ernest sat quite still. So she had seen it all ! The last person who should have done so, that dreadful little cat !

He sat in deep dejection like a pricked balloon.

But in a moment they sprang to their feet. A cry rang out from the trough of night, mournful, wild and hoarse. It was snatched up by the echoes in the forest and hanselled by them as though it were a new, strange toy.

" Drownded ! Drownded ! "

The two words arrested Catherine's heart with their

sickening, fatal sound, and, as Ernest went to see what
was the matter, she sank down on the bench again.
Enoch also heard them.   He retired to the apple-room
now in his leisure, refusing to respond to Sarah's
repentant blandishments.   He sat there in great peace,
making thatching-pegs amid the pleasant scent of
summer apples, while the storm came nearer and broke
over the house.   His unglazed window looked on the
water and the woods, and he could dimly see his aunt's
cottage which stood near the foot of the Beast Walk.
He thought how the rose-and-white figure of Marigold
used to preside over the winter tea-table, and how he
used to hurry through the wild, wet wood so that he
could see her sitting by the fire with her sewing.   He
fell into a long reverie about her and her child.   He
did not notice the darkening sky ; the mice ventured
out ; Sarah's call came unheeded from the wood.

It was not until Mrs. Gosling's cry sounded from her
garden, coming wildly across the water, that Enoch
woke to the world.

" There's ours hollering," he thought.   " The
'oman's been at it this long while, but what ails ours ? "
He listened.   Again came the melancholy lament—

" Drownded !   Drownded ! "

He sprang up and ran.

" I knowed they'd drive un to it," he thought.
"Ay, Master Jasper's broke pasture this night."

He ran beside the full stream which churned against
its banks.   Mrs. Gosling was inarticulate and wild.
She wrung her hands and wailed, her check shawl and
grey hair blown by the wind, her face running with
rain.

" Oh, my 'ouns, Enoch !   I thought you'd ne'er
come ! " she cried.   " Get un out, Enoch !   Get un
out ! "

Enoch snatched up a pole and ran downstream, for

the current was strong, and he thought Jasper must
have been carried with it. He was joined by Ernest,
competent and energetic. To do him justice, Ernest
was always ready to spend himself for the general
good. In a physical crisis he was at his best.

" What's that ? " he cried. " In the water there,
wading, white as a ghost ? "

It was Amber. But not as anyone had ever seen her
before. Wet to the waist, dishevelled, sobbing,
calling upon Jasper, she stood in the water, and her
voice was driven down the wind.

She had waited a long while for Michael. When the
storm broke, she had started to go back to the grotto.
Then that awful shriek rang out, and with a cry of—
" Jasper ! "—she had rushed to the water.

" Where are you ? Oh, where are you ? " she
called ; and the echoes, in ghostly chorus, took up the
questioning sadness of her cry. The night seemed full
of voices uttering a lament ancient as love itself. But
only the clucking of the stream against its banks
replied to her, the moaning wind, the hushing
rain.

" If you was to fetch the maister, Miss Amber," said
Enoch with his swift intuitive perception of the right
thing to do for people in trouble, " it ud be helpful-
like."

In his own heart he feared that Jasper was beyond
all help. Amber ran along the path where yellow
leaves, loosened by the storm, fell sadly from the chestnuts. Streaming with rain and brook water, shuddering with the deep horror of death, she ran blindly.
Anyone meeting her would have thought her crazed ;
for love has no thoughts for its own appearance, its
own entity, when the beloved is threatened. So, in
a world absorbed in outer forms, love is often hooted
as an imbecile. Surely on Olympus the comfortable

gods smiled behind their hands at Eros, wandering careless down buttercup ways. And we know that among his own people Christ was looked upon askance as one whom it was kinder to regard as mad.

The storm had spent its rage. The thunder had retreated into hollow caverns far away, leaving the night safe and quiet. Only Jasper was not safe, Amber thought. Only Jasper was not there to see the moon set in the clear washed heavens. The gods, who had waited around the horizon so patiently, had departed. Not one remained. The pigmy tragedy was over; leaving the little actors yet on the dim, disordered stage, they had stolen away, it seemed, in the stately silence of indifference.

Amber opened the dining-room door.
" We shall have to forgive Jasper," her father was saying. " Now Peter's gone, he must have the place. We must have one son here. It must be Jasper."
" Jasper ! " said grandmother.
" Jasper is drowned ! " said Amber, and her voice startled the drowsy walls, the lonely passages, with the emptiness of loss.

Still Catherine sat, as if paralysed, on her bench. And as she sat, Philip Arkinstall watched her from the yew-tree shade. All the evening he had been awaiting this hour. Now he heard, coming up from the water, Sarah's voice calling Enoch, Sarah's heavy feet trampling the bracken. She had heard Mrs. Gosling's cry, and was taking a short cut to the cottage.
In a moment she would pass the grotto.
He took two strides to the bench, snatched Catherine into his arms, scattered her hairpins, ripped the green silk off one shoulder. Holding her arms round his

neck with one hand, he clasped her with the other,
crushing her to him with a grip that very ably mimicked
passion.

Then he said loudly enough for Sarah to hear :

" Thank you, darling, for all the happiness you have
given me ! "

" Well," said Sarah to herself as she hastened by,
" you met kill me with a bit of grass ! 's Catherine !—
as was so mim and so prim, with her 'air all down and
dress near off ! " The smile of one completely
satiated with vengeance for many wrongs dawned
upon her rocky face.

" I hate you ! " whispered Catherine. " I'll pay you
for this, Philip ! "

" Yes, my dear. You'll pay with the gift of yourself ! "

" How dare you ! "

" I'm sorry to have inconvenienced you," he said
imperturbably, picking up the hairpins. " But you're
such a damned clever woman. A man's got to fight
with his own weapons."

" I'll never speak to you again ! "

" But you'll marry me."

" You ? " Her voice was like a knife. " When I
marry, it will be a gentleman."

" It will be me. But I don't claim to be your lover,
my dear."

" Claim ? What do you dare claim to be ? "

" Your master."

" Never ! "

" We shall see ; but I will tell you this—Sarah saw ! "

Philip Arkinstall, as he went in a leisurely manner to
help in the search for Jasper, smiled.

XX

THE MARBLE CHRIST

WHEN Catherine reached her own room, she stood transfixed in the doorway. For, at this late hour, the moon, slanting in at her window, laid the shadow of her large marble crucifix along the floor. The figure of the crucified, in contorted, purple-black shadow, stretched its arms across the room. It seemed to her that they were outspread not to save, but to grasp ; that the head was bent not in love but with the menace of a bird of prey. This Christ that she had set up in a half-conscious pose of religiosity had never been anything but a picturesque detail of her room. Now, the tortured white figure seemed to her to be real, yet not with the reassuring actuality of every day, but with the feverish vividness of a nightmare.

Catherine heard someone coming wearily and heavily upstairs. She peered out. It was Amber, looking, in the wavering light of the candle she carried, as grey and limp as if she, as well as Jasper, had been drowned. Her wet clothes and the cold night air had chilled her so that her face was almost blue. Catherine, as usual, was able to look all the things that Amber really was. While Amber only looked bedraggled, Catherine looked tragic, and she might easily have been imagined as she stood there in her white dressing-gown, to be Jasper's guardian angel.

" What has happened ? " asked Catherine.

" Jasper is drowned," said Amber. " And you are his murderess."

" Are you mad ? "

" I wish I were. I should have forgetfulness in my soul if I were."

" Then what do you mean, calling me by that evil name ? "

" Evil names are for evil people. You murdered Jasper just as much as if you had pushed him into the stream. Your spirit did push him in."

" The poor boy was crazy."

" I think the same people are responsible for what is called madness—the people, that is, who think themselves sane."

" Could I help it if he loved me ? Could I help it if they both loved me ? "

" Both ? "

There was a silence. They heard Sarah's steps go by, and the faint rattle of the silver-basket. Whoever died, the silver must be looked after. Custom decreed that it should sit on Sarah's chest of drawers, covered with a wash-leather, the plated mustard-pot outside, like a kind of Ishmael which the burglar might take if he liked. Though Sarah did not mean to go to bed, she felt that the silver would be safe in her room in the comfortable aura of ancient usage.

" Jasper and Michael," said Catherine.

" Michael ? "

" Yes."

" Do you mean that you think Michael loves you ? "

" Does a man quarrel with his best friend about a woman unless he loves her ? "

" Did they quarrel ? "

" Did Michael keep you waiting to-night ? "

" Yes."

" He was at the grotto—with me."

Amber thought—" There is some mistake ; I will
not believe it."

" Then Jasper came ; there was a quarrel."

" About you ? "

" Yes."

" You are mistaken, Catherine.   Michael loves me."

" You ! "

Catherine took Amber by the arm and led her to
the mirror.

" Look ! " she said.

Amber looked, quailed, and turned away.   But she
repeated, as if it were a charm, " Michael loves me."

" He said to-night what a nice old maid you would
make."

" If he said that, he did not mean it as you mean it."

" He was laughing at you.   Have you no pride ?
Give him up ! "

" No."

" You must.   He would only have a miserable half-
life with you.   With me "—she stretched out her
arms so that one hand touched the icy marble of the
cross—" with me he would be happy."

" I can't," repeated Amber.   " He and I could
sooner give up living, than each other."

Into Catherine's face came a look at once frantic
and shrewd.   It was intolerable to think of Amber
marrying Michael.   Whatever happened to herself,
that must not be.

" You spoke of my pushing Jasper in," she said.
" Suppose I told you that your lover—or the man you
persist in regarding as your lover—pushed Jasper in ? "

The room slipped into a darker silence, and as the
moon sank from the window, the shadow of the Crucified seemed to enlarge and engulf Catherine.

" I should not believe it."

" And if I saw it ? "

" I should say you imagined it."

Catherine remembered Ernest and his fear of her
ridicule.

" If I could bring a witness ? "

Her voice was a knife, cutting the silence with
delicate strokes. Outside, the pear tree rustled and
sighed in the wet wind that drew out of the east,
where the first grey of dawn appeared. The clocks
struck three with forceful meaning, as though to say
that Time was still unappeased, still seeking his prey
in the bodies of poor mortality.

" I should say your witness lied," said Amber.

" And if my witness was of such standing in the
world, so respected, that his witness would be taken
against that of others ? "

" I should not care."

" To-morrow, then, I shall accuse Michael."

Catherine found some relief for her misery in tormenting Amber.

" You would not try to do such a thing ? "

" On one condition I won't. Give him up."

" Catherine ! Catherine ! I never thought you
were wicked ! "

" It is not I that is a murderer."

" Oh, you are as calm as a frozen sea ! "

" You have only to give him up."

Amber groped for the matches. The room was very
dark, and she felt afraid of Catherine. She found the
matchbox, a luminous one with *Jesus* on its white surface, and lit the candles.

She looked almost old. Anyone with a spark of
pity would have waived all discussion and simply put
her to bed. But in Catherine's face, as the candles lit
it with an eerie glow, was no relenting. Cold as a mermaid languidly breasting the green water, inexorable
as a savage queen demanding sacrifice, her innermost

being looked out on Amber. Her god—a god of marble—stood unheeded behind her with tragic eyes, and dying, drooping head. He meant nothing to her, had never been real to her, any more than He is real to half His devotees. For Christianity, beautiful as it was in its precarious early days, is now too often simply a ticket of respectability that is credited by the mob.

Catherine looked at Amber with a careless scorn which veiled a devouring eagerness.

" You have only to give him up," she repeated.

" As soon tell the earth to give up feeling the pull of the sun."

" You talk quite well when you're roused," said Catherine.

" No. I am not a good talker. I only feel," said Amber quietly.

But she did not feel quiet. She was out in the wild, scarred wilderness that lies beyond the pleasant meadow-country of convention. She felt the sharp rock, cruel and cold. Catherine's soul appeared to her naked ; more sterile than the waste, more cruel than the rock, inhabiting the desolation like a white demon. Catherine the devout, she that had communicated fasting, was nothing more than a beast of prey. The two women, locked in spiritual combat, breathed heavily. Their remote selves confronted one another.

" You tortured Jasper ! You put him in a cage and tortured him," said Amber. " Now it is to be Michael."

" Jasper was foolish. He insisted on being different. He had to be made like other people."

" So you used his love for you to torture him. You made him want to die. You ought to be in hell, Catherine."

" Hell is for unbelievers."

" Are you a believer ? "

" Yes."

" In what ? "

" Jesus Christ, and Him crucified."

Amber laughed wildly.

" Don't do that ! " said Catherine nervously. ", People will hear you."

" No one but your marble god. Oh, it is right that He should be made of marble ! If He were made of anything less cold, He would disown you."

" If you will give up Michael," said Catherine, returning to her point and playing her best card, " I will give him up too."

" It is impossible."

Amber turned and went out.

Catherine was dismayed. She had not really meant to do it, though, when she remembered Michael's quiet, maddeningly quiet eyes, with their mockery, she felt that she would like to do it. But Ernest would be troublesome. Not even fear of ridicule, she was afraid, would make him bear false witness. Still, she had frightened Amber. Then, as she curled up in bed, the remembrance of Jasper came back—the intolerable remembrance of his face as she had last seen it.

" He was unhinged ! " she whispered. " It was not my fault ! "

Hark ! What was that ? The clocks were beginning again. How they growled and wheezed and rustled ! How they ticked her away from Michael into the arms of Philip Arkinstall !

She lay and contemplated her future in the grey dawn. And as she thought of it, the spirit of fear, that brooded on the rooftree of Dormer and hooted through the long night of superstition, lodged in her heart.

She looked stonily at the marble Christ, and the marble Christ looked stonily back at her.

XXI

AMBER GOES TO THE FOREST

AMBER did not go to her room. She went softly
downstairs into the hall. Her plans were made ; she
had only to carry them out. She was going to Michael.
She did not know whether Catherine's threat carried
any weight ; so she was going to Michael to make sure.
But could she do it ? She was faint and sick with
exhaustion and felt a growing feverishness coming on.
Love rose up, as it can in the most weary body, and
told her she could do it, however ill she was. A sense
of calm came over her as she went to the door. She
had a strange feeling that if Michael were here, all
would be well with Jasper. Where was Michael ?
Why had he not stayed to help in the search ? Had
he already been out of earshot when Mrs. Gosling's
cry rang out ?

While she softly undid the bolts, she heard along
the passages echoing voices. Sarah and Mrs. Gosling
and Enoch were sitting up in the kitchen, Enoch having
just come in to say that all search had been useless.
At this eerie time, down amid the elfish rustling of
the clocks in the black, hollow-sounding hall, where
dawn had not penetrated, they might have been the
voices of strange spirits.

" The body—where be the body ? "

" Gone ! Alost ! "

" Deep watter ! Ah, Dormer brook's deep watter
after tempest."

" He inna there, I say ! He inna there ! "

" Where bin 'e, then ? "

" Gone ! Washed away. Washed down to the sea."

" Gone to the sea ! "

Amber caught her breath as if she herself had suddenly been flung into deep water. As she went across the brook she felt overwhelmingly weak. She was a being who needed joy. Having joy, she could triumph over the most desperate physical ills. But when joy flickered and went out, then she remembered the grave. Now, as she went softly over the bridge and began to climb the woods, joy seemed fled forever.

She looked round her in a kind of terror, for she had come to the moment, which all sensitive people must reach at some time, when the soul perceives simultaneously the life of man—its small comforts, its upholstery of everyday—and the infinite ; when it asks, bemused and anxious, " Which is the dream ? " They cannot both be true, it seems, for they are in flat contradiction. Yet daily life is true. There it is, with its duties and meals and wordy meetings ; with its sweetness of affectionate glances and homely jests. That is no dream. Yet, when the beloved is dead, the daily life shrinks and withers ; the infinite presses in. There it is, with all its indifferent stars, fearfully real, utterly unknown. With this intrusion of the infinite there come all the strange instincts of the spirit that have no part in daily life. These also are no dream. So there the soul stands, browbeaten and stunned by antithesis, murmuring : " Which is true ? Is anything true ? "

So it is at the deathbed of a loved one. He was here but a moment ago. He is gone. Yet there are the lids ready to open ; there is the mouth just curving to a smile. But where is the love that will bring the smile ? It is here no more. The room is chill. Yet

it is indissolubly one with the beloved face. It cannot
exist without it. Neither can it, we think, cease to
exist. Here is the old inveterate antithesis again. If
too long dwelt upon, it leads to madness, unless some
merciful half-solution rides up out of chaos.

Amber was tormented by the impossibility of imagining Jasper passive. He had always been so rebelliously
himself. She felt like an actor in an unreal play.
She looked round for some convincing thing which, by
its quiet linking of yesterday with to-day, might bring
her the grief she ought to feel and could not feel. But
there were no homely things. This was no longer a
forest of familiar trees, carpeted with friendly flowers,
under known skies. It was an unknown country—that
which encircles the world of fact, holding it as a demon
might hold a crystal glass. Great pillars stood vaguely
ranked on every side. Strange avenues led away
forever. Motionless, solemn, clad in weeds of mist,
the trees stood beneath a heaven utterly sad. There
was no shadow and little light. Mournfully the slow
drops fell from the wet leaves. Mournfully an owl
cried across the grey pastures. Here and there,
against a dark curtain of massed foliage, white tormented arms were flung up, as if in appeal. They
were no longer silver birches, but creatures of the
beyond, imaging her thoughts. Those larches, what
were they ? Strange vegetation rising from unknown
deeps of mud and rock ; waving curious branches ;
bearing fruit of weird, primordial form ; standing in
a transparent, miraculous medium that men called
" air," on a ball whirling through the void. " Larches,"
" oaks ; " how impudent seemed the little words !
Amber wondered if the cave-dwellers ticketed with
their puny names the great bog plants, the primeval
beasts. The sky was no longer a blue ceiling, where
named stars went upon their ordered way. It was a

waste from which might spring at any moment wild rushing fires. All things had lost their names, their homely identity. They cried to her, with muffled, mocking voices : " You know us not ! You never knew us ! " She was bewildered, in this world where trees melted into ideas, thoughts hardened into actuality. She stood beside a dark red pillar that broke, high up, into an ominous heaviness of black, and had once been called a pine. Around her stood multitudes of other such pillars, neither interrogating nor welcoming. She stood on the threshold of the unknown. Everything seemed immortal with an ever-lastingness that cried for merciful death. The world seemed a mirage, made of nothing by a phantom, dreaming he was a god.

She looked down towards the house. It seemed no longer her home, but an assemblage of materials that might crumble at any moment like an anthill. Within, more dismaying than the fires of the sky, were beings come she knew not whence nor how ; gathered for some unspoken purpose ; full of concealed desires, hatreds, appetites. That which lay behind their innermost motive, was it friendly ? She thought it was the same thing that lingered beyond the last star in the sky, that haunted the uttermost pale tint where colour vanished. Was it personal, or was it merely naked life —nothing but matter, motion and heat ? She under-stood why thousands of lives had been spent in the attempt to solve this apparently fathomless mystery. For to know the cosmos as nothing but impersonal force is to dwell in an intellectual hell compared with which the Christian's hell is Nirvana.

It was light now, but the valley lay under a deep sea of mist. Down at Dormer would soon begin a great stir, like the stir in a hive when a hornet enters. They would wake and remember that Death had taken one of them away ; each would unconsciously rejoice that it was not he or she ; they would call to one another, running questingly up and down the groaning stairs in such a fury of vitality as might almost have roused the dead.

" But I can't believe they wanted to rouse him," thought Amber, with bleak and concentrated bitterness. " It always seemed more as if they wanted to bury him." She thought that, in the strange medley of qualities bequeathed to man by the beast, one of the most horrible was the instinct of the burying beetle. On few things does man lavish so much care as on the shovelling of his fellows into nothingness ; and a man has only to state that he is dying, and his friends will flock from every corner of the world to watch. Sometimes the throng becomes so thick that the poor soul has much ado to get out of the world at all.

From all the trees fell heavy argots of silver. Amber thought how, in the perfection of youth, Jasper's life had fallen earthwards like a spilt raindrop or a trodden leaf. To her eager temperament, the worst of Jasper's tragedy was that he had died without having lived. She had an unquenchable thirst for life, and it seemed to her a fearful irony that he should have left the banqueting hall without having tasted of the feast. She knew that she could obey death's call with equanimity if she had first lived fully. Let Life come, bringing Death on his heels if need be ; but let him come !

Life had not even touched Jasper with his rosy finger-tips before the bony, bruising hands of death grasped him. Where was Jasper now ? That soft, hesitant sound in the forest, coming down the glades from very far away—was that Jasper ? No. It was only morning stirring in the treetops, and the vacillating footsteps of the water-drops descending from the trees. That fingering of the wind in her hair, lifting it gently—was that Jasper, a wandering essence, feeling after life and love ? In the lamenting water she thought she heard him imploring her for she knew not what.

The pity of it all ! It was one of those tragedies that could so easily have been averted, she thought. Yet—could it ? Did it not grow naturally out of all that Dormer stood for ? It seemed to her not so much a gash across its routine as the logical fulfilment of its principles. She thought that with individuals and with empires such tragedies are not breaks in continuity, but simply the herd-panic at its zenith.

At last she came out on the open hills. For though Michael's hut was in the forest it was at its highest point, and the shortest way there lay across the heather. The bracken waved wild arms in beautiful abandon, not quite of summer, but not yet tinted by autumn, having attained the transparent golden-green that comes before the burning colours of September. As she walked, she watched the misty plain. Away in the east, where the land was cold and low, it seemed as if the sky had fallen—as if she was looking down on the mysterious upper sides of the clouds—thick, lavish, of a weighty whiteness. The rising sun struck the upper layers into colours of mother-o'-pearl. To the west the mist thinned and was like pale water. Upon it, with delicate dignity, the trees floated, like water-birds of faery, gravely and magically tinted. Some were brown-green like grebes, others of the ashy tint of coots, the soft grey of cygnets. The chestnuts, where the sun struck them, were like sheldrakes with their deep bronzes ; and the beeches had the glossy green of teal. The white sea was populous with these fairy creatures, floating head under wing.

It was at this moment, when her bodily self was refined by exhaustion and her spirit keener than ever before, that she felt for the first time within the thrilling poignancy of beauty a sense of intimacy—as if she were beginning to know not only the face of beauty, but her essence. She knew, in the belated silver owl that passed hurriedly, as if ashamed that the eye of day should behold its quest, something more than a bird of prey, something wistful, immortal, kind. She knew in the silver spire of Dormer Church, suddenly smitten by a lancing sunray, something less than an oracle—something often pathetic, but withal lovable. As she watched the long vermilion clouds in the east, and the luminous intervals between the colours (for, as in a rainbow, so in a sunrise, though they inundate one another ever so gently, there is an interval between them, where it often seems that beauty dwells) there swept into her half-expectant mind a vast, all-hushing peace. It was not personal ; but it enfolded personality. It enfolded everything. A sigh, contented as that of a tired but comforted child, went up from the pale earth to the pale sky. But whether the bracken sighed, or the forest, or she herself, Amber hardly knew. She only knew that every tree and leaf and meadow shared with her in a stupendous quietude where only the miraculous seemed possible.

She saw the strong line of hill above Michael's dwelling lit with sunlight, shining like a wedge of unpolished silver. The rough cart track that led to it seemed like a silver road for the chariots of almighty love. She thought this place was like the land of heaven, where silver-footed creatures wandered, bemused with joy. Love was the core of the morning ; the unreasonable, unreasoning beatitude that nestled in it as a germ does in the rosy pollen ; the central

fire round which all paler fires whirled. There seemed
no disloyalty to Jasper in this love. The mist slowly
ascended in lilac wreaths and veils. The hilltops
flowered like purple pansies, and the serene sky seemed
to soothe the earth like a father's hand.

Amber's ideas of God were vague and shadowy.
The moment she tried to materialize them, they
vanished. But now she felt, with a shock of reality,
that there was more here, on this airy hill, than could
be seen or touched or heard.

She knocked at the Shepherd's Hut, and Michael,
shirtsleeved, with a kettle in his hand and a light of
love in his eyes, opened the door.

XXII

FUNERAL PREPARATIONS

On the morning after the storm, Mr. Greenways, having sorted the letters, was sitting in the sun, piping like a blackbird. He was a cheerful soul, and while he produced, with puckered brow, pleasant little trills and grace notes, he had a sense of deep content. But he stopped immediately at the sight of Enoch's face and the tremendous black bow that Sarah had tied for him. It may be said that, although this stood out to his ears, it was unable to rob him of dignity.

" The old lady ? " queried Mr. Greenways.

" Mas er Jasper," said Enoch.

" In the flush of life ! Ah, when I piped at Miss Ruby's wedding, I knew I piped for trouble. Was it at the Wallows ? "

" No. In Dormer brook. Drownded."

" Laws ! When's the funeral ? "

" We hanna found un."

" Not found un ! Does Mallow know ? "

" I'm going after Mallow now."

" If there's ought to find, Mallow'll find it," said Mr. Greenways. " Trust the Law."

When Enoch had gone, Mr. Greenways pondered awhile. Then he bethought him to dispatch youths to various quarters to bear the tidings.

Meanwhile Enoch went to Mr. Mallow.

" Somebody drowned ? " said Mr. Mallow, turning the words over on his tongue as if he rather liked them.

" Ah ! " said Enoch, with his pine-tree cadence, " drownded dead and never found."

Mr. Mallow fetched a pair of handcuffs.

" We'll find un," said Mr. Mallow, " *and* the murderer."

" There's no murderer," said Enoch. He was troubled by these dark happenings. They were to him, as to all contemplative people, so many axes felling the trees that grew in his soul.

" No murderer ! " Mr. Mallow eyed Enoch as if he suspected him of fraud. " There *must* be a murderer ! "

The Dormer kitchen was full of the smell of burnt porridge, which showed that something was wrong. Sarah never burnt anything except under the influence of strong emotion.

As they came in, Mrs. Gosling and Sarah were folding a great flapping sheet.

" What's that ? " asked Mr. Mallow briskly.

" A winding sheet," said Mrs. Gosling. " God send the poor young gentleman's found ! "

" Found ! " said Mr. Mallow, looking squarely at Jemima's grave. " I'll lay I'll find un. *And* the murderer ! "

" Master Jasper fell in 'isself," said Mrs. Gosling. " I seed un."

" Woman ! " said Mr. Mallow. " When the Law comes in, your eyes go out."

" There was a man once," said Mrs. Gosling, " wanted to find the murderer, and I partly think he *was* the murderer."

She did not like Mr. Mallow's curtness. Mr. Mallow said he would see the family.

"They're going in to their breakfasses, poor things," said Sarah protectingly. She was mothering everybody in this crisis. She was the kind of person who could make even crime homely, and create in a house riddled with ghosts a reassuring atmosphere of the commonplace.

"Let 'em enjoy their victuals on this day of days!" she said, "and take bite and sup yourself, Mr. Mallow!"

"Well, I don't mind if I do taste a bit of flesh-meat!"

"Anything that's breathed, Mr. Mallow likes!" said Sarah admiringly. "None of your snibs of vegetables nor snabs of eggs!"

"You can partly tell when folks be fed o' that'n," said Mrs. Gosling, ready to make peace. "Poor measly things they be!"

"Ah! But Mr. Mallow likes a tuthree pounds of juicy steak," said Sarah.

"Ours did too." Mrs. Gosling spoke with melancholy pride.

"Anything as the life's been took off violent," added Sarah. "I could tell Mr. Mallow anywhere for a brave fellow."

Mr. Mallow received this ovation as if gold and frankincense and myrrh were his by right, and fell to on the meal. He being incapacitated for conversation, it was kept up by the others.

"Mr. Mallow'll find out what there is to find out. He loves crime. I partly think 'e hankers for crime."

"Mr. Mallow'd make as good a chief constable as one here and there," Sarah remarked. "He's got it on his fingers."

"It's to be 'oped Master Jasper'll be found," said Mrs. Gosling. "Such a beautiful corpse he'd make!"

She did not judge people by the world's standards in

proportion to their usefulness, lovableness or beauty ; nor even according to their wealth or the number of their progeny. She judged them solely by their nascent gift for making good corpses.

" I said the same to young Jim Cardingly as went for a sailor," said Mrs. Gosling, " ' A beautiful corpse you'll make," I says.

" ' I'll diddle you yet, Mrs. Gosling,' says he ; and, sure enough, he took on soft and went to Paradise the watery way. ' Lost at sea and never found,' says the paper. ' Obstinate to the last ! ' says Anne Gosling."

Here the dining-room bell rang, and Sarah went to the call like a hen to her chickens.

When the clocks in their leisurely way struck twelve, there seemed to be something more sardonic than usual in their dilatory enunciation. The house had become a seething hive. Sarah, in her excitement, was laying dinner an hour too early. Mrs. Gosling, in the kitchen basting the beef, kept murmuring : " ' In the midst of life we are in death,' " smacking her lips gently because the text was so suavely in her own vein. Mrs. Cantlop had come to condole. She sat opposite to grandmother, with her heart—as usual —in the right place, and her bonnet—as usual—not so. Mr. Cantlop lurked in the shadow of the Welsh dresser, where, being so very thin, he attained the effacement which to him was fulfilment. Sarah flung the cloth across the table with a sound like wind in a sail, and dealt out the knives and forks with her habitual air of disillusionment. Did she not know as much about the knives and forks—their nicks, their flaws, the two with loose handles—as she did about the people in the house ? But to-day there was also something of the high-priestess in her manner.

There were so many people in the room that she had difficulty in getting about. In the general tumult

no one had so far missed Amber. The Rector sat by
Mrs. Darke, and such fragments as " When He
maketh up His jewels " . . . " sardine stone . . ."
were audible. These left Mrs. Darke cold. Solomon
sat in his arm-chair and once or twice shook his head,
murmuring :

" Both gone ! Both lads gone ! "

Grandmother, hearing this, spoke her thought aloud.
" I'm alive ! " she said.

Except for occasional sobs from Mrs. Cantlop and
texts from grandmother the room was quiet. A few
scuffles occurred when Sarah fell over Mr. Cantlop
as she might have fallen over one of the cats. Ernest
sat moodily in the window. He had spent an unpleasant half-hour with Catherine. She had mocked
him unmercifully. " Portrait of a parish priest in the
rôle of a satyr ! " she had said. Being not very highly
educated, she had said " satire." Ernest, even in his
misery, had corrected her. He had also permitted
himself to murmur : " Jezebel ! " Afterwards he
had given his verdict as to Jasper to the family.

" Jasper is in an intermediate state. I have prayed,
and I know."

The Rector had expressed no opinion. He was
one of those rare beings who, being full of a gentle
faith, never dogmatize.

There was a double knock. " Church bells and
organ ! " Sarah announced.

Mr. Dank came in, followed by the ringers. They
were the first-fruits of Mr. Greenways' activities.
When should the " Dead March " be played ? When
should the muffled peal be rung ?

Solomon thought he would wait to decide until Mr.
Mallow came back from his examination of the stream.
So Mr. Dank sat down just inside the door, and the

ringers sat down just outside, such being their own idea of their subtle difference in rank.

Hardly had they done so when there was a sound of wheels, and the activity of Mr. Greenways became again apparent. Everyone beheld Mrs. Griffin's gig, the horse in a lather ; Mrs. Griffin's dressmaker, in complimentary black ; Mrs. Griffin's little boy, almost intoxicated with excitement, looking, in his neat round collar, much more like a cherubic illustration to an epithalamium than a mourner ; Mrs. Griffin herself, benignant, bland, sympathetic, looking as if she knew that life and death were a blend.

" The black ! " cried grandmother. " They've gotten the black ! "

They staggered in with their loads, like bees when pollen-flowers abound, and began to spread the black materials over the table. Master Griffin sat with the ringers in the hall, where he eyed the animals' heads and feet, and played cat's cradle with a bit of black tape.

" ' Mourn, mourn for Jerusalem ! ' " said grandmother, trying on bonnets at the mirror.

It was at this dramatic moment that Michael and Amber came up the drive.

Catherine saw that Michael's arm was round Amber as they came in. Like a gunshot, without her own volition, came the words : " He pushed Jasper in ! "

They all seemed frozen in their seats. Michael stood and looked at Catherine, and she confronted him with blazing cheeks and eyes in which was no shadow of relenting.

" I saw Mr. Michael running down the 'ood far enough away when Mrs. Gosling shriked," said Sarah.

" What were you doing ? " asked Mrs. Darke.

" Looking for my intended, mum."

" She torments our Enoch cruel, mum ! " said **Mrs.**

Gosling, who had been talking to the ringers. " Even
meals he canna be easy at, he's that nervous, staring
round like a frightened coney."

" Well, well, never mind that ! " said Solomon.
" Did anyone else see what you saw, Catherine ? "

She turned to Ernest, who looked as if he wished he
were as small as Mr. Cantlop.

" Say what you saw, Ernest ! "

But at this moment Michael and Amber broke into
helpless laughter, and even as the family still stared
and Mrs. Darke murmured, " Mad ! " there at the
window stood Jasper.

Catherine fainted. Whether the faint were real or
simulated, it served her need, for it saved her from
taking any further part in the scene. Mr. Mallow,
entering with the handcuffs, stood aghast. Ernest
looked pained, for this was not the intermediate state.

Mr. Mallow bent over Catherine.

" It's not fracture nor a lacerated wound," he said,
" nor stroke, nor a foreign body in the ear " (he remembered Jemima). " What took her ? "

Solomon shook Jasper by one hand while the Rector
shook him by the other. Mr. Cantlop stole from his
corner, gave Jasper a surreptitious pat on the back,
and vanished again. Mrs. Cantlop enveloped him in
her complimentary half-mourning. Eight eyes looked
in from the hall, and Master Griffin made such a mess
of the cat's cradle that it had to be discarded. Mrs.
Griffin began very tactfully to fold up the black.

" Not my bonnet ! " said grandmother.

Jasper surveyed the room—the chairs littered with
rolls of black ; the table laid for dinner ; the crape ;
the black kid gloves and black-edged handkerchiefs.
He looked at the faces in the room with an inscrutable

expression. He felt as if he were his own disembodied spirit. He thought : "Self-destruction may be the one sane action of a lifetime." To look at Catherine, white on the sofa, was exquisite torture, knowing as he did that she was a hollow shell. The room, all the familiar things, gave him the sick distaste that a man feels for a room where he has been desperately ill. He would never sleep again under the shadow of the old gods of Dormer. Everything seemed paltry, savourless, twice-told. He wished Death had given him his sable livery, his dole of tears, swept him up in his pageantry.

" You've forgotten the coffin," he said, and, turning, went out into the hall and up into his own room to pack, leaving Michael to explain. " He fell in, and I pulled him out," was all that Michael vouchsafed. The Griffin party and the ringers melted away.

" Then Michael took him home," added Amber, " not thinking anyone had seen him fall in. For when Mrs. Gosling called out, he had just run down the wood and jumped in. He had seen Jasper fall in higher up. So he did not think we should be anxious, as Jasper stayed with him that night before, when it rained."

" Where were you ? " asked Mrs. Darke.

" I went to Michael's."

" Not knowing Jasper was there ? "

" Not knowing."

" Then if Jasper had not, by chance, been there——"

" We should have had to be married," finished Michael. " We'll consider that Jasper was not there."

Catherine, who had been " brought round" by Sarah, got up at this.

" You may all like to know," she said, " that I have promised to marry Philip Arkinstall. I am going to stay at the Keep to get my trousseau."

So she made a dramatic exit against heavy odds.

XXIII

MR. CANTLOP ACHIEVES FAME

" YOUR wedding morning, 's Amber," said Sarah,
" and may the course of true love go smoother for you
than for some ! True love's a treasure ! " She wiped
her eyes on her sacking apron and felt that its harsh-
ness was as her own fate. For Enoch had been hard
to mollify since the unfortunate accident of the letter.

" A sore man ! Neither to drive nor to lead ! " she
reflected.

" You deserve to be happy, Sarah," said Amber,
stroking the muslin folds of the dress in which she was
to go to Michael.

" Desert's a beggar, 's Amber, generally speaking,"
said Sarah. " When people's intendeds be like horse
and mule——" She was so overcome that she went
" to rouse up the old lady."

Grandmother wanted her to wrap up a present for
Amber. It was a plaque on which was painted a
ptarmigan, head downwards.

Returning to the kitchen, Sarah found Mrs. Gosling
already busy.

" Ah, Sarah ! " said she, " a wedding, when it *is*
a wedding, takes the eye ! With the half-dozen bridesmaids giggling, the mothers fighting each the other
like wild cats, the bridegroom champing to be off
(ours champed terrible when I was wed. A meek
manner had ours, but a great sperrit). There's

bridegroom hollering for coachman; and coachman lashing up, very fresh; and even parson a bit fresh— leastways in the olden days. But this! No champing, no maids and men, no coachman, and nobody fresh! Give me a funeral, say I! And a funeral we met ha' had, but for Mr. Michael lugging Master Jasper out. We met ha' had great black feathers waving, and crape without stint, and old men walking two by two, as grievous as the gun-dogs! I'd liefer a funeral than an outing! I mind when old Mr. Mucklewick deceived me sore that way. He went into a swound, and they took un for jead. So they made un a coffin. He was allus bone-idle, was Mr. Mucklewick, and he stayed in that swound till they came to nail un down. It was touch and go, then! But he stirred the little finger, so they knew their trouble was for nought. 'Poor Anne!' says he. Always one for a joke was Mr. Mucklewick!"

"Well, auntie!" said Enoch, coming in, "your breath's your own to spend and squander. But I wouldna waste so much of mine all at once, not in a week of years!"

He took the pails to the dairy, where he was run to earth by Sarah.

"Mr. Michael said to 's Amber," she remarked, "in the little drawing-room (as I couldna help but hear, being dusting in the big un), as folks that was married wunna married if they didna love each the other. Eh! I did laff!"

She looked at Enoch to see how he took this.

"Outlandish notions, folks get," she added.

"I dunna see as its outlandish."

"Well," said Sarah, surprisingly and firmly, "I love you, Enoch, and so I tell you straight!"

She advanced with the streaming skimmer in her hand. He backed towards the door.

" We'll walk out from this day on," said Sarah.

But from the passage, with the sound of retiring boots, came Enoch's voice : " It wunna be able to be done ! "

Sarah was obliged to comfort herself with the beautiful rendering of " The wings of a dove," by Mr. Mallow at the wedding service. Mr. Cantlop was there—a shadowy sexton, with a whisper faint as the rustle of leaves, hovering in the dark corners, smuggling people into their seats with the air of a conspirator, and handing them prayer-books as if they were ill-gotten gain. Mrs. Cantlop's bonnet towered and shone, lustily outfacing the colours of Death and Hell. Grandmother insisted on wearing the funeral bonnet. As Amber came down the path on Michael's arm in the sweet September sunshine, he whispered :

" Handfasted now, eh, little girl ? "

" I would have trusted you without," she answered.

It was at the wedding breakfast that Mr. Cantlop, accidentally, unintentionally, alarmedly, attained everlasting fame.

He covertly stuffed into Amber's hand a shabby little bag, which, when she opened it, contained some dull pebbly things.

" To make a necklace," explained Mr. Cantlop apologetically, and disappeared into his glass. But the Rector behaved strangely. He started ; stretched his neck like an eager hen ; came round the table ; snatched up the pebbly things ; shouted :

" My God, Cantlop ! You're not a poor man any more ! "

Swear not at all ! " said grandmother.

" Where did you get them ? " cried the Rector, shaking Mr. Cantlop in his eagerness.

"An old man, very ill," murmured Mr. Cantlop.
"Looked after him. He gave me those. No value.
Make a necklace."

"Have you any more of them?" shouted the
Rector.

"Another bag."

"Give it here! You're a rich man, my dear
fellow."

"What are they?" breathed Mr. Cantlop.

"Diamonds!" said the Rector. "It's a good thing
you didn't know, Cantlop. You thought they were
valueless, and so you kept 'em. If you'd known their
value, you'd have lost 'em."

"You must give those back, Amber," said Michael.
Amber obediently did so.

"Keep 'em!" said Mr. Cantlop distractedly, "oh
keep 'em."

"She's my wife now, Mr. Cantlop, and I'm vowed
to poverty," said Michael.

"Suppose you keep one or two, just to rent a cottage till you start work in earnest," said the Rector.

"Very well, as a loan," said Michael. "Thank you
kindly, Mr. Cantlop."

Mr. Cantlop beamed, blushed, coughed, murmured
something about a hiccup, and fled.

XXIV

A FOREST BRIDAL

MICHAEL took his bride home without pomp or ceremony, leaning on his arm, walking under the green roof of the woodland. The forest and man, who dwells within the forest, sleep. When they wake they wake together. The forest slumbers; its green walls are the walls of a palace enchanted, far gone in spells. Every tree has its own dream; the flowers drowse with eyes open or closed, and the dew gathers insensibly on their heavy eyelids. All things have an air of suspension, as if once, long ago, they were awake—moved freely with their large gestures; spoke in their own esoteric language; and were then tranced in the gracious attitude of their last waking moment. When the leaves fall, the trees loose them as a sleeper drops his book. Inanimate nature sleeps without pulses. Her creatures go their dim ways in hypnotic ambulations. So, when in this spell-bound place the soul wakes, a conscious entity, it is afraid in its loneliness. But as it stands under the frescoed arches, a creature small but vital, the spell is broken; all nature wakes with it, rises with it. The flower's eye is no more vacant; the trees stretch their arms in the luxury of waking; the forest sings with multiple voices; the supine earth finds a soul.

So it was with Michael and Amber. Arms were stretched forth in welcome. Flute notes fell from

276

thickets. The eyes of bird and insect, the dewy gaze of a few late flowers, peered on them with new meanings. Along by the stream the willows, clad in silver-dusted feathers, meditated like stately birds. Willows are of all trees the most mysterious. It is said that they were the first of trees, that before a bird sang or a bee quested for honey the world was full of willow forests. There the wind went in spring, a visible golden wave, deeply laden with yellow pollen. There, in the glistening air, with none but their own silver tongues to break the silence, the willows waited. They waited for the insects to come to their yellow aments; for the birds to flash in and out, making low music in the dusk. But they awaited also the perception which should complete their creation. The flowers that bloom unknown for a thousand years only exist when at last one flower blossoms under a perceptive eye. For that flower the pollen was launched spring after spring, the nectar gathered, the seed rounded. So the understanding of beauty is a priesthood. Amber and Michael gave to the forest almost as much as they gathered from it, as they wandered in the warm and mellow harvest weather.

The shadows were richly blue, of the tint of a chaffinch's head. There were breakers in the standing corn, where Philip Arkinstall rode up on the reaper which rose beyond the tall wheat like a ship over the horizon. From every nook in the forest came to meet them the benignant scent of wet moss. The very hills were mossy in the sun. They were like brown star moss; pale yellow sphagnum; bright green, red, green-white, acorn-coloured, or purple moss. They lay in clear and gentle colours under the periwinkle sky, and far off in the south a green-tinted rain-storm wandered along their sloping sides.

A quintessence of the whole year's sweetness was

distilled upon the cool air. The atmosphere was of
the unmixed gold of summer's maturity, yet the landscape lay in the colours of childhood—swimming rose,
sapphire, mauve, frail gold, and again rose—all
gathered within the dark-blue silence of the horizon.

Vague rumours came over the plain, murmuring the
vast content of summer's end. Yet the air was quick
as April is with the scents of growing things ; with
warm poplar resin, and the smell of earth and leaves
churned up by rain ; with the fragrance of the late
white clover that came to meet them like a friend.

The sheep, clean and white, fed in mown pastures,
and the geese, wild with the hint of autumn in the air,
went with a flapping of white wings to the rain-wet
grass.

Already there had come in many trees a faint
penumbra of gold, and over all things lay the beauty
that brings tears. The lovers came to the Birds'
Orchard and sat beneath a tree hung with little
painted apples.

" I wish I could be beautiful for you," said Amber.
" I wish I had Catherine's eyes and hair ! "

" What colour are your eyes and hair ? " asked
Michael. " I'll be damned if I know ! "

" The rudiments of courtship have not been taught
to you."

" Your spirit shines so, I can't see your features.
Crude soul, that's what shines."

" We must pray for a great deal of crude soul,
then."

" The windward side of an April orchard, that's
what kissing you is like," said Michael.

So they sat, ringed in pale fire ; for them bloomed
red roses that had in their petals no essence of decay ;
to them spoke in low, melodious voices, the birds that

roost in faery forests. Softly and slowly the fragrant evening fell around them. The plain slept, and over the rosy plough-lands, the quiet forest, the golden, ever-stirring wheat, were drawn thin, dusky veils. As the silence deepened, a thrush began to sing somewhere in the woods—an autumn thrush, more plaintive than those of spring. The music ascended like spirals of light smoke, and the soul that haunts the depths of the forest began to spin from itself the frail thread of beauty.

Over their hut, as they came towards it, stood a white cloud like a shield of silver.

As they came to the door, there was Jasper, pale and wistful, but smiling ; and there by the fire was Ruby, with Ernest junior (domed even at this early age with Athanasian dignity) on her knee.

" I brought her for the day ! " whispered Jasper. " It's supervision that's wearing her out."

Jasper was going to live at the Keep and work for his exams. Mr. Cantlop had insisted upon paying the expenses of these. He had also paid for Peter's and Marigold's passage to America.

" We're going now," said Ruby, who understood that there might be men so different from Ernest that a woman would like to be alone with them.

" You must stay to tea—or supper," said Amber. She thought Ruby terribly pathetic. " What a dear baby ! " she said.

" Is it ? "

" Yes. A darling ! " said Amber, determinedly seeing only baby and not Ernest.

When the sound of Jenny's feet died on the soft green turf, and the shrill complaints of Ernest junior were hushed by distance, Michael and Amber stood beneath a spreading larch tree, watching the sunset. The west was a lake of luminous crocus yellow, clear and translucent as water. In this, like green lilies, floated minute flakes of cloud. Among them, peaceful and motionless, lay water birds of soft grey cloud, sleeping among the lilies with folded wings.

In the woods it was already dusk, and, as they looked down towards the plain, they saw lights spring out there, shining between the interstices of the branches like glow-worms.

" Amber," said Michael, " what are you going to do with your life ? "

" Give it to you and to—all this."

She waved an arm round the dark horizon, whence a fresh wind came.

" I have a confession to make, Amber."

She smiled and waited.

" These things may not content me. I knew it to-day, when Cantlop and the Rector were hobnobbing about our cottage. Think of it ! They and Arkin: stall, your father, all of 'em, just the same, year by year. And out yonder—the world."

He looked at Amber keenly. The expression he had expected darted into her face—surprise, almost agony. So might a devout Catholic look, being excommunicated. Michael, watching her, wondered if she would pass the test. It was characteristic of him to test her thus, through pain. He was a hard man ; hard to himself, to the world, hardest of all, perhaps, to the woman he loved. Not even on her wedding day did he spare her, chiefly because he so greatly wished to know how much she cared for him. She had the shuddering air of a tendrilled plant torn from its support. He waited. No crisis of the struggle was hidden from him. Her face was clear and familiar to him as a flower's nectary to the bee.

She clasped her hands, hot with the stress of passion. For the love of nature is a passion for those in whom it once lodges. It can never be quenched. It cannot change. It is a furious, burning, physical greed, as well as a state of mystical exaltation. It will have its own.

Amber thought of June mornings when polished birds with flaming yellow bills made large tracks in the dew-white grass. She thought of the subtle changes of the seasons, breathlessly fair, not one to be spared. She remembered dawns that bloomed like a hedge of roses above the amethyst hills, and the bank of white violets which had never missed her yet in April. These things were her home, not Dormer. As one saying good-bye to home for ever, she sat with drooping head. She felt in her fingers the stalks of all the flowers she had ever picked—hyacinths, cool and brittle ; smooth cowslips ; hollow mallows ; warm comfrey. She heard in her heart the individual leaf-song of every tree. These things were of her essence now. But Michael also was of the forest. These things belonged to her ; but she belonged to Michael.

She looked up at last, and found his eyes on her. With a catch of the breath she said :

" Of course, Michael. We must go—away."

Her voice trembled into lostness.

Michael sighed. The tension had been almost unbearable.

" You love me enough to be willing to go ? "

" I have said so. You are stern to-night."

" You're a very beautiful woman, Amber. And if we go, I'll make it up to you."

He spoke with self-reliance, having enough insight to know that the man a woman loves can make up to her for anything on earth.

" What fairing shall I buy you, out in the world, Amber ? "

" Nothing."

" Is there nothing that will repay you—the delights of big cities ?   Finding yourself ? "

" No."

He was silent.   Around them the forest took up its night-spinning of multitudinous little sounds.   Sigh and rustle and soft footfall, ruffled feather, falling of early seed vessels, and that dream of a sound, the stealing of dew on to every leaf and blade and mossy bed—all blending in a vague half-music.

Michael brooded on the leafy layers below them, on the glow-worm lights which were all of the world that he could see.   While she groped intuitively, he saw the situation starkly and clearly.   The temptation to let this moment pass, to let the crisis remain unspoken, to let their lives go on with the important things tacit, unexpressed, took hold of him fiercely. But he had never treated life in this way.   He took a little medallion out of his pocket, and striking a match on his boot, held it before her.

" That ? " he asked.

" Yes, Michael."

" In poverty and discomfort ?   In crude places beyond the sea ?   In the squalor of big cities ? "

" You make it all very hard, Michael."

" Life is hard."

" Well, then, yes ! "

" Risking death ? "

" Michael, Michael ! Let me be happy to-night ! Let me ! "

She was crying.

" Risking death ? "   His voice was harsh.   " Do you think I shall let you say ' Yes, yes ! ' in your eager way, without first making you realize ? "

" There are some things in life that cannot be bought except at that risk, Michael.   They are worth it."

Her voice sank in the purple silence. The little medallion of the Madonna and Child slipped from her lap.

" Don't think I care about it at all, Amber."

" No ? "

" I'd just as soon—not."

" What a dreadful lie, Michael ! "

He looked up with the shyly guilty air of a small delinquent. She loved that look.

" And so brazen ! " she added, stroking his hair. Michael knelt on the moss with his arms about her. He was silent, but the forest, with a deep and solemn murmur, spoke his heart.

XXV

GRANDMOTHER HAS AN INSPIRATION

THE house of Dormer was very quiet after the lovers left it. Even Ernest was gone. Sarah, coming down from putting Mrs. Velindre to bed, said : " She's very sullen, Mrs. Gosling."

Mrs. Gosling was lugubriously washing up. Not only had it been a shabby wedding instead of a grand funeral, but Marigold had written to say she would not take the money, but was going to live with Peter.

" All that money to slip through the fingers, Sarah ! " she said. " Give me a sup of spirit."

Upstairs, grandmother looked very small in her large bed, very withered and puzzled. There was something she wanted. She moved her lips, but the only words that came were :

" Perverse ! A perverse generation ! "

The feeble glow of the nightlight and the flicker of the small wood fire lit the room vaguely, lighting up a feather fan in one place, a stuffed bird in another ; throwing into sudden relief the watch-stand with its skull and hour-glass, and the white, round face of her watch. It was a comfortable room, she reflected ; but it was crowded. It occurred to her that there were so many things in it that there was no room for her. Hour after hour, being too much excited by the wedding to sleep, she lay and thought of all the things in this room, in the drawing-room, in the hall. The clocks, the portraits, the nodding idol, the stuffed animals, the Bibles and prayer books in their special bookcase all these things seemed to crowd on her till she could not breathe. She felt at enmity with them. She wanted to get rid of them. Lying there in the increasing darkness, she heard Solomon and Rachel come up ; heard their muffled voices praying as usual ; and the chink of Sarah's silver-basket. She thought of calling Sarah to remove the crowding things that troubled her. But Sarah was gone before she called. She had an idea. She would look in the Bible. She lit the candle and opened the Bible. Her eyes fell on a heavily underlined text.

" Burning and fuel of fire."

That was it ! There was her answer ! She looked round triumphantly. Now she would show them !

She got up, took the candle, and went downstairs. The house was full of noises—the rats, the clocks, the rising night-wind, the little death-watches, ticking till the landing was like a clockmaker's. If anyone had met grandmother they would have been likely to faint with fright. With her huge nightcap, bare feet, and angry face she made a quaint picture. She lit a bon-fire in the drawing-room, and another in the hall. Then she went back to bed very happily, feeling that she had removed all annoyance through the inspiration of a text. Upstairs, they all slept. Downstairs, the little fires crackled and blazed under the amazed eyes of the ancestors, and the glassy ones of the stuffed birds. The nodding idol disappeared in a welter of flame. The ancestors curled up in their frames.

The rising moon laid the black shadow of the house on the lawn for the last time. Inside, it was already hollow. And now, within the shadow of the lawn, another shadow seemed to gather and stir and grow, so that what had been a quiet pool of darkness became like water when the wind goes over it. It consolidated, and then began very slowly to flow across the lawn. The rats were leaving Dormer, coming from cellar and attic and from their haunts in the thick walls. They passed away in the direction of the churchyard like the shadow of a cloud. The lower windows were all illumined now, and Enoch, who was wakeful, having the sense of impending calamity shared by animals and poets, saw the angry, red glare.

When he arrived at the house, all the clocks that remained were striking with solemn tones the hour of twelve, and from the kitchen the cuckoo hooted wildly. Enoch smashed a window and got in.

" Sir ! " he cried, hammering at Solomon's door, " Dormer's burning ! "

" Save your mother, Rachel," said Solomon, " while I loose the gun-dogs."

Enoch thundered on Sarah's door, which seemed to deprecate this rude disturbance of a maiden's bower. Within, all was in its usual order, Sarah's clothes neatly folded, the silver-basket palled in its wash-leather.

Sarah woke, and heard Enoch's voice, but the cotton-wool kept her from distinguishing the words.

" Enoch taboring at my door, and it midnight ! " she said.

She had heard of lovers doing such things in the old days when there were rope ladders ; but that it should happen to her ! She smiled in the darkness and wondered what Enoch would do next. She decided to be very righteous, moral and self-respecting.

" Sarah Jowel ! Sarah Jowel ! " cried Enoch.

" Ah ! I hear, never fear," murmured Sarah.

" Get up, woman ! " shouted Enoch.

" What a belownder ! It's no use you shouting,

Enoch, for I'm a self-respecting woman," she said,
" and let you in I never will.   I'd die first."

" Die !   Of course you'll die !   You'll be roasted if
you're so pig-headed ! "

" Now don't you make such suggestions to me," said
Sarah, " for I wunna listen to 'em."

She took the cotton-wool out of her ears to listen
better.

" I tell you Dormer's burning ! "

" Oh, is that all ? "

It seemed a small thing to hear that Dormer
was on fire when she had thought Enoch was on
fire.

Enoch carried grandmother downstairs, looking, in
his large embrace, like a Red Indian's doll.   Her dark,
pleased, slightly malicious face was lit by the red light
as they passed through the danger zone.

" I did it !   I did it ! " she cried.

" Most a pity if you did, mum, as you can boast of
it," said Sarah.   But grandmother only laughed her
rustling laugh.   Enoch set her down in the church
porch, where she huddled like a winter bird, only her
eyes alive, with their old look as of unknown creatures
stalking in their depths.   She surveyed the blazing
house with complaisance.   Then she said :

" A burnt offering to the Lord.   Hannah Velindre
shall be called blessed.   Dormer's falling ! "

There was something prophetic and portentous about
her voice ; but as she met her daughter's eyes—frozen
and scornful—it trailed away.   Her   concluding
" I did it " had a childlike tremor.

" She must be shut up," said Rachel.   Her eyes
brooded on the house, that shone like a firework picture.
The chimneys lit from below, seemed made of solid
gold.   Every window was illuminated as if for a festival.   They summoned with ironic hospitality to a

feast of death, where that wild creature, fire, was host
and reveller. As one by one the squares of daffodil and
red and primrose sprang out of the blackness, they
seemed to be saying that every house not lit by love is
desolate.

Enoch, coming through the wicket, met Sarah with
her arms full of salvaged goods.

" Did you send for the Silverton engine ? " asked
Sarah.

" Ah ! but I doubt it's too late. The bitter old
place'll faal."

He returned to the house and came back to Sarah
with something in his hand, which he presented to
her.

" Woman ! " he said.   " Your world ! "

" Oh ! " cried Sarah, " what's a world ? I want you,
and so I tell you straight ! "

" Softly, Sarah, softly ! " said Enoch.   " It wunna
be able——"

" What did you save it for if you didna mean keeping company ? "

" It was to be instead of me.   It'll be company for
you.   It'll outlive you and me.   ' The grass withereth,'
but the like of that never gets broke."

He spoke without irony.

" Enoch Gale ! " said Sarah, " do you mean to tell
me, after the coaxing and the driving I've been obliged
to do, and the promises you've almost give me, that
you're going to creep out of it again, you miserable
man ? "

" I saved your world."

Sarah was swept by a wave of hatred of art for art's
sake.

" So I'm to have this, am I ? And it's to outlast
me, is it ? I'll learn it to outlast me ! "

She lifted the round varnished thing, with its jubilant

colours, and flung it, crashing, at the feet of the negro boy.

" What a furious, ravening woman you are, Sarah ! " said Enoch.

Sarah, whose equilibrium was upset by the fire, flung her arms round his neck.

" It's like the 'ymn, Enoch ! " she said. " ' All the vain things that charm me most——' I've given it up for you, Enoch ! You canna say ' no ' now ! " Enoch started like a trapped rabbit.

" It wunna be able——" he began lamentably, with a very red face, less from embarrassment than from the constriction of Sarah's muscular arms, which were firm as her resolve.

But Enoch remembered Marigold's maytree freshness—all her rose and gold and white—and he hardened his heart against Sarah.

" —to be done ! " he finished, freeing himself by a dexterous twist. He backed away towards the safer regions of the fire. Sarah followed, still a good deal upset.

" You've broke my spirit, Enoch," she said. " And Mallow must mend it ! Mallow's a disappointed man since Mr. Michael turned out not to be a murderer. I'll marry Mallow ! "

Nothing was heard in the churchyard but the roar of the fire and the cropping of Mr. Arkinstall's two goats. He had voted himself the right of grazing the churchyard, and they were tethered beyond the yew-trees. Their grotesque, bearded shadows stretched across the graves, black and stark. Grandmother clapped her hands as a chimney fell. Into her strait, emotionless life had come an impulse, the first for numberless years. She rejoiced greatly.

Over the house stood a pillar of smoke, towering into

the sky and flattening out into the shape of a Druidical altar.   Behind it the dark trees of the Beast Walk were scarlet from the reflected glow, as if they too were burning.

Rachel was stunned as a long-caged animal is at the sight of open doors.   She would never hear the solemn, deathly night sounds of Dormer again ; never pace her grey bedroom.   Grandmother had destroyed it all. Here she was, shivering, outcast, lonely, the house she trusted in dissolved, the restrictions that upheld her removed.   She had lived according to the ghostly will of the house until her faint desire for freedom and development had died.   Freedom was a dream ; when it had gone, she slept the better.   And now, here she was, with nothing between her and the stars.   She was exasperated.   She put her hands on grandmother's shoulders and shook her till her ringlets swayed. " I'll lock you up ! " she said, and loosed her.   Grandmother sat crookedly, in her grey tippet, against the wall.

Rachel awaited a harsh word.   None came.   Only the leaves lapped upon the silence, wave upon wave, with a sound of peace.   Only the pearl-grey dawn began to build very slowly, with an architecture at once mighty and sweet, a house of many vistas.   This immense freedom, opening majestically and relentlessly around a cowering soul that did not want it, held a kind of irony.   For Rachel Darke did not want it.   She wanted the old vampire dwelling.

She nudged her mother.

" Wake up ! " she said.

Grandmother fell in a stiff heap at her feet.   She lay there like a broken idol that no man remembers. She was never to go tapping round with her stick again. It is ill to look upon the old gods in their last pitiful downfall.   With a vertiginous horror Rachel knew that her mother was dead. Brown, wrinkled, hard, the old face lay, smiling in the secure knowledge that Hannah Velindre was to be called blessed.

It was at this moment, when dawn brooded like a silver-grey pigeon over the world, that two odd figures appeared in the churchyard. A hint of light from the east revealed them as William and Amelia Cantlop. Amelia had been awakened by the red light or by some instinct of disaster.

" Dormer's burning, William, my dear ! " she said with composure. Real disaster found her possessed by a deeper self that slept within the feckless, frustrate Amelia and woke when people were in trouble.

" Brandy, my dear," she said.

Mr. Cantlop cunningly decanted it, Mrs. Cantlop collected wraps, her idea being that people's clothes would be burnt off their backs and decency outraged. They set forth, Amelia's bonnet not even attempting a union with herself ; only the strong corded strings prevented it from darting eagerly skywards. Mr. Cantlop stole along in the shadow of the hedges, noiseless as a homing owl. They seemed more at home in the wide morning than Rachel, for they had no possessions except a mere living.

" She's dead," said Rachel.

It was as if some poor wandering ghost had spoken of another ghost. The goats looked up sharply, like bearded men consulting on a knotty point.

From its height the forest contemplated them. It had its own preoccupations, its dreams of bronze and copper and clear gold. It was cold to the death of humans and of houses. For the god of the forest is not a following god ; not one that stands at the door and knocks. To those that seek him in the forest he gives a welcome. To those that sleep he speaks no word. They may lie in their mole-like chambers for ever, and slip from slumber into death.

The autumn wind, gay and eager, flutteerd Mrs. Gosling's apron as she went into the church to keep vigil beside the dead. Then with a swift onrush it broke upon the forest, where the lovers woke as day enlarged the world.

THE END